A Semester Abroad

Ariella Papa

FOR LE RAGAZZE.

The same night whitening the same trees.
We, of that time, are no longer the same.

-Pablo Neruda
"Tonight I Can Write the Saddest Lines"

GENNAIO

1.

As the plane began its descent, I was fighting sleep. My head bounced from side to side on my neck as it had for the entire seven hours of the flight. I hadn't wanted the dream to come. I sat in darkness that night as around me people snored. I wasn't startled by the flash of light from the shades the flight attendant opened in the morning. But even still, he remained behind my eyes, the boy I was leaving behind.

For a minute, I lost the battle with myself and dozed, long enough to get the image but not quite sure I was dreaming, half believing that it was real.

I dreamt that Jonas was touching me the way he did. He started with my ankles, grabbing on and worked his way up. Over my legs, hesitating momentarily on my hips, he looked at me, waiting, as always, to get permission to break my heart. I smiled at him, encouraging. I reached to touch his shoulder, the other hand searching for his hair. It was good. He came to me.

But when he got to my shoulders, he was no longer there. The plane bounced as the wheels dropped. I was not with him in the room that would be our only venue. I was going to Siena. I was about to start the process of my escape.

This happened many years ago when I was barely twenty. I was not quite enjoying my youth or the freedom that came with it. When I stood to walk off the plane my shoulders hunched over, my steps were shaky. In those days, I often clasped my hands together in front of me, scared that free they might strike someone or reach out for an unwelcome embrace.

At any minute, I might find tears coming to my eyes. I had stopped trusting myself. If you held a mirror out to me with a smile, I would have shaken my head and walked away.

In Brussels, I had to check in again, so that I could continue onto the flight to Florence. But I couldn't find my ticket or passport. I panicked. Kneeling on the dirty airport carpet, I searched all the compartments of my brand-new backpack, tearing out the crumpled clothes I had tossed in when I packed frantically the morning of my flight. I denied help from my family, who tiptoed around me. I refused to get out of bed and pack before that, saving it to the last minute, not really thinking through what clothes I would need for five months.

My pajama pants went flying out along with three socks I hadn't bothered to fold. I could hear the sighs of the people behind me as they almost stepped on one of my shoes. I grabbed it out of the way quickly and looked up apologetically. I was just a girl taking up space in the middle of the floor. They had their documents ready. I couldn't find mine. My heart raced and sweat formed on my forehead. My breath became gulps. I looked at the guard.

"Miss, you must locate your papers. If you cannot locate your papers, you cannot board the plane." His harsh accent scared me. It was like German with a twist of French, elegant and sinister at the same time. Maybe I had seen too many movies about foreign interrogations. I felt like a drug smuggler about to get pinched. I wondered if everyone could hear my heart beating. There was sweat rolling down my back; my T-shirt would absorb it before they saw it through my sweater. I searched again the compartments in my new bag. I bought this monstrosity so I could travel farther and farther and farther away, but now I might be sent back.

"Miss, your papers!"

Would they send me back so soon? Could they? I explained that I was a student with the university. All of the students in the program should be on the flight. I wasn't sure if my English was making any sense to anyone.

"Miss, we cannot hold the plane. You must find these documents." His voice was louder now, scarier. Could he see the circle of sweat around the collar of my shirt?

I stopped. Thought. I could feel Crazy sneaking up behind me as she had so many times before I left, trying to seduce me with the release that she claimed would make it all okay. I knew it was my mind, but Crazy followed me everywhere I went those days. Like the stalker I had forbidden myself to become, she was there for me, in every shadow, every doorway, around every corner. She lurked, she taunted, and she waited

3

for me to give in. I didn't want that temptation here. I couldn't allow her to catch me this time. I'd spent far too much time considering her seductive offers. I didn't trust myself. I didn't want her to find me. She had caught up to me once, took me into her sweet embrace and tried to prove to me how easy it would be to let go, but I fought her. I ran. Still, I had to get farther. Away.

Where were the documents? They could not be in the suitcase that was checked through because I showed them when I boarded the plane. It was right before I turned to my parents to wave goodbye. Their smiles were big, forced. On the way home from the airport, they would avoid talking about why I had come home early for Christmas break and hadn't come out of my room for almost three weeks.

If they sent me back, it would not be Jonas waiting to embrace me. No, he was locked up with someone else. If they sent me back it would be to the other one I ran from. *If they send me back Crazy will take me in her arms and never let me go.* That terrified me.

I ripped open the back of the bag. It wasn't a compartment, but a place to hide the straps to turn the bag from a backpack to a carry-on. And there they were—my precious documents. I was still kneeling when I thrust them up to the guard's stomach. He handed them over to the flight attendant, but he watched over her shoulder to make sure they were in order. I crawled around collecting my belongings, as other passengers grumbled in various languages. At last they nodded for me to go ahead. I got to my feet, slung on my backpack and continued my journey.

They did hold the plane for me. Several of the other girls smiled at me as I walked down the aisles. Their smiles were suspicious and not returned.

The first word I said in Italy was *grazie* to a customs agent in Florence who fingered the visa in my passport and said my Italian last name assuming I could speak Italian. I had studied it, but when he heard me thank him, he knew I couldn't speak. I hadn't yet learned the right way to work the *e*. Italians take all the letters in every word and give them the respect they deserve.

Arturo met us at the gate and began to herd us to the bus. He was our chaperone. He was a grad student, a sweet-faced man who was studying the neighborhoods of Siena, the *contrade*, for his thesis. He was speaking slowly in Italian, but still I couldn't understand. I looked around at the faces of the other students, doubting they could understand either. I was edgy and tired and that boy named Jonas returned to my head, giving me some stability, something I was used to. The idea of missing him calmed me only because it was something familiar; the only recognizable feeling I had in this country of strange words and people smoking in front of NO SMOKING signs. I wondered if anyone would ever speak to me in a language I could understand again.

We piled onto the bus, maybe forty of us. I hesitated before taking the step on. It was too late to go back. But again I thought that maybe I should return home. I doubted. I didn't know what was ahead or if I had the energy. I felt the anxious stare of someone behind me and stepped on.

On the road to Siena, Arturo announced the housing in English. I was hoping to be placed with a family. I would learn more that way and assumed that they wouldn't really understand me or hold me accountable for anything. I felt that I could hide in a language I didn't really know. Instead, Arturo revealed I would be rooming with three other women; a pale girl who was saying things in Italian to no one in particular, the blonde girl I saw painting her nails on the plane and her less blonde friend with great posture and a bulky sweatshirt bearing the name of our university. We would live in an apartment. Arturo said something in Italian. I glanced at the other three quickly. Only the pale girl nodded smugly, understanding.

"It's inside the walls," said Arturo, clarifying in English.

And in moments, we all saw those large gray walls that once protected Siena and behind them a zebra-striped building that I knew from brochures to be the Duomo, the cathedral. Beyond it, a salmon-colored tower, Torre del Mangia. I had one orientation class with Arturo before I left. He called himself Arthur then. He explained that Siena was a still a medieval city. He said the mentality had remained. We would find that the people in Siena were closed to us, like the walls that protected their city. They had their own traditions, centuries old, but he reminded us that the locals would note whatever we did. We, the *stranieri*, the foreigners, would always be seen.

I rallied myself out of my dorm room for that orientation two months earlier, without even my roommate, Kaitlin, reminding me. I had known that Kaitlin was going to Paris second semester, and I didn't know how I was going to make it without the one friendly face I still trusted. So I listened carefully to my

Italian teacher when he told us about the semester abroad and went to the orientation in the student union.

It was the first time I saw Arturo and pictures of Siena. The town was beautiful and full of sun. I learned the story of how Siena had once been a political power in Tuscany in the thirteenth century. It had rivaled Florence long ago. Then, eventually, Siena became the sleepy town that it is. And Florence thrived.

That's when I decided to come here. I wanted to live inside those stone walls, behind a fortress. I believed they could protect me, too. And I wanted to come because Arturo said that in spite of this loss, Siena remained beautiful, proud and trapped in time. It kept its dignity somehow.

That was for me.

In Italy there always seems to be some random holiday sneaking up on you when you least expect it. A *festa*. I arrived in the country on a *festa*, though I didn't feel like a holiday or remember how to celebrate. It was the feast of the Three Kings. L'Epifania. Nothing was open. We were lucky to get cabs, Arturo said. Only small cars were permitted in the city, beyond the walls, through the skinny gray cobblestone streets. It was freezing; that's what I noticed as I put my bags in the tiny cab.

My new home, my home for five months, was supposed to be welcoming and warm. The sun was shining in all the brochures. The reality, as I watched the driver shove our bags into the tiny trunk and encourage us to get into the car with words I didn't understand, made my teeth chatter.

Turn back, I heard Crazy whisper. Imagine the bed

in your room at home. Your parents will leave you alone to wallow with me. All of this is going to be too hard.

But I didn't know the words to work my body back over the road, to the airport and onto the plane. And I thought of my parents opening the door to their lost daughter and wondered if their first thought would have been for me or for checks that had already been cashed.

So I got in the cab with the pale girl and our squished bags. We took off through the walls. The cab raced down the skinny streets. The buildings were so close to us. I wondered how we weren't hitting them. There was no room for a mistake. I glanced at the speedometer. He was going almost a hundred! Kilometers, I reminded myself. It wasn't as bad as it felt. I tried to glance up at the gray and brown stone buildings that made me feel like I stepped back in time, but from my vantage I couldn't see the top. From my vantage point, I couldn't see the bottom.

I had a quick twinge of claustrophobia, but that came more from the girl, Lisa, than the tight pass through the city. Lisa spoke Italian the entire time. I didn't know if she was saying the right words, but her accent was crap. Even I could tell that her vowels didn't flow like Arturo's or the cabbie's. But she wouldn't shut up. The cabbie was just nodding and not responding. She filled every space with her droning voice. I should have admired her efforts for trying out the language, but it had been a long flight and I wished I could will her to stop talking.

I glared at her. She had long *Brady Bunch* hair, but it was a mousy brown instead of sitcom blonde. There was a half moon of pimples below her chin. If I could reach over and erase them, I thought, I could make her normal, I could make her shut up. My mind was wandering out of control again. I needed sleep

The cab stopped in front of what would be our building on a street called Stalloreggi. Via Stalloreggi 6. The other two were already there. Janine and Michelle. They went to my university. I could tell what dorm they lived in by looking at them. They lived in Sullivan with football players and sorority sisters waiting for the rush. The blonder one looked me up and down. I had already forgotten which one was which, just that one was taller and one was blonder. I suspected that the blonder one had the upper hand. But I was jealous of both of them for having each other.

I lugged my suitcase up the stairs because those two jammed all their suitcases into the tiny square elevator. My body ached from sitting for so long, and going up the stairs made me sweat once again.

"Wait till you see it," said the blonder one—Janine, maybe. I wanted to make sure that my reactions to everything she said were correct. Her gaze was intimidating. I barely registered her looking me up and down before she was staring into my eyes. I wasn't exactly sure what I was dealing with, but I knew that I was being sized up.

I climbed up to the third floor. The hallway was big, full of alcoves and wood. The apartment was way in the back. When I opened the door, I gasped. It was simple but prettier than I ever could have imagined. There was a tiny kitchen, the wooden desk in the hallway, the cherrywood cabinet full of plates. The dining room window looked out over all these rose-colored brick rooftops and beyond that what looked like the countryside I had seen in so many pictures.

There was no microwave and no television. There wasn't even a telephone. I was finally somewhere else, somewhere far from what I knew.

"Imagine no telephone. Hello, it's 1995 and here it seems like 1885," one of the blondes said. But I didn't mind. I wasn't expecting any calls.

"More like 1295," Lisa said, correcting. "Because that's when Siena was a real force to be reckoned with."

The smiles on the blonde girls' lips told me everything I needed to know about what they thought of Lisa. I knew I hadn't said enough yet to give them impression of me. I didn't want to say any more. I inspected the rest of the apartment.

There were two bathrooms, both with bidets, a strange toilet-like contraption that I didn't understand. The bathroom in the room Michelle and Janine took was the one with the shower. Lisa started making a stink about this when Janine came in with three of her bags.

"We took the double room. We figured it would be cool if we bunked together." Janine said as if she was doing us a favor. She looked at me for help. She determined that I already understood that Lisa wasn't cool. If I wanted to enjoy my stay here, I would know whose side to take. "We knew you guys didn't know each other and we thought since we did..."

I felt so lonely then. And that was nothing new except that for the first time in months, in almost six months, I was not lonely for him but for my roommate, Kaitlin, for a friend. I had already almost accepted that I would never be with him again, but I hadn't prepared myself to feel so friendless.

All three women stared at me, waiting. I knew that

I didn't want to sleep in a room with Lisa or either of the other two. I wanted a friend but did not see that in their eyes. I would rather have my own room, no matter what the size or proximity to the bathroom.

"Look, I don't care about the bathroom. I'm sure we're all going to have to work it out with the shower. I'll take the back bedroom. I don't mind." I said. It was smaller, but it had the window. That meant the room Lisa had, although bigger and closer to the showerless bathroom, was the one that was basically a hallway. Anyone using the other bathroom would be walking through Lisa's room. I would always walk through her room on the way to mine

I went back to my new room without waiting for protest or permission from the strangers that were my new roommates.

It didn't take me long to unpack the little I brought. I folded half of the things I hadn't bothered to at home and hung up some of my wrinkled shirts on wooden hangers. I surveyed my room, a box with faded flowery wallpaper and a thin pink blanket on a tiny bed. I hadn't had any pink in my room since I was eleven. There were two scratchy brown blankets in the dark wood armoire where I put my clothes. I took them out and threw them on the bed. The pillow was pitiful, but I folded it in half and lay back on the bed. There were chips in the ceiling paint. I am going to be staring at these chips for the next five months, I thought.

If only I had a picture of him in that secret compartment that hid my passport. Or a picture of us. It would be proof that the person I cared for existed. I didn't need reminders of him, but I yearned for something tangible.

I thought about the first time he kissed me.

We were lying on my bed. That was not new for us to lie together, holding each other and not doing anything else. It was one of those funny dorm things people did in college. We slept bundled tight together for many weeks until it was almost comical that he hadn't kissed me. But one night, that night, he did. He kissed my forehead first, my ears and then my chin. I held my breath expecting to be disappointed. Waiting so long for something almost guarantees that it won't be as good as you expected.

But it was better.

When he kissed me, I felt that this boy had been born to kiss me. That he knew how to kiss me in a way I hadn't even known I wanted to be kissed. I didn't say that, though. I just kept kissing, wanting to go as long as I could.

"Wow!" He whispered at last. Him, not me. "I could kiss you for a long time and never get tired."

I was so happy about that and didn't think until much later that our definitions of a long time might be two different things.

But he was kissing someone else as I lay in that tiny bed in Siena. Someone he kissed before me. She had endured through it all. It didn't hurt so much to think of him kissing someone else as to think that those lips *could* kiss someone else's. How would those lips fit to anyone else's? They should slide off another's—never quite matching, never quite locking in.

But they did.

My first night in Siena, Arturo came to pick everybody up at our doors for dinner. We walked up and down the hills through the narrow, windy, carless streets of this tiny medieval town. We were a group of foreigners, a caravan of *stranieri*.

We ate pizza with a crust like a crispy cracker with *rucola* and *pecorino*. I had heard of the salad green arugula but never tasted it and it was delicious and spicy. The cheese also had a kick, it was made from the milk of a sheep.

There were about thirty of us in the exchange group. The number was less than I originally thought when I got on the bus. Though more than half of the group were people from my school, I didn't recognize anyone because my university was so big. I liked that about it, that you could get lost, that you could avoid certain people or always meet someone new.

Some of the kids, mostly ones from the private schools, spoke Italian. I followed the gist of their conversations but didn't attempt to speak this language. It all seemed a bit pretentious, like they were exaggerating the accents. Lisa was one of them; she kept speaking to Arturo, showing off for him.

"I don't even speak Italian. I took French," said the taller of my two blonde roommates to no one in particular. The other one stayed in, claiming not to feel well. I suspected she was planning ways of making an entrance. "I just came for the trip. I just came because Janine said it would be cool."

Right, this was Michelle.

"They're going to give us a test on Monday at the university. They'll put you in a class that suits you," Lisa, who acted like she knew everything, said. She turned to Adam. "I knew before I came that I was going to wind up translating a lot for my roommates."

Adam was the guy with the biggest accent. Lisa wanted to impress him. He had mentioned several times in English and Italian that he had spent a summer in Rome. She continued talking to him in Italian. While her accent was bad and American, his was an exaggeration of vowels. They were posturing for each other and for us.

My head was spinning. Part of me wanted to go back to that little room that would be mine and crawl under the thin pink blanket and not worry about speaking to or knowing anyone. But instead, like everyone else, I drank glass after glass of Chianti and hoped that things would improve.

2.

I slept through Saturday morning into the early afternoon, waking in the tiny bed with my mouth feeling dry. I grabbed my watch and tried to calculate the time difference. It was after one or maybe after two; I was having trouble remembering how many hours ahead we were.

I got up and I stuck my tongue out at myself in the foggy mirror in my room. My mouth was stained purple, like I had been on a Popsicle bender. But the slight throbbing in my head wasn't a brain freeze. I tried to remember if I did anything stupid, but I didn't even talk to anyone.

I dreamt of Jonas again. He was standing in nothing but his boxers, his body long and lean. His stomach and the muscles in his upper arms were perfectly clear. He was still tan from the spring we spent together. I could see the freckles on his shoulders, but this was just a dream. He was above me on a terrace in one of the arched windows with deep red shutters open around him.

Every building I passed yesterday had shuttered arched windows, and in my dream he stood in one. He was yelling at me, yelling at me for leaving, for being who I am. I could not make out all of what he was saying, except that he was telling me that I was wrong about everything.

It would have been nice to believe that. To believe that there was some excuse for all of this. But in reality, there was no reconciling the Jonas I believed in with the truth of the one that existed.

It could drive a girl crazy, and it almost had. It still could. But so far in this country, I was okay. There were things I hoped would distract me. The newness of everything battled old memories. Maybe Crazy got stranded in Brussels.

I left the apartment quickly. Lisa was still asleep. The blonde best friends were nowhere to be found. I didn't shower. I was not ready to be naked yet.

On the street, I studied the buildings around me, worrying that I would not be able to find my way back to Via Stalloreggi. I considered for a split second going back in. But that was foolish. I couldn't hide forever. I needed to explore the city, see what it had to offer, discover if the brochures told the truth.

I walked through the town, circling the piazza, the center square. I hadn't expected it to be so cold, although it was January. For some reason, I believed the brochures of Siena with pictures that had probably been taken at the height of summer. I hadn't packed my heavy jacket, hadn't wanted to waste the space. I regretted it. I would have to buy a new one, though I couldn't. I was on a budget, and food was more important.

The scent of crackling fire surrounded me. It was a cross between a campfire and the Italian restaurant I went to back home. Behind the tall stone buildings people were cooking and laughing. They were cozy. They were not lonely.

I thought of how I would describe it in letters back home. I had to mention the hills, the way I braced the front of my feet as I went up and down the random slopes of cobblestone streets. I would describe the dark shutters of windows that Jonas would never be behind. I would compare the color of the buildings to one of my pale peach shirts. The streets were narrow and windy with the piazza the center of a spider web.

Around me, people walked. They knew where they were going; they had a purpose. The women were well put together. Their hair and makeup were perfect, and in their stylish wool coats, they weren't cold. I couldn't focus long enough on the bits of conversation that drifted by me to make sense of it. They shouted *ciao* at each other. Even those *ciaos* sounded different to me, like it was two syllables, the end ringing out harder, almost a howl. I formed my mouth into an *o* and said ciao, letting the end ring out, quietly to no one but myself.

I called my parents collect, to say that I made it safely. I vowed to be grateful for everything. I did a good job of convincing them that I appreciated the sacrifices they made, saving the money to get me here. I thanked them for all of this and told them how lovely the city was. I tried to convey how certain I was that I would be fluent in a matter of weeks.

I didn't tell them how cold I was. I didn't say that I felt trapped in the lack of language or that I didn't feel particularly close to my roommates. They had always maintained I should stay with a family. And I certainly couldn't have mentioned that as I walked the Italian streets I should be enjoying, the name of an American boy was just below the surface, repeating over and over like my mantra.

At last indoors in a coffee shop, I stood and tried to remember the system. The men behind the counter were handsome. They held themselves taller. They had the confidence lacking in American boys. They didn't hunch their shoulders or jut out their chins. What would it take to forget him? Try and replace this set of memories with another. It's what you were supposed to do. Forget. Move on.

I ordered my cappuccino, unsure of the words and my pronunciation, but the man understood me and placed a cup before me on the bar. For something to do, I added sugar and swirled it into the foam carefully, watching it dissolve.

Older men surrounded me, watching. No one was really openly looking at me. No one was a real threat. The cappuccino warmed me, but it took only so long to drink. Then I had to pay. How to say this?

"*Pago?*" I asked the man, hesitant again. He leaned closer, smiling. I repeated myself, feeling my eyebrows knit closer together. He said something in his language gesturing toward the door. He nodded at me to see that I understood. I didn't but pretended that I did, to get out of it. I managed a smile. I nodded. Fortunately, he began helping someone else. He did not return to help me. I was helpless.

I couldn't figure out how to settle it, what to do. And so I left.

On the street, I was frustrated. I looked ahead five months and wondered if I would ever be able to speak to anyone. What if I could talk only to the women I lived with? What if I starved? Worse, what if I had to rely on Lisa? What if I somehow got grouped with her?

I was warned about this. This was the program to go on if you really wanted to learn the language. No one speaks English in Siena. It's what I thought I wanted.

Then I heard it. English, American English, drifted toward me on the street. I turned and saw the short brown bob of Olivia, a girl who was in my Italian class for two straight semesters. We studied for an Italian final once and we compared our programs' Financial Aid packages. Now she was in Siena with a group of Americans.

"Olivia," I shouted. Olivia looked up at me and then, like some sort of long-lost siblings, we rushed to each other and embraced. I couldn't believe how happy I was to see Olivia, to hug a girl I barely knew. She was smiling, too. I was something not quite known but familiar. The last time we saw each other was over coffee in the student union, and now we were standing in a medieval town. It felt like a miracle.

Olivia told me where her hotel was. She used the Italian word for hotel, *albergho,* giggling. The hotel was further down the street from my apartment. She and her group would live there for three weeks before going on to Florence. She introduced me to four people from her program, and I forgot their names immediately, my brain was already full of the people on my trip.

"We have to meet up with our group," Olivia said. "Do you want to meet up later at the Barone Rosso?"

"Sure," I said, trying not to sound desperate. If I could have, I might have held her leg and dragged along to keep my eye on something familiar. "Where is that? What is that?"

"I'm not sure where it is." Olivia laughed. "It's a bar. I'll give you the address."

When we said goodbye, I was thrilled to have a plan for the evening with someone I barely knew.

I turned into the Piazza del Campo, the town square surrounded by stores and restaurants. Inside the piazza, there was a narrow pink tower, Torre del Mangia. It was the tallest thing around, nothing beyond it but gray sky. There were steps to the top. Arturo told us that it was bad luck to climb the tower as a student; you must wait until you finished your studies to climb. I couldn't imagine what it would be like in five months at the end of May when I could climb the tower. I wondered if I would be able to make any sense of this language by then.

After the tower, I looked to the shell shape of the piazza fanning open and up. It was there on the sloping ground that everyone sits or stands and gossips and watches. I walked up, looking for people. I was looking for Jonas for some reason, thinking there was a chance he could be among these strangers, even though he was still across an ocean. But maybe if I sat down and waited, he would eventually some day pass by.

Instead of Jonas, I ran into some of the people from my group by the white fountain directly across from the tower. They were sitting on the pink tiles in spite of the weather. I joined them and felt the chill through my jeans but decided to stay. Of all the people in the cluster of them, I only remembered Lucy's name.

We all reintroduced ourselves. Lucy told us about her apartment outside the walls of the city. For some reason Arturo couldn't explain to her, she was not matched up with anyone from our group or a family. Maybe it was because she was older. She was way into her twenties with the oily skin of a teenager and a kind smile. She lived with other *stranieri*, a Brit and a Greek. There was something reserved about Lucy that I liked immediately. Another guy, Tim, was also older; he had been in the army before becoming a student. Pam was from the Midwest, and she spoke in non sequiturs, pulling out a menacing shot of adrenaline, that she instructed me to plunge it into her heart if a bee ever stung her.

"Are there bees here in Italy?" Pam asked in her friendly accent. I shrugged and looked to see if anyone else knew. Pam didn't wait for an answer. Instead she asked, "Do you know where to get some hash?"

The piazza was the meeting place. Another bunch of the kids from the group showed up. We traded names again and information. Where we would take the placement test for the university? How hard was it going to be? Where does someone shop for food? What about toilet paper? The climate eventually bested us, and we decided to go to a café for panini. It was Lucy's idea. Lucy spoke with an authority about this city that I envied.

My *panino* was delicious. It seemed impossible that a sandwich could taste so good. I ordered one with speck. I had no idea what speck was—I still forget sometimes if it's beef or it's pork—but my life has been better for trying it that day. It was delicious. Lisa showed up with Adam. They sat with us but insisted on speaking Italian to each other. They brought the optimistic vibe down. We all knew that was what we were supposed to do, but I was overwhelmed by everything and happy to not have to try hard. We were caught up in excitement for a minute over our prospects, instead of fretting about an unknown future in a little-known language. With their arrival, that minute was over.

Instead of joining their conversation, most people stopped talking and stared blankly ahead. I felt myself pulling out, wanting to go back to my room and close my eyes and try to remember Jonas's face again. I was trying to remember it there, but the language distracted me. At last, Pam obliviously interrupted Lisa and Adam to ask if they knew where she could get hash.

The table laughed, and I doubted Lisa knew what hash was. I felt a breathy voice in my ear.

"This is really something else isn't it?" It was Lucy, smiling.

"That girl is my roommate."

Lucy offered me a cigarette. I didn't really smoke, but I took it, happy for another smile.

My mood turned again.

Janine and Michelle were home when I got back. I stopped at a *tabac* to get postcards and stamps and to get away from Lisa. For some reason they sold stamps at a candy and tobacco store according to reports, from the other kids in my group.

It took forever because I tried to do business in Italian and the woman behind the counter kept asking me to repeat myself. She kept saying *cosa*? and *non ho capito*. I could understand her, and I didn't believe she couldn't tell what I wanted. I was holding postcards. I knew the word for stamps and the word for the United States. I double-checked it in the damn *dizionario*.

It would have been comical if it weren't happening to me. I questioned whether I was even in the right place, but the cigarettes and postcards made me believe that I was. I waved the postcards around again and again, pointing to the box where the stamps went. Finally, she handed me the stamps I needed and gave me a sigh when I counted my change, trying to figure out if it was correct.

I never went back to that *tabac* again.

Lisa returned to the apartment right after me and looked at me suspiciously. Janine and Michelle were there in sweats and sneakers. I was finally learning to tell them apart. Janine's sweat pants sat low on her hips, revealing stomach, the top of a thong. They said that they spent the day running around the city. They found a supermarket and bought a ton of supplies and food. They even cleaned up the place. They scrubbed the floor. Then Janine asked Lisa and me for money. It was a little presumptuous, but since they got stuff like toilet paper and dish soap, and dealt with whatever communication difficulties on their own, I gave them 25,000 lire, the equivalent of around seventeen dollars. Lisa demanded to see the receipt and then handed over only 15,000 lire.

"I'm on a budget and besides, I don't drink milk."

"Well," said Janine, "we just got stuff I thought everyone could use. Milk does not equal 10,000 lire."

"Well, no one talked to me about it before hand." When Lisa talked her eyes kind of fluttered underneath lids that were half closed. It was as if she had already explained whatever she said and couldn't believe that she had to go over it again. I thought Lisa was one of

23

those people who don't really understand how to interact with people and thus she was a little intimidated by Janine, who was more than a little intimidating. Michelle left to fix instant coffee in the kitchen.

"Look, Lisa," I said. "It was cool of them to go shopping for us. We need that stuff. We're all on a budget, right? Why don't you just give her some more money and in the future we'll all do our own shopping."

Lisa sighed. She got another 5,000 out of her purse and handed it over to Janine. "This is all I have right now."

"I just think it's pretty stupid and cheap," Janine looked directly at Lisa for a full second, "for us to all buy our own toilet paper. And if we want to keep this place clean, we're going to need soap and shit."

Michelle's tentative voice came from the kitchen. "Maybe we should make a list of supplies and take turns buying it."

"I think that's a good idea," I said.

Lisa looked annoyed again. Janine grimaced at me behind her back, and I tried not to laugh. In her own way, she would be just as bad but more entertaining.

"Look, Lisa, I can't see how you have a problem with that. We are living together we are going to have to make some sacrifices," I said.

"We have to wipe our asses," Janine said cracking up everyone up. Lisa laughed the loudest but nervously.

We sat around the dining room table for the remainder of the afternoon. Lisa brought some Italian book she had and kept thumbing through it, saying words and their definitions to us. Janine wanted to talk about the boys she had seen on the trip to the grocery store.

"Do you have a boyfriend, Gabriella?" she asked me.

"No." I answered without hesitation. I wished Jonas didn't flash into my mind.

"Well, I do. I have more than one," Janine said. Michelle laughed. She knew all of Janine's stories, the way Kaitlin and I knew each other's. And she listened the way we did, as if she hadn't heard it before.

"It's not exactly going to stop her," Michelle said.

"Doesn't sound like it." I said, smiling. I wanted to get along with them, but I was cautious. I had been through it all already. The first few weeks of college when you think everyone in the world is your best friend, you get close and then you realize you are nothing like them. I already sort of sensed I wasn't like them. I didn't feel I could be like anyone. Jonas had zapped my emotions, I wasn't sure I wanted to invest so much again.

"American boys suck," Janine said. That I could agree with. "Bring on the Italian men."

"*Uomini italiani*," Lisa said. I looked at her. She mistook my expression for not understanding and relished the thought of explaining to me. "Italian men"

"Yeah, I got that one, thanks." I said.

"Whatever," said Janine and inexplicably lifted up her shirt to flash us her red bra.

I met Olivia at the bar Barone Rosso. It took me forever to find. I got lost off the main streets and meandered around for a while, not wanting to embarrass myself asking for directions with the wrong words.

We sat upstairs. Downstairs, a band was singing songs in Italian and English. All the Italians were singing the words to every song. They sang with passion, their voices traveling into the upstairs section.

One of the boys from Olivia's group drank a big mug of beer called *birra alla spina,* which cost 7000 lire. I bought that because it was a cheap way to get drunk.

I dodged the crowd in the bar and the women with the trays. These women wore short skirts and held the trays of drinks high above their heads. They said *permesso* as they tried to get past patrons. Their voices rose above the music and the singers, repeatedly punctuating the sound of the bar.

Upstairs, one of the guys from Olivia's group, Kurt, began talking to me. He raised his eyebrows and held my gaze, flirting. He laughed about my big beer.

Then Olivia came over and introduced Suzie, her roommate from the program. Suzie was thin and tall. She had a thick mess of brown curly hair. And when she arrived, Kurt turned his attention completely to her. He did not look at me again. He acted as if he was waiting for Suzie the whole time, just practicing on me.

"He was talking to her on the plane. He came to our room before dinner to hang out with her," said Olivia in a type of explanation. I tried to explain that I wasn't the slightest bit interested in Kurt. It was just something to do.

"Don't worry about it. He's not my type. We were just talking."

We drank for a while, taking the scene in, smiling at everything. The boys in Olivia's group reenacted scenes from their favorite movies. The girls danced to the songs on the jukebox. The Italians who were upstairs were watching and whispering even though we wouldn't have understood them in their regular voices. I liked that neither Olivia nor I needed to talk. We could just hang out and chill.

"Do you smoke?" I asked Olivia.

"Sometimes."

I laughed and said I sometimes smoked, too, when I drank. I held up my beer to indicate that I was, in fact, drinking.

"Will you help me smoke one if I can bum it?"

Olivia nodded.

Beer brave, I walked a couple of steps to a table of Italian boys in leather jackets of varying colors. Hesitantly, I pointed to the pack on the table. "*Cigaretta?*"

"*Prego*," said one of them, holding the pack out to me. The other three shot out their lighters like it was some kind of standoff at the end of a Western. The boy who was the quickest draw smiled as he lit my cigarette.

"*Grazie.*"

"*Prego*," three of the boys said and the other, the one who held the pack out to me, said something that made the rest of the table laugh.

"I think he called me a *fumacina*," I told Olivia when I retreated to her corner, offering the cigarette. "Do you know what that means?"

She shrugged. I wasn't sure if I was being made fun of. But it didn't matter.

I hoped I had found a friend of my own.

Michelle found me upstairs with Olivia and her friends. Michelle hugged me with the affection only a too drunk girl can find. She lost Janine in this bar after a marathon of other bars, she explained slurring. The details were hard to understand. It seemed to me that Janine might have purposely lost Michelle. I doubted she would have wanted to hang, as we did, upstairs drinking big cheap beers. Janine wanted something more exciting. She wanted action.

When Olivia was ready to leave, I hung behind with Michelle to look for Janine. I didn't really want to, but it seemed the right thing to do. Downstairs, the bartender said. "*Quella bionda è andata via.*" He flicked his hand several times. I squinted my eyes as if I could understand better by seeing better. He laughed at me, which was no longer a surprise, and dumbed it down in my language. "You friend go."

I understood some Italian words that night. I thought I heard one of the tray women sitting at the bar saying *quella bionda*, the blonde, as the bartender referred to Janine. As we turned to leave I heard her laugh and say *putana* and *americana*. American whore.

I walked unsteadily arm in arm with Michelle back to the apartment through the empty streets. There were lanterns with dim white light flush against the side of the buildings, but the streets were still dark enough to see the stars.

It was like Michelle was sleepwalking. Her eyes didn't focus on anything, but everything was hazy for me, too. I hoped I was going the right way.

When we finally reached the apartment, it was freezing. Michelle went straight for the refrigerator. She pulled out a tub of Nutella. She found a spoon and started shoveling spoonfuls of the hazelnut-chocolate sauce into her mouth. She did not even taste it. She was a savage, eating it ferociously. A little bit fell on the floor, and Michelle crouched on the ground and wiped it up with her hand. Then she ate it. She was a junkie. She didn't care where the fix came from. She just wanted the Nutella high. I watched her, stunned, shivering.

"You're hungry, huh, Michelle?" It was all I could think to ask the girl who was turning into an animal before my eyes.

"Yes, and it won't stay closed," Michelle said, twisting the top of the tub off again. She had abandoned the spoon now. She was reaching in with her fingers shoving them into her mouth again and again. The chocolate sauce fell out of her mouth onto her pretty pink shirt. She didn't care. She rubbed the stains with the back of her hand, licking it. Any minute, she might peel off the shirt and suck on the material to maximize the taste.

I didn't want anyone else to see her like this. I didn't want to see it. I was embarrassed for her. I didn't know her. I didn't think I should see this part of her.

"Well, I'm going to bed, Michelle, good night."

"G'nigh." Michelle said, barely looked up from the tub. Her teeth and lips were covered in brown chocolate sauce. She was moaning with the delight of having the freedom to eat like this.

I walked through the hallway that Lisa slept in. Her face was turned into the pillow. She was awake, I thought, and crying. Lisa hadn't gone out. No one had asked her. I had thought about it and decided I didn't want to be saddled with entertaining her. I didn't want Olivia to associate me with her, because I didn't really like her. So there she was crying in her bed and I felt guilty. But I was too tired and drunk to see if she was okay.

I climbed into my little bed. I didn't bother to brush my teeth. I was careful not to let my hands touch my body. The last thing I wanted was to remind myself of his touch. Many nights I went to Jonas's room after a night like this, with my lipstick smeared.

"Did they love you for your mind?" he asked me about all the nameless boys I met. He wanted to remind me that they didn't. He wanted to show me again how different he was from the rest. I was waiting for him, waiting for him to kiss me.

But he didn't kiss me, not that night. I was used to nights of just waiting and not being kissed. He reached across to wipe off some of the lipstick on my mouth.

"You know your lips are a beautiful color without all this crap."

I couldn't look at him, then but I could feel him looking at me, feel his words spread through my body out into my legs.

It was too much.

"And hers?" I asked, meeting those eyes again in time to see the hurt. He got up and left his own dorm room.

He was not going to her. She was sick. She was far away and I was there. But now she was well. She was back and I was gone.

Just fall asleep, I told myself, don't think. For once. *This scene is too weird and you have drunk too much to deal.*

I drifted off, but then I felt the chill in the air, the blanket being pulled back. I started to smile a bit, in anticipation, but it wasn't him. It was Michelle, smelling of booze and burps and chocolate that was certain to stain my shitty pillow.

"They're doing it," she said. "Janine and some guy. Going at it in my room."

"Shit." I moved over as much as I could in the bed to let Michelle in. I could hear the distant sounds of sex, the screeching of the bed, thumps. A woman was moaning, a man speaking a language I didn't really know yet. Michelle promptly fell asleep, taking up more of the bed than seemed possible and staying that way, a stiff rock, for the rest of the night. Not even my bed was my own anymore.

This is only the first whole day, I thought, and tried to imagine what the next 150 would be like.

3.

The Università per Stranieri di Siena was across the Piazza del Campo from the apartment at Via Stalloreggi 6. It was there that I spent some of the most frustrating moments of life. But unlike my apartment, the *universita* always had heat.

There were two buildings to the school, with a small piazza between them. The school was for *stranieri,* meaning foreigners, not just Americans. It was full of people from all over the world. The only language we would ever share was Italian.

Each time I walked to school from the apartment, sometimes with my roommates, sometimes without, I worried that I would slip down the steep hill into the *campo*. When I came back up and out the other side of it, I worried that one of the little cars or motorized bikes would hit me on the narrow streets. Small commercial cars were the only cars allowed beyond the walls and then only in the morning. In the small window of time they had, the drivers sped around like demons. There were times when I don't know how they missed me at the very last minute. But they were the experts; I was the *americana*.

My first day at the university I bombed the placement test. I was never a good test taker and I was nervous about speaking Italian. In my individual interview, I couldn't seem to raise my voice when the proctor asked me about American film. He wanted to put me in the first level, the level for beginners, but I pleaded with him for placement in the second. Even though I barely understood anything, I had taken Italian for three semesters. I couldn't be a beginner. It was a matter of pride.

"*Posso fare secondo. Voglio secondo,*" I said, not even sure if I was speaking the right words as I begged to get into the second level, whether I was making my case better or worse.

He looked over my written portion again. Thankfully, there were a lot of multiple-choice questions. I smiled the biggest smile I had at the proctor and said, pronouncing every syllable, "*per favore.*"

When he sighed and started talking in fast-flowing syllables I still wasn't sure of my fate, but I kept my face calm and nodded. Then he handed me a piece of paper with my class on it. He had given in, and I was in the second level.

And so I found myself in Signora Laza's class. Many days I watched the sun stream through onto the white walls and had no idea what the hell was going on. I kept telling myself that it was all part of the experience, but *non ho capito* became my party line to the *professoressa*. I sat next to Lucy, which was helpful.

I didn't understand a single complete sentence throughout the entire first class. Maybe I should have accepted defeat and gone to the beginner's class. None of what I learned in class seemed familiar from my last semester of Italian at school. That last semester I had skipped many classes, and Italian was the last thing on my mind.

Each day I understood a little bit more, but there was never a moment that I felt relaxed or comfortable. Every day there was a *pausa*, the break that would be customary in the three-hour-a-day lesson. I drank my cappuccino and wondered if it was ever going to get any easier. Luckily, I mastered the art of ordering cappuccino by the first week. That was my small victory.

Lisa was bitter that she also got placed in the second level. Apparently, she expected to get into the third level but didn't speak Italian as well as she thought she did. I wondered if my being in her level made it sting even more. I should have been above enjoying that, but I wasn't.

Janine got the first level and Michelle, who had never spoken a word of Italian, was able to avoid the placement test all together and just go into the beginner's class of the first level. For our first week Michelle's default was *"Mi chiamo Michelle. Sono americana."*

It was almost impossible to be comfortable in the apartment those first few weeks. I was always shivering. A warm bar was always preferable to a freezing apartment. The heat in my cold stone building came on in the evening and shut off somewhere in the middle of the night, leaving me to swim around my tiny empty bed for warmth. I started leaving my clothes out on the bed, so I could change under the covers.

Some nights, I lay on my bed, pulling the scratchy brown blankets around me, trying to take the lesson in. I studied my Italian grammar book and tried to concentrate on the *esercizi* in *suffissi speciali*. Mostly it felt futile. *Futile.*

I would have done anything to be able to veg out in front of TV with a bowl of microwave popcorn and a down comforter. I didn't know how I was going to handle not having a television or a telephone. I wanted to get away, and now I was away and isolated. There didn't seem to be much else to do. No distraction from learning the language. Right.

I fell into a pattern with my roommates. They remained strangers to me for the most part. We occasionally met at the kitchen table in various stages of eating the meals we prepared for ourselves. I began cooking for myself once I was brave enough to order bread at the *forno* and learned that I wouldn't have to talk to anyone at the Coop supermarket, though it was closed in the middle of the day and on Wednesday afternoons.

They were not roommates the way I had been with Kaitlin. She was a friend who made me think that a roommate was someone who shook you awake when you hit SNOOZE too many times before a midterm, who shared clothes and confidences. I was spoiled by Kaitlin. She always had a smile when I needed it.

There were little things I liked about them, though. Janine was a performer; she thrived on attention. She had a way of holding court, exaggerating the frustrations we felt with no idea of what was going one. She made fun of herself trying to act out a blow dryer in the tiny department store Upim because she couldn't think of the word.

Lisa kept herself separate from us. Maybe she was homesick for the boyfriend she claimed to have. Janine speculated that this boyfriend was gay when it was just the three of us, following it up with, "Oh, no, I didn't!"

I thought I could hear Lisa crying at night sometimes, but I didn't know her or what to do to make her happy. I tried what I could. The one time I asked her to come out with me she said, "I don't know how it is in *your* second-level class, but I have a lot of homework in my class." I shook my head and walked away.

Lisa was the queen of passive aggression. I knew she was the loser of the bunch. That gave me a bizarre protection but also a sort of sick feeling in the pit of my stomach.

I went out with Michelle and Janine a few times. It was never like the casual nights I had back at school with Kaitlin. Those girls took going out for a drink to a new level. I was always underdressed in my tight knit shirt and jeans. They got really dolled up and it worked; they got attention. I often felt like a third wheel except for the times that Janine got hit on. The slightest interest from a man would make Janine turn away from us, leaving Michelle and me with nothing much to say to each other.

Janine brought a lot of guys home those first weeks. All of the freedom intoxicated her. She skipped a couple of classes to the horror of Lisa. Janine hobbled around in the mornings with her body looking sore and her hair a tangled mess.

"Just needed to get the cat patted," she said, smiling and heading back to bed.

Too many random men came into our apartment. This wouldn't have happened if I stayed with a family. But at least Michelle started taking the small couch in the dining room and not my bed.

At times, I wished that I lived alone. I yearned for quiet when I wanted silence and not the laughter, the crying, the issues these women had and the smells of their bodies. I knew it wasn't healthy to want to be by myself, but I did. Who knows what would have happened to me if I had been left to my own devices in that apartment?

I found my friendship with Olivia. I was scared to hold on to her too tight, though I wanted to. I spent nights with Olivia and Suzie going to bars. No one in Siena spoke English, except the men at the bars where we went every night. There were disparities between night and day. At night, I laughed and drank without worrying about my accent or whether or not I was using the correct tense.

Wherever we went, *milatario* came out of nowhere to join us. These boys in the military had their own strong scent, button-down shirts, ironed jeans hemmed at the ankle and nice leather shoes. They smirked at everything we said. Their names were things like Pino, Allesandro and Armando. Olivia started a list of names and hung it in her hotel room. Every night she added to it or noted repeats. Mauro was the most popular name and Paolo was a close second.

With Olivia, it was all good, though. Fun, funny and distracting. She was more my speed. And she had a way of making me cheerful. She was full of plans and happy to be in Italy. I began to enjoy the way Olivia's voice got raspy when she had too much to drink. We smoked and ordered more alcohol to help communicate with those bold boys who talked to us. It was easier than class. The bartenders always understood what I wanted, unlike the rest of the shopkeepers.

I would have felt like a third wheel with them if it wasn't for the developing relationship between Suzie and Kurt. One night Olivia and I followed Suzie around the town hoping to run into Kurt "accidentally".

"I've had enough of American boys," Olivia whispered to me as Suzie turned purposefully into the piazza. "We're in Italy now."

As if to confirm it, I stopped in front of the tower. I grabbed Olivia's arm and pointed up. Around us, everything was spinning, but the tower above loomed large and stable, behind it twinkling stars. We looked at a picture of this tower back at school when we discussed programs, when we didn't know each other. But it became our reality. I looked to see that Olivia felt it, too. I wouldn't want to experience that moment alone.

"We're here. We're really here."

"We're in Italy," Olivia said, getting even happier. She was jumping up and down; she was drunk. She was hugging me. Suzie was on the other side of the *campo*, but we didn't mind. "We're really here."

During the days, in spite of the harsh temperatures, I spent a lot of time just walking on my own, following the curves of the steep narrow streets until I could find my way back home from almost any point. I found a café on the other side of the *campo*. The proprietor at this café was a bleached-blonde woman who stood behind the bar with tight jeans stretched over her stomach. The proprietors said *dimmi* when people came to their establishments, but this woman made it sound sexy and confident.

This became my place where I could sit at a table and write in my journal. I wrote letters to my friends back home and to Kaitlin, who hadn't yet left for Paris. I sent them the address at the school, Università per Stranieri di Siena, because none of us could figure out how to get mail at our apartment.

Of course, I never wrote to Jonas. Well, I wrote to him, sometimes, but I never sent the letters.

To my friends, I tried to sound happy. I said optimistic things, things I didn't necessarily feel about learning the language. I wrote about the colors of the buildings, the way I felt like I had stepped back in time. I invited them to come visit me, made plans to meet up with some of them in foreign capitals. I wanted everyone who watched me slip into a depression to know I had been cured of him. I wanted them to believe that I was over my addiction, rehabilitated.

One night Olivia and I went to the cinema. Suzie was at last having her night out with Kurt. The movie was my suggestion. I saw the theater on one of my walks. I liked the idea of sitting alone in the dark surrounded by people. We chose some British flick neither of us had seen.

Almost as soon as the film started, I realized that it was a mistake. They don't subtitle in Italy; they dub. There was no respite from Italian, no translation. Maybe if we went to see a blockbuster with more action than dialogue we would have been okay, but of course the movie was really talky and all the talking was in a language I didn't really understand.

Other people did though; everyone got it but me. They were laughing all together at the same moments, sharing. I looked at Olivia. She had a thin smile on her face. Maybe she understood some of it; maybe she didn't. This was the worst idea. I was crawling out of my skin.

Then there was a *pausa*, just like class, we got a break. I turned to Olivia. I hesitated, our friendship was still too new to do anything bold, but I thought that if I stayed and watched the rest of this movie I didn't understand, I might just lose my mind. "I think I have to go."

"You do?"

"Yeah," I said. "I'm sorry, but I mean, do you understand this?"

She shrugged. "Not really, not much."

I nodded. I wanted to go but couldn't move. I liked her enough to want approval.

"Okay." She said at last.

We were out of there.

Back on the street we walked in the direction of her hotel. What a ridiculous night. Though I felt free, I thought, What now? Will I just go back to my dark frozen apartment? Would I stare at the walls, wishing again for a television? No, I would spend the night remembering every little thing I could about Jonas, the good and the bad.

We were coming to the street of Olivia's hotel. I didn't want my night to go the way I thought it was going to. I thought Olivia could probably find other better plans. I worried again that she wanted to keep watching the movie, just not alone. It was now or never.

"Do you want to grab a drink?"

"Yeah," she said it so quickly that we both laughed. I felt a little better.

Janine told me about this bar. It was where she met the second guy she hooked up with. By now, she had lost count. It could have been a gay bar for all the good-looking, well-dressed men who were inside. There were few women, and I suspected they were tourists and foreign students like us.

"We're outnumbered as usual," said Olivia through gritted teeth.

"And underdressed yet again," I said. "Let's get a drink."

We ordered cocktails from the unfriendly waitress who banged the menus in front of us and swept them quickly away when we placed out orders. Olivia got a plate of fries. They were served with mustard and mayo. We started to scarf them up, but they were burning hot. We swallowed the last of our drinks to cool our mouths. We ordered more drinks and asked for ice, but in Italy ice didn't really exist. What we got back was puny slivers of barely hard water in our glasses. We drank it up. The roof of my mouth was burned. We experimented with fries and mayo.

"I like mayo, but this is pretty gross," I said.

"It's kind of cooling my mouth out, though," Olivia said, blowing out her breath.

"Will you be okay if I go to the bathroom?" I asked, looking around at the men who were circling us.

"Sure," Olivia said. "Hopefully, I'll be here when you get back. Good luck."

"Thanks. I'll need it." I never knew what to expect from the bathrooms. Sometimes they were just a hole in the floor. This one wasn't so bad. There was a toilet, but no seat cover. I drank a little water from the sink, knowing it would be a while before the waitress came back.

Outside the bathroom, there was a man leaning against the jukebox. His eyes widened when he saw me. I thought he mistook me for someone else, but when he waved, I said hi. He looked confused and asked if I was English.

"No, I am American," I answered in Italian. He was staring at me so intently that I couldn't tell if I was making any sense, but I continued. "I am studying here."

"Yes," he said in English. This man was dust. His skin and his hair were almost the same light-brown color. Only his eyes burned like the end of the long ash on his cigarette. They were light gray with specks of hazel close to the pupil. I shrugged and walked past him back to the table where Olivia was finishing off the fries. I grabbed one of the last ones.

"Sorry," she said. "I was starving. Was it okay?"

"Yeah, it was fine. Don't go yet, though. If you have to go."

"Why? Did you make a friend?" I rolled my eyes. She looked up over me. "Is he wearing a yellow sports coat?"

"Shit," I said and he was at our table with three of his friends.

"I am Gaetano. This is Dino, Giovanni and Paolo." More names. I held my hand out to each of them, unsure if I wanted the customary kiss. Olivia got the kisses from Dino and Paolo and both of us were confused about protocol. "May we sit?"

They didn't wait for us to say *prego*. They just sat. Olivia said, "Oh, okay," but smiled when Dino winked at her. They were all students, not *milatario*. Dino could speak English better than most of the men we met. He ordered more drinks for us. When I looked at Gaetano, he was staring at me. I smiled politely.

"You are very beautiful," he said in Italian. I laughed. "Why do you laugh?"

"You are funny. That's very funny." These were words I was able to say.

He was almost thirty. He told me in Italian that he was going to be a doctor. He wasn't from Siena. He was from the south of Italy. He said that like he was talking about a different country. He told me a lot, and I wasn't sure I understood everything. I knew that he was trying to talk slower so that I could understand. I was listening to the tone of his voice more than trying to understand the words he said. His voice was a part of the larger sound of language in the bar. I began to feel a part of that sound. I became a piece in this Italian puzzle.

But after we got the next round, I was tired of trying to speak his language. It happened that quickly. I grew frustrated with trying to make sense. Moments earlier, I was happy to be a part of it, and suddenly I would give anything to be talking to some frat boy in English, to not have to think.

I looked at Olivia. She looked like she was having the same problem despite Dino's command of English.

She suggested we play a drinking game. Great idea but what? Asshole would be too hard to explain and besides we didn't have cards. Quarters could be turned into lira, but did we want to start throwing money around a bar? Then I thought of it.

"The sign game," I said.

Olivia nodded. "Thumper, right?"

So we demonstrated the sign game. In the game, everyone makes a sign with their hand: thumbs, bunny ears, hang loose, whatever. That is your sign, and when someone makes your sign, you have to make it again and then pick someone else's sign and do it right away until someone messes up or can't think of a sign and has to drink. We exaggerated gestures when we couldn't think of the words to explain the rules. It was tough to demonstrate with only the two of us. Dino tried to translate, but the other men were yelling that he wasn't quick enough. They were yelling what they thought were the rules. They were all just kind of yelling.

We played a lightening round of the game with each other and then decided the Italians were ready.

We played this game for a couple of hours. Giovanni kept fucking up, and the others yelled at him, trying to explain, pleased that they had the knowledge of the new fun foreign game. They kept yelling the word *subito* at him. As I watched them explain it to him, I understood the word *subito* meant right away, right now, immediately, without having learned it in class or looked it up in the dictionary. The Italians wanted everything *subito*. It was better than any lesson Signora Laza could give me.

The game served its purpose. It got us drunk. It broke the ice. Olivia's smile got wider and wilder; her laugh grew less nervous and more confident. She made up a lie about a boyfriend, so that she could relax. I did the same thing. I didn't give my fake boyfriend a name, but I looked Gaetano directly in the eye so he would understand that I was not interested. I had a *ragazzo* and didn't want him.

The group broke off into little conversations. Olivia and I were not able to talk to each other. Occasionally the Italians said something to each other in a harsh language that was a southern dialect. I was flattered that they thought we would understand standard Italian. The dialect sounded sort of similar to the language I could barely understand, but the accent was harder like German and the ends of words were cut off.

I talked to Giovanni, who I liked because he seemed to be the most confused, the least sure of himself. There was something endearing about that. Then Gaetano said something to him in dialect. Although all the dialect was rough, this was an outright command. Giovanni stopped talking to me immediately, and I realized that Gaetano had somehow claimed me. His friends respected that.

Eventually, Giovanni excused himself and I tried to get into the conversation Dino and Paolo were having with Olivia. But Gaetano took the opportunity to talk to me. He asked where my parents were from, and I told him where my grandparents were from. It was a simple enough conversation to understand. What he was really asking was what part of Italy I was descended from.

"So you are from the south, too?"

"Well, I'm an Italian–American."

"The north and south are different you know. The south is better." Dino, who was from the north, said something to Gaetano that I didn't understand. Gaetano ignored him and continued. "People here don't like the people from the south, and we don't like them."

"You like Dino."

"Dino is different. He is good."

"I see."

"For me you are Italian."

"I am. Italian-American."

"Your mouth is like the south. And your dark hair and eyes. Like the women of south Italy." I didn't know what to say to him. Dino winked at me and switched to English.

"The men of the south are all criminals."

"Are you a criminal?" I asked Gaetano.

"No," Gaetano said with a wry a smile. "Sometimes, the men of the south who move north have to do things that are a little illegal."

"Like...criminals," Olivia said. I laughed feeling nervous, and Gaetano said something else to Dino that I didn't understand.

"You know Gaetano is priest?" Dino asked. The Italians at the table cracked up. Gaetano wanted to speak English now. They all did; they all wanted to show off the little bits they knew.

"Are you a priest?" I asked. This was starting to get weird. I wasn't sure what was worse, having a criminal or a clergyman looking at me the way he was.

"He say this because I live with monkey," Gaetano practically screamed for emphasis.

"You live with monkeys?" Olivia laughed. "In a zoo?"

"Are you a zookeeper?" I asked.

Dino corrected Gaetano in Italian.

"He live with monk, not monkey," Dino explained. I shrugged, not sure if this was a joke. "How you say where live monk?"

"Monastery?"

"Yes, yes. I live monster with monk, no monkey," Gaetano said. The Italians laughed again. Paolo began making monkey noises. Olivia and I looked at each other waiting for the punch line.

"No, is really," said Gaetano, nodding. "I live 'ere. In monster."

"Okay, sure." I guessed it was like a dorm.

"So we mus' go your *casa*," Gaetano said, winking a gray eye at me. The Italians thought this too was funny. Gaetano translated for Giovanni. Giovanni turned a little red.

"We are not going to go to my apartment ever," I said. Then I switched to Italian, for the benefit of anyone who needed clarification. "*Mai.*"

The waitress brought another round. It was the last round for us. It was after two. The boys conferred in dialect. They were trying to plot ways of making us stay. We wouldn't stay. We needed to go back to our beds and sleep. We used sleep as an excuse.

"*Andiamo via,*" I said. "*Siamo stanche.*"

Confused, they followed us out. They said they wanted to walk us home. They asked us to go dancing. They asked us to go to a hot spring. To each request we shook our heads. We continued to tell them that we had to leave. We were tired. They didn't believe it.

"Why?" Gaetano asked. Everyone seemed to be waiting on me.

"We're not going to get in a car with strangers." I said, using a word I learned in class that day, *sconoscuiti*. I could tell immediately I hadn't used it right. Gaetano was genuinely offended that I said that. He claimed not to be *sconoscuito*, whatever the damn word meant. He insisted that we go with them to the hot springs.

"He says it's nice for tourists," I told Olivia, not sure why I was translating.

"We're not supposed to be tourists," she said.

"They probably want us to go skinny-dipping," I said.

"Let's just go home," Olivia said, starting to walk toward the *campo*. She waved back to the guys. "*Ciao!*"

"Wait," said Gaetano, walking over to us. He looked at me. "You call me."

"I can't." I said. "I don't have a phone."
"She 'ave none in 'er *albergho*?" He pointed at Olivia.

"You can give it to her," I said. He wrote down his number and handed it to me. I took it and gave it to Olivia. I had no intention of calling him.

"To the monster," he said, pointing at the paper. "You call me."

"The monster, yeah. Scary," I said as Olivia laughed. I grabbed onto her sleeve. The rest of the boys kissed us on both cheeks, and Gaetano got too close to my mouth. I moved away quickly and tugged Olivia down the street. We shouted *ciao* at them, letting the end ring out like the Italians did.

We walked down Via di Citta, arms linked as if we were Italian women and Siena was our city.

4.

I set rules for myself, so it would be easier. One was not mention his name. It was an old rule, started by my friends when his girlfriend, Mono Girl, came back. They stopped bringing him up. They thought they would protect me. But they didn't realize that conversations for me became yet another waiting game. No matter who I was talking to or what I was doing, I was waiting for a clue about him.

But in Siena, no one knew me or him or anything. If I didn't mention Jonas, if I didn't speak his name, I told myself things would be fine. In Italian, the letter that started his name didn't exist. I told myself, He will not exist for me here. But whenever I looked at the poster of the Italian alphabet in my classroom, the first thing I thought was that something was missing. I had to stop it. If I could manage to get through a day without relating everything back to him or us, this would all be worth it.

But, it was so hard to walk those narrow streets.

The couples stopped everywhere to kiss each other, to heat each other up. The men looked at the women in a way that broke my heart. Their love was on display. These couldn't be the same men who wanted to fuck blonde *americane* in my apartment.

I couldn't help picturing the two of us on these small streets. Sometimes he came up behind me and placed a hot hand on my neck. I saw us together in the kissing couples. I closed my eyes to envision him pressing me against the gray walls, more persistent than he had ever been. My skin shivered against the stone from where my shirt was lifted by his hand.

These were the images that would do me in. This was Crazy trying to trick me.

I should have listened to Kaitlin that day when Jonas came up to us in the student center. I was helping her work on a mural with her art class. I couldn't draw, but I was letting her boss me around, enjoying the sight of her red hair tied back, fingers pointing and wiping paint on her jean cutoffs. All I had to do was keep filling in the sky with the cobalt blue paint it had taken Kaitlin hours to decide on.

Kaitlin ran a tight ship, and she went to pester one of the freshmen about his choice of color for one of the parts of the mural. She left me alone with Jonas.

I knew him through friends. I knew him from parties. He lived in my dorm. I chatted with him about our plans for the weekend.

"You, uh, got a little something on your face," he said, gesturing to his own. He smiled at me. I don't think we ever really looked at each other before that minute. I don't think we saw each other the same after that. I don't know why, how it happened. I could feel the paint on me, but I wiped the opposite side of my face.

"Other side," he said.

"Oh," I said and overshot so I was scratching above.

"No, here," he said, shifting his book bag and touching my face for the first time. I smiled at him.

"Are you going to the cafeteria soon?" I asked hoping it would sound casual. "I could use a dinner break."

"I, uh," he hesitated. In that hesitation, I understood how out of reach he was. In that hesitation, I was hooked. "I actually have to go to a screening for class."

"Okay," I said, hoping it wouldn't sound devastated.

When he was gone, Kaitlin was at my side. "You know he has a girlfriend, right?"

She didn't think I was that kind of girl. I didn't either.

I still don't.

"I heard she took the semester off. Besides, it was just dinner." I said. I ignored the face I knew she was making and went back to filling in the sky.

Olivia was leaving for Florence. Her three weeks in Siena were done. She would live with a family. She and Suzie agreed to be roommates in Firenze as well.

Olivia and I went to the Duomo because she wanted to go to the cathedral one more time before she left. My group had already been to the Duomo twice. I knew more about architecture, the painters the Lorenzetti brothers and the ancient tribe of Etruscans who founded Siena and their legacy than I ever could have anticipated. Everywhere I turned I encountered a fresco by some famous painter that Kaitlin would have loved. It was mostly lost on me.

As Olivia walked around the cathedral looking at the artwork, I could see that Olivia's group had also been inundated with "culture." We started pointing things out to each other, trying to outdo each other with our respective facts about what statement the artist was trying to make through Mary and baby Jesus' expression. We speculated as to why Jesus was sometimes a sour-faced baby and sometimes a mini adult in Mary's arms. We tried to keep straight faces as we spoke as academically as possible. Then I started making up facts about the artist Giotto and Olivia lost it, drawing stern looks from the Sienese women praying in the pews.

"*Andiamo*," Olivia said, laughing hard. "I'm hungry."

"I could eat a fresco," I said as she pulled me out of the Duomo and we stood giggling on the steps.

We found an *osteria* behind the Duomo. The people in the restaurant were so friendly to us that we knew we wanted to stay. We didn't even need to look at the menu before deciding to sit down. The host led us downstairs into a cave. He sat us in a private alcove.

"It's beautiful," I said, looking up at the cool brown walls.

"It's like an Etruscan tomb," said Olivia, not meaning to invoke the game again. The waitress brought us glasses of prosecco for no reason. I looked at Olivia, confused, but when Olivia shrugged, it was good enough for me. We clinked our glasses together and said "chin chin" like we heard the Italians say in all the bars. I drank the bubbly white wine and smiled.

We ordered crostini and bruscetta and declared it the best we had ever had. Olivia ordered a bottle of Chianti, and we each got some sort of pasta that we didn't quite understand. There was no rush to this meal or to any meal I experienced in Italy. Olivia confessed a secret that she hadn't even told Suzie. She kissed one of the *milatario* that she and Suzie met one night at the Re Artu bar when I was out with Janine and Michelle.

"How come Suzie didn't, you know, see you kiss him?"

"I waited till she went to the bathroom. Now he's off to Sicily."

When the plates of pasta came we ordered another bottle of wine and I was sure that we were glowing from sulfites and happiness. We each took a deep breath of our food and sighed, then smiled, realizing we did the same thing. Olivia got a type of ravioli, and I got thin, small, twisted pasta. We both got sauces made of truffles. The pasta was not drenched in sauce but barely coated. Still, it tasted heavy and rich. It was heaven.

"This meal tastes of everything that is good in the earth," I said, knowing it would make her laugh. I felt this urgent need to communicate with someone who understood me in my language.

Olivia told me that Gaetano called her hotel the day after we met him.

"I don't know why. We weren't even that nice to them," I said. I was jealous that she had a phone, something to keep her in touch with the outside world. She didn't have to hope as I did that people remembered me when I ran into them on the street.

"It's not how nice we are; it's how *bella*." She accentuated the syllables. "You have no idea how hard it is to try to talk to these people over the phone. They just keep saying English words over and over like they have that disorder."

I giggled. Olivia was becoming beautiful to me. I was getting too accustomed to her looks, to the mole on her lip, her straight dark bangs and the scar on her temple. That was how I could gauge the strength of our friendship. Her features were no longer strange but familiar and comforting.

Olivia wondered what would happen if Suzie and Kurt keep going at the rate they were. "It's not like school; I can't just run down the hall and sleep in someone else's bed."

"Have they done it yet?" I asked.

"No," she rolled her eyes. "They haven't even kissed. She's one of those."

"A prude," I said.

"Virgin," she said.

"Wow," I said. "I can't imagine she will be much longer in this country with all this," I gestured to the wine.

"I know," Olivia said, mopping up the last of her truffle sauce with a piece of crusty bread.

For dessert, we had cappuccino and tiramisu and *zuppa inglese*, rolling each creamy dessert flavor around our mouths. I was falling into a food delirium. We asked for the check, but they brought us *cantucci* and *vin santo* instead. We were already feeling drunk, but we dipped the little biscuits into the dessert wine. When *il conto* came, it really wasn't all that expensive.

"We could come here every week or at least every time you visit," I said, hoping I didn't sound as desperate as I felt. Maybe she wouldn't return. Who knew what Firenze had in store for her? I might be left with no one to laugh with, trapped in someone else's language.

Olivia invited me to go to the bar Re Artu with her for a last drink with her group. I didn't want to spend time talking to all the people that were leaving. Besides, my tiny bed was actually inviting with my belly full of this much food. But I walked her around the *campo* over to the bar. The streets were crowded with people walking *in giro*. These walks *in giro*—basically just walking around the town—were the pastime of the Italians before they went to their bars or café. We stopped in front of the bar.

"*Ci vediamo presto*," she said. We will see each other soon. "It's only an hour away on the Pullman or train. You have the number. Call in a few days."

And it saddened me a little that the first thing I thought was that I didn't know if I could handle the conversations that would be involved in getting those Pullman or train tickets. Getting to Florence was another maze I would have to run through.

"*Si, certo*," I agreed, smiling. We hugged goodbye, and she went into the bar.

I started to walk home and noticed that a group of people was gathered outside a *paninoteca* on Via Independenza. There were two men fighting viciously. I couldn't see their faces but I saw Dino and Giovanni in the crowd. They spotted me as I went over to them. They kissed me on both cheeks before turning their eyes back the fight.

"*Hai visto Gaetano?*" Dino asked, gesturing toward the fight. I followed his gaze and realized it was Gaetano holding on to some guy's nose, drawing blood. He looked like an animal and had a nasty scratch on his forehead. The friends of his victim pulled the nosebleeder away.

Gaetano bent at the waist, put his hands on his thighs and breathed out. Dino called to him, and Gaetano looked up to see us. He came over immediately, practically panting, his breath coming white into the brisk night air. Dino said something to him in dialect, and Gaetano nodded. He didn't kiss me; he was bloody and sweaty. He took a cigarette from Giovanni. "How are you, Gabi?"

"Fine, and you?" In English, I would have made a joke about the fight he had gotten into. In English, I could try and be a little witty in lieu of this situation. In Italian, I was a dumb girl who didn't say much and kept her voice low.

His answer made his friends laugh, but I couldn't understand him. I assumed he said something like, "I'm good, but you should see the other guy."

"What happened?" I asked. In the distance was the sound of sirens. It was *polizia* or *caribinieri*. I still didn't know the difference. Only their tiny cars were allowed to come down those streets at night. Gaetano took my hand. He was still holding it when his friends said that he needed to leave.

"Will you call me?" He asked this twice, in both of our languages

"*Gaetano, dai!*" His friends were anxious. They started to tug his dirty sleeve. He was still holding my hand. He wouldn't leave until I answered.

"Will you call me?" I didn't want to, but the dumb girl who couldn't say much and found it necessary to smooth things over answered to appease the anxious friends.

"*Si.*"

"*Sicura?*" Was I sure? Of course not. I didn't have a phone. I had nothing.

"*Si,*" I lied. And then he smiled and ran off with his friends, leaving me alone on the suddenly empty street.

I crossed the *campo* before the *polizia* arrived.

5.

Janine had a boyfriend named Roberto. She met him at the *enoteca*. He was from Sicily, and he had a car. He could also speak English, which made life a lot easier for Janine. He was the ideal boyfriend for her.

One night, I was sitting at the table in the hallway working on my *compito* when Janine came up to me. I looked up from my homework. She didn't say it right away, but I could tell almost immediately from the bright smile that she wanted something.

"How's it going, Gab?" I hated to be called that. Michelle in some of her relaxed moments had taken to calling me G, but Gab I hated. I didn't say that, though.

"*Bene.*" We used the little Italian we knew like slang in the house.

"What are you up to *stasera*?" Janine liked to inflect all the Italian dramatically.

"Tonight? Not much. I feel sort of sick." Almost a month of cold weather had taken its toll on me. I was sniffling and my head felt stuffy.

"Oh, that's too bad," said Janine. She put her hand on my shoulder. I wanted to believe she genuinely felt bad for me, but I saw the gesture for what it was, a means to an end. "Because I was going to see if you want to go out with me and Michelle and Roberto and two of his friends to that club Tendenza."

"I probably shouldn't." Though actually moving, dancing, not just sitting sounded good.

"C'mon, don't be a nerd." She made one of her funny faces. "I'm not going to ask Lisa."

She wouldn't care so much if it weren't to please a guy. But I did want to check out that club and it would be easier to go in a car. I could be resting in America, hiding in my bed as I had in the past. Now I was in Italy, and I reminded myself that I shouldn't miss any experience. "All right."

"Nice, G," Michelle said walking through the hallway. She was eating an apple. It was probably one of the only things she ate that day. I suspected that Michelle puked in my bathroom so Janine wouldn't hear it. Michelle trailed the scent of perfume behind her. That smell reminded me of Kaitlin. It made me think of times when I was happy and we went out together, just to have fun, not to prove anything or to drown any sorrows.

"Yeah, it's going to be kickass. So I was wondering if I could look at your clothes and see if I want to borrow anything." At last, Janine made the real request.

"Sure, check it out. I might want to check out your stuff, too."

"No prob, Gab," said Janine ready to begin her search-and-recovery mission. She was already in Lisa's room when she added, "If you think you'll find something that fits you."

I heard Lisa giggle. Lisa thrived on any insults that were not directed at her. Janine hadn't invited her out, and Lisa was going to be bitter. It was worse that Janine decided to model all of my clothes that she liked for Lisa. Lisa complimented everything. She was hoping for an invite, hoping at last to get out of the life she has chosen, sitting in our empty apartment, studying hard to show off to people who didn't like her.

I tried on everything I liked in Janine's closet, too. My larger chest stretched out Janine's sexy cheap tight black shirts. I defiantly buttoned up a red wraparound skirt. It was a little tight around the hips, but I didn't care. I didn't appreciate her comments.

I settled on one of her dresses. It was tight and gray but styled like a schoolgirl uniform. I could wear my own black shirt under it, and it would fit me even shorter than it fit Janine. I felt like looking good tonight.

I went back into my room for more primping. I shut the door so Lisa, who was pacing nervously around the apartment, could not prey on me. She kept sighing and mentioning how she needed to work on her American celebrations essay, hoping if she sighed loud enough, someone would give her another option. It didn't work. At last, Lisa came sheepishly into my room. I continued lining my lips.

"So you're going out with them." From the way Lisa said *them*, I knew she had already glorified them. They were the cool kids she was never going to be. I began applying the gloss with more care than usual. I considered wearing eyeliner.

"Mmm-hmm."

"Did they ask you?"

"Well, I didn't just tag along. I don't do that." I turned to Lisa, holding her eyes. Her forehead was full of acne. It had to be stress.

"Can I come?" No one with any sense of pride would ask this when they are so obviously not wanted. Is she liked somewhere else, I wondered. Is there anywhere this girl has friends? I finished my bottom lip before answering. I almost pitied her. She was just trying to impress Janine when she giggled at her comment. I should be the bigger person. I should understand that she was lonely and desperate. But I wasn't a saint or a psychiatrist.

"I don't know, Lisa. It's not my thing. It's Janine's. It's her boyfriend. You should ask her." I tried to make my voice softer, kinder. She looked at me, pleadingly. I tried not to think about all the times she corrected me and acted like a know-it-all. "All right, I'll come with you."

"C'mon," Lisa left my room in a hurry, glancing back to make sure I followed her out through the kitchen into the better bedroom, where Janine and Michelle slept. Michelle was checking her face out carefully in the mirror. Janine was in the bathroom. I pretended to need to borrow some perfume. Lisa asked Michelle if she could go out with us. Maybe she wasn't as socially inept as I thought; she was picking the nicer one.

Michelle was nervous, not sure how to answer, but she didn't have to because Janine emerged from the bathroom. She was dressed more conservatively than she usually was for going out. Roberto liked Janine to dress like this. Janine said he was traditional. He wanted her to be modest, even though he liked the fact that he could fuck her the first time they met.

"You can't come, Lisa, there just isn't room in the car," Janine took charge while giving me a quick look up and down. She turned to Michelle. "Do I look okay?"

"You look good." Michelle said, for once barely giving Janine any attention. She wanted to look good tonight too and kept shifting her outfit in the mirror.

Lisa looked at me. Again with the pleading. This was where I was supposed to intervene. Fine.

"I'm sure we can make room in the car," I said. I looked over at Michelle. She let herself meet my eyes for exactly a second, before glancing quickly at Janine and then back at her reflection.

"Do you want to switch with her?" Janine asked me. "I mean, there is only so much room in the car."

"We can sit on laps," I tried. I was starting to fret that I was going to lose my chance to get out of this freezing apartment.

"That's with sitting on laps," Janine said. She smiled at Lisa. "Next time, Lisa. Gabriella is already ready, anyway. Maybe sometime we'll go out when it isn't a school night."

A good woman would offer to stay with her. A better one might switch. But I was neither and the idea of staying with her in the frigid apartment or, worse, staying by myself was more than I could take. I looked at her and tried to convey my apologies.

Lisa left the room. Janine had already moved on.

"We should have drunk something before shouldn't we? Now we'll be totally sober," she said, looking at me because she thought like everyone else that I had some sort of high tolerance because of the big beers I bought. "Fuck it, they'll buy us drinks."

They were waiting. Roberto's friends were both shorter than Michelle and me, but we were instructed to sit on their laps in the backseat of the tiny car; Gennaro (under me) and Mauro (under Michelle). It was true enough about the room in the car. All the cars in this country seemed smaller. But I liked being packed into the car like this, the smell of the male cologne, testosterone. My sense of smell was sharpening. I was picking up not just people's scents but their intentions.

The Tendenza was like nowhere I had ever been. It was a giant warehouse space with people dancing everywhere. Even Michelle and Janine, who went clubbing at home, were in shock. Everyone was given a number when they went in that they had to put on. The bouncers pinned the numbers close to our breasts, and the Italian boys put drinks in our hands. Roberto unpinned Janine's number and put it on the waistband of her skirt, the skirt she borrowed from me. We downed our first drinks and got others at the bar before heading onto the dance floor. The Italian boys paid for everything

The numbers were projected on a screen, and if you saw your number, you had a note waiting from an admirer. It was a literary meat market. The club was blowing purple smoke onto the dancers. The Italian boys were delighted. They kept saying "*è bello, è bello, no?*" They loved it. I wished I could say *surreal* in Italian. I thought that it was probably something obvious like *surealistico* or something, but if it wasn't I would have to try to explain it to them. They would want to understand me; it would be complicated. Sometimes it was better not to even bother trying to communicate unless you had a lot of time.

Janine started dancing seductively against Roberto. The rest of us danced on the outskirts. I liked these boys, liked that they didn't try to get too close. Michelle and I danced closer together. There were also scantily clad professionals, mostly women, who were dancing on a stage in the center of the club.

I felt Janine's hand on my shoulder. She was pointing up toward the screen with the numbers. I looked at the number pinned to my shirt. My number was flashing across the screen, and there was Michelle's, as yet no sign of Janine's. I was really curious about what the letters might say. Michelle couldn't contain her excitement.

"Come on, G, let's check out our letters." Michelle was drunk already, but her enthusiasm was clear and contagious. She pulled me over to the bar for another drink and then onto the stage, where you got the letters. It was mobbed, but we each found a pile of letters for our numbers. I translated the letters for both of us. They had a common theme, *I saw you from across the floor. You are beautiful, I would like to meet you.* As I read these to Michelle I put on a fake Italian accent and we both laughed, hysterically.

Janine ran over, pretended to look annoyed.

"I got one of those letters. Roberto is pissed. He's so Italian."

"Look, G, our numbers are up again," said Michelle, smiling. "Let's check our stash."

We both had bigger piles than before. Janine had three. I translated these again in the same accent. There were some new admirers and some from the last batch who were upset that we didn't respond. Michelle enjoyed this a little too much, and Janine took her lack of letters a little too personally.

"It's because I have to wear my fucking number on my skirt. He'll be mad if I don't." Janine was making excuses, trying to convince herself more than us. Michelle nodded.

"You should get another drink, Janine, and then you won't care what he thinks." She didn't sound as sympathetic to Janine as usual. Michelle was different tonight, more independent, no longer simply Janine's appendage. "Let's get another drink, G."

When we got back to the guys, they looked at us sheepishly. I accused them of writing the letters, but they denied it. They asked us if we want to smoke hash.

"Do we want to smoke some hash?" I translated for Michelle.

"Sure. I mean I guess. I never smoked hash, have you?"

"Once," I said, "it fucked me up. Though it may have been because I was doing a lot of other stuff. But I think it can really fuck you up."

"Let's get fucked up." Michelle said, widening her eyes. I had the feeling that she would have been up for anything. "Let's do it."

And so the four of us went off into a little dark corner with a low lounge. We smoked a cigarette laced with a bunch of hash. Homemade by Gennaro. We passed it around. Mauro taught Michelle how to inhale it.

The last time I smoked hash, I was a wreck. I literally could not move. This time I began to feel a haze, but it worked with the lights and scented smoke that filled the club. I suspected from Michelle's expression that she felt the same way. We went back to the floor and danced together, not speaking, not smiling, just moving. This was the closest I had ever felt to Michelle. Those times we sat awkwardly together in bars we lacked this energy that floated between us as we danced now

When Janine found us, I didn't care about anything. I realized that I usually was aware of my looks around her, because of the way she always looked me up and down. Now, when she did it, it meant nothing. I just wanted to get back to dancing. I couldn't focus on her face. Michelle could handle it.

"We're gonna go. His ex-girlfriend is here". Across the dance floor I saw Roberto talking furiously to an Italian girl with long brown hair. She had that regal look that I noticed on some of the women in Siena.

"Are you guys ready?" Janine expected us to be. I nodded, assuming that Michelle would want to leave. But Michelle hesitated.

"I'm having fun, Janine. I don't feel like watching you guys fight all night. G, don't you want to stay?" I didn't really want to get involved, but I wanted to stay. I was getting fucked up, and I didn't want to feel Janine's bad jealous vibe.

"Well, how are you guys going to get home? Roberto has the car."

"There's a bus. Pam took it she told me," Michelle said.

Janine shook her head and said, "Pam." Information not shared between them. It might have been the first time that Janine realized that Michelle was her own person and not just a sidekick. Maybe the first time for Michelle, too. "Fine then. Stay."

She walked away from us. I looked at Michelle, but Michelle betrayed nothing, she looked like any other pretty fucked-up foreign girl. So Michelle and I began to dance again.

"We are leaving," said Mauro to Michelle. It was half a question. I started to translate for Michelle, but she understood him.

"We aren't leaving," said Michelle in hesitant Italian. Mauro, the spokesperson, turned to Gennaro to confer. They were confused. Michelle said her next sentence in English but slowly loudly, using her hands. "We are not going. We dance. Janine and Roberto go away to fight and..." Here, she shrugged her shoulders, making us laugh.

"We stay, too," said Gennaro, suddenly confident in his language skills. He grabbed my hands and led me back onto the dance floor. "We dance."

And we danced to the electronic music peppered with dirty English phrases. We danced and smelled the sweet sweat of everyone in the club, and even though we saw our numbers going by again, we didn't bother to check the letters. Our minds were heavy from the hash, and we could only concentrate on dancing. It was wonderful to be this far from my thoughts. I could have done this every day. I was dancing in the purple smoke, and everything fit together.

When the lights came on in the club, my feet were killing me and my mouth was dry. I begged the *barista* for a glass of water. I shared it with Michelle like it was some great dance prize. I hadn't really thought through how we could get home. I just believed that Michelle was certain of the bus. It was not like me to take someone else's word for it. I only agreed to get away from Janine.

"So how are we going to get home?" I asked. "Is there really a bus?"

"There was. I don't know how late it runs," Michelle said. I didn't think my feet could handle the walk home to Siena. I had no idea where we were, just that it took us twenty minutes in a car. I wondered if I could find one of the couches and pass out until morning.

Gennaro and Mauro brought another guy over to meet us. He was dressed formally in a suit and tie, his face was sweaty and he kept wiping it with a handkerchief.

"I am Sandrino." He shook both of our hands and kissed us on both cheeks. I wasn't sure I was in the mood to be charming.

"Sandrino will port us home in *macchina*," said Mauro in his broken English. It was all going to work out. Sandrino had a car, God love him. Michelle and I smiled and said, *grazie*. I tried to show my appreciation by working the e in the word as I had heard the Italians do all month.

In the car, Gennaro and Mauro insisted that they resume positions with us on their laps, even though there was enough room in this car not to. We maintained our pairing by name. This satisfied everyone. Gennaro and I sat up front with Sandrino. I rolled down the window, stuck my hand out into the sky. I slipped off my shoes, and Gennaro called me *americana* and said something to Sandrino that I couldn't understand.

I heard Michelle and Mauro in the backseat; heard Mauro enjoying whatever was happening. Sounds of zippers and elastic. Michelle would puke this all up later. Another finger in another hole.

But I would be fine if I kept my face to the window, turned into the blackness of the night. Then I wouldn't have to see what they were doing. I wouldn't have minded kissing Gennaro, he was sweet enough, but then I would have had to turn my face. Besides, I liked the way it was, his hand tightening and releasing on the space above my hip, fingers close to my breast. He whispered in my ear, against my neck, soothing the ring from the club's loud music. I was *bella* and the song was *bella*, no? That was what he said. And I believed him for a minute that everything was beautiful.

The last time I smoked hash back at school it was a dirty brown ball in a pipe. It was not cut with any tobacco. I could not move then. Kaitlin propped me against a wall and I stayed. I watched Kaitlin drinking and dancing, getting on with her life. I knew that if anyone came up to me against the wall, Kaitlin would be over immediately. I put my trust in Kaitlin.

Kaitlin took me home that night. I asked Kaitlin why Jonas didn't care about me anymore. It was the only time I said something like that. The only time I admitted to anyone how much I hurt. Kaitlin shook her head. How could she explain it? Hadn't she tried to warn me? She stripped off my clothes, leaving on the bra and panties he would have taken of. She let me stay in her bed, the bottom bunk in the dorm room we shared. I wanted Kaitlin to climb in next to me, to feel someone else there, but Kaitlin climbed to the top. She never answered my question. Maybe there was no answer

Sandrino dropped us off in Piazza del Mercato. Kisses all around and Mauro got out of the car and tried to impress us with his English. He said hi to both of us as we left, thinking this was a true translation of *ciao*. Michelle and I didn't bother to explain it to him but laughed all the way up Banca di Sopra. The city was empty. It was ours.

We stopped at the statue of the she-wolf and took off our shoes.

The cobblestones were freezing. We ran giggling through the streets. Bruised and blistered feet against stone. Our sweat dried cold on our skin. We smelled freshly baking bread, and we peered through a window at a baker. When he waved at us, we scampered off. We didn't feel like ourselves. We had too good a time with strangers. We, too, were strangers to each other.

In the apartment, we drank more water and I left Michelle alone in the kitchen to find and eat whatever she would.

In my room I felt lucky that I was back in my bed, that Sandrino had a car, and that I was in this country far away from anyone who really knew me. I was happy that for a little while, with my head turned out to fresh air, I felt beautiful.

I fell asleep before I could hear any of the noises from my roommates that might make me sad. I fell asleep before Crazy could remind me that I wasn't okay after all, that I never would be again.

FEBBRAIO

6.

Sometimes in the mornings a ghost awakened me. This ghost was tricky. He convinced me over and over again that he was really there. Breath against my ear, fingers clutching my arm, hand moving up the inside of my leg.

Wake up! Wake up!

I refused, shook my head, sometimes I cried. I never wanted to open my eyes. I didn't want to find it was the draft from the window, a twisted blanket, my own hand. I begged him not to bother me, to just go away. The ghost continued. *Think of how nice it will be, me here with you, here in your bed. Don't you want to see me? How much fun could we have?* And I fell for it always. Holding my breath, I opened my eyes expectantly to see I was alone, of course. It was only Crazy up to her old tempting tricks.

He didn't come every morning, but he did come. And I began to feel a sense of normalcy in that bed, whether he was there or not.

I wished that Jonas was one of those boys I could have hooked up with and gotten over like it was nothing but a warm end to a happy night. He wasn't, though. Things started slowly, and I found that I liked him, talking to him, the way he phrased things, the random song lyrics he sang, always meeting my eye. The time I asked him why he was a history major and he sang, "You don't know your past, you won't know your future."

After that time in the student union when he turned down my dinner invitation, we had a class together. On cold mornings a bus ran from our dorm to the class at 9 A.M. It took longer to get to class on the bus, but you avoided the cold. It was one of the prerequisites everyone had to take. It was a dumb class that pretended to be about biology, but was really a way to get us info on contraception and STDs.

I waited for him on those mornings, letting buses pass until the last minute, but he always came. We sat together and talked. Our travel mugs of flavored coffee scented our ride. Side by side, I made him laugh and he made me laugh and I don't remember most of the things we said to each other, just the laughing.

And then one morning, I overslept and hustled down to the bus stop as a bus passed before me. Cursing, I thought about running after it, trying to catch it at the next stop, but nothing said he would even be on that bus. Why should I be out of breath when I got on the bus at the wrong stop? When the bus passed in front of me, I looked at the bus stop and there he was waiting. He was waiting for me, too.

"You looked worried there for a minute," he said.

"I was," I admitted.

"Don't worry." We stood so close to each other then, grinning. I should have been worried, but I wanted to believe.

And then I knew that everything wasn't just on my side and it was only a matter of time, if I waited as I had all those mornings, something would happen between us.

There were no buses in Siena to make the frigid five-minute walk to school any easier. The days slipped into a little routine. It was not exactly a comfortable routine, because I never knew what sort of unanswerable question was going to be presented to me and in what ways I would make a small fool out of myself, but at least I had an idea what the day would be like.

I dressed quickly in the cold. Sometimes when I had a lot of time, I made an espresso in the *macchinetta* loading it with sugar, but mostly I drank instant American coffee in the morning. Michelle, who lived on coffee, showed me how to make it taste better by loading it with cinnamon. For the rest of my life, I will call cinnamon *canella* the way we did in that apartment.

I was learning to cook for myself, too. My meals were simple, pasta with fresh vegetables or vegetables on the pizza crust I got at the supermarket. I relied heavily on the delicious Tuscan olive oil. It made everything taste better. I stopped at the COOP supermarket once a week to stock up on basics. Every other day, except Wednesdays when everything was closed in the afternoons, I went to the *forno* for bread or the *frutti vendolo* for vegetables. I tried not to say too much and double-checked in the *dizionario* how to ask for exactly what I wanted.

Sometimes, I felt normal, almost hopeful. But other days, because of the weather and because of the strange looks people gave me when I spoke, I felt like an alien. Sometimes, several people would gather behind a counter and try to guess what I was talking about. Once one of the men at the *frutti vendolo* started speaking to me in German, assuming that was my accent. When I explained that I was *americana* and not *tedesca*, he looked at me like I was just stupid and didn't even understand my own language. The easiest thing to do on days like that was to hide out in my room, write in my journal and contemplate what I would make to eat the next day and if I would feel better.

But often, I couldn't take the cold apartment. I felt stifled and so I walked in spite of the weather. My walk was no longer my own. I used to walk with confidence. Jonas said he could see me all the way across the quad. My walk was something he liked about me, and now I didn't have it anymore.

Instead of swinging my arms, I clasped my hands together. I didn't trust Crazy not to sneak up next to me and take my hand as she once had. I didn't trust my actions. I no longer believed I could gauge who people were. My instincts had failed me before.

My roommates and I usually didn't go to class together. Janine cut class and had a habit of trying to convince everyone else to do the same. Lisa was always early. Michelle ran in the morning to avoid the attention she got from men when she ran in the afternoon, so she was always late.

I felt like my class was pointless, that I was never going to learn the language. The words I heard, the grammar rules were all white noise floating around me.

I wondered if babies felt like this when they didn't know what the adults were saying.

I liked my *professoressa* Signora Laza. She was *sienese sienese*, truly from Siena. Her neighborhood was the *contrada* of *bruco*, the caterpillar. She prided herself, as most Sienese did, on her *contrada* and on the fact that in Siena, the Italian language was truest. While other regions had dialects, the Italian they spoke in Siena was closest to standard Italian.

Signora Laza must have thought I was pretty dumb. I was never a bad student in my language, but in her class I dreaded being called on. When I had to read aloud, it was a disaster. Signora Laza constantly corrected me, looking at me over her glasses. It was humbling to be one of the worst students in her class.

In the language lab, we all wore headphones, listened to lessons, and repeated words into microphones. We sat in our separate cocoon of desks, connected to our weird audio players. It was bizarre and Big Brother-ish. Signora Laza could listen in to whomever she wanted, and her voice often came into my headphones, correcting my pronunciation. I was always on edge and ready. I constantly snuck glances over my partition at the top of Signora Laza's head, but she was busy bent down, trolling for mistakes. And there was no warning when she would get to me. I was a language experiment gone wrong.

In addition to Lucy, there was another American, Pete, in my class, but he wasn't from my group. There was a Greek opera singer, a beautiful aging German car saleswoman, a married artsy Japanese couple, three Koreans and two women from Spain. I tried to talk to them all at the obligatory *pausa* where we went to the café for cappuccino. I was constantly amazed that we could communicate in a language that belonged to none of us. Though I wanted to get to know all these new faces, I mostly spent the *pausa* chatting with Lucy and trying to secure from her that I understood what was going on.

After the *pausa*, class went quicker. Sometimes we had a surprise quiz that I suspected gave Signora Laza a thrill. And then class was over by noon and I had the day to myself unless I had my culture class with the group.

The culture class was led by Arturo and was either an hour and a half lesson on Sienese culture and history or a brisk walk to one of the myriad freezing churches to stare at frescoes and Gothic architecture.

Kaitlin would have loved it, she was an Art History major, but to me, it was all dates and names and different meaningless design eras. Sometimes I wanted to block out all the facts that were constantly provided. I would have been just as happy to walk around and look at the churches without knowing anything. I would have liked to stare into the eyes of the various depictions of Mary and Jesus and try to draw my own conclusions.

Slowly but surely, however, almost by osmosis, the names of these artists became ingrained in my head. I could have led a tour around Siena and wowed people with my knowledge. But as far as I knew, no one was coming to visit.

Everything came to a boil one day when I was sitting at the dining room table trying to conjugate verbs into all the nineteen different tenses. My quiet was shattered by the sounds of pots crashing onto the floor.

It was Janine, who had discovered Lisa's dishes in the sink and threw them across the kitchen.

"Lisa, you fucking *porca butana*, can't you clean up your shit?" I had to give Janine credit, she spoke Italian for shit, but she knew how to curse in a variety of dialects, thanks to the men she fucked. Half the time I had no idea who she was calling what, but she managed a convincing accent.

Lisa ran out of the hall that was her room. She was shaking and on the verge of tears. She was not used to conflict. This kind of venom and volume intimidated me, too. "I was going to clean them."

"Fucking when?" Janine screamed. "You need fucking twenty pots to make that shitty canned soup you buy, and I can't even have a plate of pasta."

"Could you guys lower your voices? I'm trying to study," I said. Janine barely glanced at me.

"I'm sick and tired of everyone being such a slob around here."

"I clean my dishes," I said. This was true most of the time and luckily, had been that night. "And be careful with those pots. I don't want to have to buy more."

"I know, I know, you're on a budget," Janine said, smirking. I shook my head and turned back to my book, trying to decide if I should just go hide out in my room like Michelle was doing.

We had been letting things go for a while at Via Stalloreggi. Anonymous messages were left around the apartment about the state of cleanliness. Our floor was sticky and dirty. Occasionally, one of us got fed up and bitterly cleaned up for someone else. I knew this row had been coming for a while. I just didn't want to deal

"Well, you take toilet paper out of our bathroom so you won't have to buy it," Lisa said. She sounded like a child tattling to her kindergarten teacher. This comment was directed as much to me as to Janine. I was supposed to rise up and join forces against Janine.

"You are such a cheap ugly bitch, Lisa," Janine said before I could decide whether or not I was going to join in. Then Janine stomped to her room and slammed the door. Lisa looked at me for a second and then went to the kitchen to clean up all her pots and wonder if what Janine said was true.

After that, we had a tense house meeting to set up a schedule for cleaning and supply buying. We divvied up responsibilities and vowed that everyone would clean their own dishes. We stuck to it for about three days before we all started slipping.

And someone started stealing food. We were all buying our own food. And we all complained of food theft, but someone was lying. It wasn't me. It could have been Michelle, who was always making excuses not to eat. I doubted that it was Lisa because she had an annoying habit of asking to sample whatever anyone was eating. Whether it was a freshly made meal or a piece of bread that I was certain she knew the taste of, she wanted to try everyone else's food. Behind her back we called her the "Can I have a bite?" girl.

I started thinking about carrying my food around in my backpack the same way I carried my journal, but it seemed a little extreme.

Every day, I longed for letters from home. Finally, the first group came in a giant batch. I get seven letters at once at the university. They were all sent on different days; two were sent ten days apart. I got news of Kaitlin settling in to Paris and other letters from friends back at college.

From then on, I got mail a lot. Sometimes letters came twice a day and at other times there was nothing for days. *Sciopero,* said the constantly changing person behind the desk when there was a drought. They used the word for strike as if it could explain away anything.

"How can they go on strike so often?" I asked the roommates.

"All of Italy goes on strike all the time; it's very political here," Lisa explained pretentiously. She fancied herself in touch with the political climate of Italy. She flaunted that she read *Espresso,* the newsmagazine, while the rest of us—when we had extra money—picked up Italian women's magazines that gave you freebies like lip gloss. I didn't believe that anyone in Italy understood the political situation, including the Italians.

My roommates resented all the mail I got. Sometimes, they checked under my name at the *università* and reported I had four letters waiting. I started to enjoy sitting at the table with my letters piled beside me, fingering them as Janine sipped cups of tea, watching me because we had no TV. In a way, I flaunted the letters. It was proof that people back home missed me. It was almost a challenge to the rest of the roommates. A reminder that eventually we would be home and I would be back in the circle of people who loved me. I didn't like those thoughts I had, but this weird female way was becoming a part of my world. I was turning again into someone I didn't know.

In the letters I wrote back home, I focused on only the good things. I described how beautiful my apartment was and my classes at the *università*. I told them that people were nice. That really meant nothing, it was so abstract, but I knew this was what my friends wanted to hear. I mentioned that I was constantly at a bar or eating a delicious meal. These little tidbits I would like to get back to Jonas. I want him to hear in passing what a good time I was having, how wonderful it all was.

I wanted to believe that across an ocean, I could still affect him.

One day, Gaetano was waiting for me outside of the *università* on his *vespa*. It was freezing, and I wondered how long he'd been there studying the *studenti*, looking for me. His leather jacket couldn't possibly keep him that warm.

"*Ciao*." I said.

"You didn't call." He revved the bike.

"I know. It was Olivia that had your number. Remember? Because I don't have a phone." I offered him excuses in my muddled, confused Italian.

"*Quanto sei forba*," he said and I didn't understand. "Let's get *panini*."

"I have to some stuff to do," I said, trying the Italian. "Plus, I need to do my homework."

"Dinner, then. I can help you with your homework," he said slowly so I would understand. "I will pick you up at your apartment at eight."

Before I could think of a reason not to go, Lisa was beside us, speaking to both of us in Italian. She was managing to work the *passato remoto* that she learned in class into the conversation, even though it didn't seem appropriate. When I looked at Gaetano, he rolled his eyes, which made me laugh.

"*Devo andare via, ragazze*," he said to us, making an excuse to leave. He looked at me. "*Ci vediamo stasera*."

"Okay, see you tonight," I agreed. Lisa reminded me of all the reasons I didn't want to be home. "I'll bring my homework."

He came early and laughed at my bare feet when I opened the door. Michelle and Lisa had just gotten into a fight about Lisa making a mess of the stove. A large part of the fight consisted of slamming pots and sighing. I couldn't wait to get out the apartment.

"I'll just get my shoes," I said, leaving him in the dining room to be interrogated by Lisa, who perked up at the prospect of showing off more Italian. He looked me up and down, approvingly when I came back to the kitchen, but I ignored it.

He took me to a brick-oven pizzeria on Viale Cortatone, near the Upim department store. We ordered a pizza with a fried egg on top, and he got a bottle of wine. He stared at me the whole time, even when he was eating, but he spoke to me in a way that I could understand. He spoke slowly, pausing to see if I followed, attempting to find the English word when I didn't. He used his hands a lot.

He described his medical studies. It seemed kind of easy compared to what I thought American universities were like. He didn't have class all the time. And it was hard to believe that someone who chain-smoked the way he did could ever be a doctor.

He told me about his town in the south of Italy. It was at the arch of the foot, he said (well, showed me, tracing the boot that is Italy on the white tablecloth with his fingers). In his town, life was simpler he said, people were kind and more open than people up north. There were never any plans made; you just saw people walking in passing, *in giro*, and you were happy about it.

"You must see my country," he said. I was confused about how he said the word; I thought meant country, *paese*, to mean his town, but after awhile I got it. To him, it was a whole different country; he wanted me to understand that. He raised his fork up at me as he chewed; he was holding it in his left hand. "You don't want to see my country?"

"Sure, but you know," I spoke Italian slowly, trying not to say it wrong, "I have a boyfriend."

"I know."

"Okay, good. So you understand I just want to be friends right? That's okay. If we just go out as friends?"

"I have no friends that are women only, girlfriends." I looked down at my pizza. This was a mistake. I should go home. It was too bad because I was starting to have fun, starting to follow. He was an attractive man, but I wasn't ready to be with anyone yet. I just didn't know if my body could stand to be touched by anyone else. I didn't know if my mind could handle another relationship.

"You know why American girls come to Italy?" he asked at last.

I wanted to say in my most sarcastic way, "I have no idea." But I didn't know how to convey that the way I wanted, so instead I said something I was more used to saying, "No, I don't know."

"There are three reasons," he said, holding up his thumb and first two fingers. He paused, trying to play up the drama. I didn't say anything. "Do you want to know?"

"If you want to tell me." He laughed and shook his hand at me.

"The reasons are..." He cleared his throat.

"Before I die," I tried to say or something like it. I could tell he understood what I meant. And I was glad to, at last, get my point across in another language.

"Number one to buy shoes," he said.

"I understand that."

"To say they have." I shook my head, rolled my eyes.

"And finally," he switched to English so I could really understand, "to fuck Italian boy."

I took a sip of my wine. I wondered if I was ever going to get my homework done.

"What do you think of that?" he asked. He was quite satisfied with himself.

"I don't know." The place we were in was too nice to be talking about this. "Who told you that? An Australian?"

"Well, what is your reason?"

"If you want me to pick one from those choices, I guess, for the experience. I'm Italian-American. I wanted to see this country."

"This isn't your country. Your people aren't from this country."

"*Stesa*." I said, certain I was screwing up.

"It's not the same," he said correcting me. "They are different. Completely."

"Okay."

"I could teach you."

"I don't think so."

"And your roommates? *Quella bionda*? What's her reason?" I didn't know what he heard about Janine. I wasn't sure what I should tell him.

"You know if you are foreign or from the south everyone knows everything in Siena. They talk." Then he cursed in dialect.

"I haven't done anything they could talk about." I said.

"Not yet."

I wasn't sure how to say I wouldn't. I still wasn't comfortable in *futuro*. I shrugged my shoulders. I held out my homework worksheet. "Do you want to help me or not?"

"*Allora*," he took the worksheet and filled in the answers.

"No, can you explain it?"

And he did. He went over each question with me, explaining the reason for each answer slowly, so that I understood. And I did understand. I actually got it. The rules made sense for a change. For a little while, the tension I felt around him lifted.

We split a dessert, *torta della nonna*. He kept touching his pack of cigarettes, his finger running up and down the side. It was making me uncomfortable, just like the way he kept looking at me. I felt like he was trying to figure me out. I had already been figured out. It wasn't pretty. I wouldn't let it happen again. I didn't need anyone else looking me in the eye. I asked him for a cigarette, so he would stop.

"You can just take what you want," he said. He handed me a smoke and held out a silver lighter for me.

"*Grazie*," I said, letting the *e* ring out a little more at the end. He laughed and I thought I messed up again, over-accentuated if that was possible to do in Italian. "What?"

"You Americans always say thank you. You must not say thank you to your friends. You want to be friends? For your friends it must be a gift for them to give to you. To say thank you is unnecessary. Never to your friends. Okay?" He said friends, *amici*, with a smirk.

"Okay."

When I finished my espresso, I took another cigarette without asking.

"*Brava*," he said. This was the first of many lessons I would learn from him.

We left the restaurant. I was ready for bed. I felt the wine when I stood. He parked his *vespa* somewhere outside the walls and asked me if I wanted to take a ride. I still didn't trust him.

"No, I'll just walk back home."

"Okay. I'll go with you." We started walking together; we cut through the *campo* and up the hill, chatting the entire way. I was surprised to carry on the conversation for so long. It was easy to understand him. It relaxed me or maybe it was the wine. It was cool to be out with someone, to be able to talk and understand this language. It was not just another night in a bar drinking or sitting at home wishing, again, that I had a TV or some other distraction.

At my *portone*, he kissed me formally on both cheeks. "*Okay, bella, amica, ci vediamo.*"

"*Ciao*," I said waving. Then I decided to test my sarcasm in Italian. "On second thought, I guess I wouldn't mind a pair of Italian shoes."

He laughed and called me *pazza*, crazy, kissing me once more on each cheek.

I rushed up the stairs, trying to beat the electric timer on the light as usual. And, for once, I did. I was smiling and out of breath when I walked into my apartment.

"Looks like someone had a little *sesso* on their date," Janine said from the dining room table. For once her schoolbooks were spread before her. Lisa was eating a package of cookies, shoving them into her mouth one after another. I could hear Michelle listening to some female singer behind the closed door of their room. It would have been nice if one of them were Kaitlin. I just wanted to get some girl talk.

"No, no sex, it wasn't like that. It was just nice to go out, you know, talk one-on-one to one of them. We're just friends."

Janine, who had appointed herself an expert on Italian men since she slept with several of them, raised an eyebrow and said, "Do Italian men know how to just be friends?"

"Do American?" I asked.

"Well, I had a little friendly *sesso* tonight with a hot Italian who didn't want to be friends. Now I have to conjugate verbs." Make that more proof for Gaetano's theory, I thought. I heard the kettle in the kitchen, and Lisa got up for some tea.

"Make sure to put enough sugar in mine," Janine shouted into the kitchen at her. I watched as Janine's hand, a toad's tongue, reached across the table to take one of Lisa's cookies.

7.

A sickness started slowly in me. All of us in the group were coming down with one thing or another, because of the weather and the lack of heat in all the old buildings. I woke up one morning with my head feeling congested and heavy. I coughed throughout my language class, drawing annoyed looks from my classmates and Signora Laza. I couldn't help it. The cough bested me. It could not be controlled.

I didn't eat much because I couldn't taste it. I bought canned soup from the store and heated it. I took a lot of naps and stopped going out at night. No matter what time I went to bed I felt exhausted. In the morning, my eyes were sealed shut.

I didn't want to go to the doctor. I was scared, and I wouldn't even know how to find a doctor or how to describe my problem. I considered asking Lisa for help, but decided against it. I just need more sleep, I told myself.

So I carried my sickness with me, bringing bits of toilet paper from the *università* wherever I went. I was disgusted with myself and I hid out in my room away from the rest of the dirty apartment and the dishonest food thief.

I didn't miss class, though. I was there to learn. I owed it to my parents. Maybe I needed a break from partying and this was a way to focus on learning, though I could barely stay awake to do my homework at night.

It was on the way to the group class that I saw Gaetano again. It had been over a week since our dinner. I was bundled up with a scarf wrapped around my head, and my jacket that was not warm enough.

He called to me, as I almost walked by him. I stopped to talk, but I didn't want to be out in the cold for long. I yearned for the warmth of the *università*. My head was so congested. I couldn't think straight enough to worry about what he thought. I told him that I was cold and sick. And then I asked him if he could get me anything from the hospital, any drugs. He was a medical student after all, wasn't he? He said he would try, but he didn't really have that kind of access.

"I must get to my class," I said in my Italian.

He smiled at my bad accent, worse from the cold. He told me that he would be at the Barone Rosso on Thursday. I nodded, said that I would try to make it.

In class, Arturo called on me and I could barely hear him from the pressure in my ears. My throat hurt when I tried to answer his question about which Lorenzetti brother painted the depiction of just and unjust governments. I had a fit of coughing in the middle of my answer, and I had to start again. I was required to answer in Italian, no less. Arturo corrected each grammar mistake I made, rolling the *r*'s and the *l*'s in the word *frattello* tauntingly. I raised my voice above the cacophony of coughs of the rest of the class. More than half of us sounded like death. I had to keep saying my answer again and again until it was perfect. Except for my accent.

On the way home, I stopped with Janine and Michelle at the *trattoria* across the street from our apartment. I hadn't been out to the stores all week, and I had nothing to eat in the house except for some olive oil and old bread. When I sat down I began to feel sick. I ordered *tortellini in brodo* and both girls looked at me.

"Is that all you are going to have for dinner," asked Michelle, who would eat a few leaves of lettuce and claim to be full.

"I don't think I can keep anything else down," I said, truthfully. My face should have conveyed my sicknesses. They nodded and changed their orders so that they got even less than me, so that they would not feel like pigs compared to me.

I ate two tortellini and tried to sip some of the broth. They cleaned their plates and finished my soup, shaking their heads as if I was not eating it because I didn't like it. I gave them 8,000 lire and told them I had to go to bed and I would leave the front door open for them.

In my bed under the scratchy blanket, I peeled off everything but my underwear and a tank top. The room was cold, but I was sweating. It was only nine o'clock. I spent that night between sleep and wake. I was hypersensitive to everything happening in the house, to Janine staring at her face, plucking her eyebrows, to Michelle quietly puking my tortellini into our bidet and to Lisa crying into her pillow. I even heard the rustling of a bag of biscuits in the kitchen. The food thief struck again.

I heard all of those things, and they disturbed me. I could not rest because of them. I was not sure if everything was a dream, but every time I thought I might sleep peacefully, something else pulled me out of it. I tossed and turned all night, flinging off my covers and then desperately trying to get them back. When the travel alarm clock beeped in the morning, I shut it and stayed in bed for two days. I was missing a quiz and missing the trip to look at Saint Catherine's finger remains in the church, but each time I went to the bathroom, I felt so unsteady.

The roommates, when they were there, brought me juice and water. They asked me if I wanted anything. They didn't know me well enough to force me to drink or to eat the way Kaitlin would have. She would have made me soup by now.

What if I never got up? I had never felt so sick.

I didn't communicate this to my roommates. During the day when I spoke to them I said I just needed rest and asked Lisa, who was, in spite of herself, in my level, to get my homework.

Jonas came to me during the night. He spoke words I couldn't hear. All the things we said on the bus he said in a low whisper, just out of my reach. But he touched me. And his touch on my skin brought my fever up.

It had been almost a year since I walked into the room where he blew pot smoke in my face. It was after he waited for me at the bus stop. He invited me to a party, Kaitlin and me like it was no big deal. She raised her eyebrows when I asked her but put on her lipstick and came anyway. She was good like that. She indulged me when she knew better. She never said I told you so.

That night he danced a circle around me without picking up his feet. I knew that he had a girlfriend who lay sick in bed across the country in her hometown, but still her influence was strong. He kept his dancing circle wide enough that he was just out of reach, at least for a little while. He laughed when I passed the joint the second time and blew smoke in my face, smiling. I just inhaled his breath.

And then, we were together all the time. At a party in the corner, just the two of us. Somehow we never ran out of things to say. His roommate had a girlfriend, which made it almost obvious that he could stay with me when Kaitlin was at her boyfriend's. We were just friends, though. It was all cool. There was a girlfriend we were supposed to be thinking about, but she never came up. She was sick and not getting well. I didn't worry. He said don't worry. I believed him.

In the bed in Siena, I could not focus on my thoughts. They were slipping away from me, but it wasn't sleep. My resistance was weakening like his faraway girl. I knew her name but I always called her Mono Girl. I created a face for her because she had only been the back of the hair the one time I saw them walking together. I was behind them. She didn't see me, but he did.

My friends also called her Mono Girl. I'm sure her friends called me something worse. I'm sure she hated me. I never hated her. I envied her. Our only connection was Jonas.

There is always someone else, isn't there? Two of the worst words in the English language. I couldn't think of how to say them in Italian in my sickness, and at that point I probably couldn't have figured it out right if I was well. But there was always someone else in the mind of the person you want when they should be thinking of just you. There was always a reason for them to be guilty, preoccupied. There was always an excuse not to give you all of them. Mono Girl was someone else. And then maybe now, somehow, I became the "someone else" that he thought about. And she had to deal with my shadow the way I dealt with hers.

Maybe not.

"What does she look like?" I asked Kaitlin when Mono Girl returned, the next semester able-bodied and ready to pick up where I left off. I wasn't sure I wanted to know.

"Nothing like you," Kaitlin said in a way that made me love her all the more.

In my crazy fevered visions, I gave Mono Girl the face of Santa Caterina, whose fingers I didn't get to see at her church in Siena. I was sweating, imagining Saint Catherine and Mono Girl and I were one falling into ecstasy as that parasitic boy crawled inside us. What good did the ecstasy do you if your fingers wound up preserved away from your body? With my fingers still attached, I wiped the sweat from behind my knees. *I cannot stop these images. I'm helpless.* In Italy, I didn't know who would care.

The weirdest things went through my mind. They were strange enough for me to know that I was delirious. I remembered that first night when he stayed over my dorm room, how we just pretended to fall into it, because it was easy, but down the hall a woman was sitting outside a door. Kaitlin and I called her the Stalker. She was obsessed with a kid on my floor. She waited for him. She banged on his door in the middle of the night, but the he never opened up.

I must have told Jonas about her when we came in. I must have whispered that she was a stalker disapprovingly. What did he say? I can't remember. I only remember how Jonas shrugged when I told him he didn't have to sleep on the floor. Why do so many things from the past go out of focus? You don't know your past; you won't know your future. I told myself I would never be like the Stalker. I didn't understand how someone could go so crazy.

And I fought it. I ran from it. But as I was sweating and sick in that bed Crazy was catching up with me. I was going to give in.

"What are you going to do when she comes back?" I whispered. I thought the answer was simple. Remember, I was trying not to be worried. For some reason I thought there were promises in words and kisses. I thought listening to someone's breath as they slept and feeling content meant more than it did.

"I don't know," he said. "This is so crazy."

He smiled at me all the time, until she was back and then I never smiled. I didn't want to be the Stalker. I didn't want to be the Someone Else. I just wanted to be me, with him, like I had been.

But one night Crazy found me. The night started too easy. It was the end of the semester. I thought I had begun to accept that Mono Girl was back. If I could hold out another few weeks, I would be away from it all. I would be in Italy. I was starting to study for finals and write papers. Kaitlin was studying, too. It was her class on Native American art. I peered over her shoulder as I walked to our mini-fridge. There was a portrait of an Indian in vibrant colors. I looked closer at the picture.

"What's that on his face?" I asked Kaitlin about the deep red color.

"It's a hand. They think it means he killed someone with his bare hands. I guess it's a reminder. I'm not sure if it's pride or shame."

I nodded. Pride and shame I understood. Crazy seduced me at that moment. She made it all make sense. She had been beckoning me. And maybe all the stress wore me down. With her hand in mine, I snuck to his floor. I pressed my ear to his door. *Know your past*, I wanted to shout. *Know me.* I covered his wipe board with question marks.

I couldn't breathe that night. I was holding my breath. But I must have at some point, because there was noise. I thought the squeaks were the sound of the marker on wipe board. Then I realized that it was me and I had no longer confined my question marks to the wipe board, I had covered his door with black lines.

When he opened his door, he stood there, blinking at me. He didn't stop me when I pressed the marker into his forehead to draw a question mark. He had killed me somehow, killed something, and I wanted to remember. I wanted him to remember. Pressing. I pressed the marker into his skin. I hit and slapped and spat. I found ways to hurt him. He stood there and took it all. Was that pride or shame?

I wasn't sure why I stopped or what I said. When I got back to my room, Kaitlin tried to clean the ink from my hands. I was in a daze. She wiped the sweat from my face. She didn't ask me any questions.

"I am not a violent person," I said. I was starting to cry.

"I know, Gabriella, I know. You aren't." She gave me some Nyquil and tucked me in once again.

I asked to take my finals early so I could get home, get out. I didn't see him again to see if the marker had actually been permanent.

That was as low as I got, that was right before I left.

"I am not a violent person," I whispered in that sick, small Italian bed, clutching my hands again. If I held them, Crazy couldn't take one. But maybe she could help me find him again. Let Crazy comfort me. *I will give in if that's what it takes.*

And it worked. I brought him back.

Jonas turned on the lamp and heard me groaning for him. It was real. He was speaking to me loudly. But it was Italian. I was squinting into the light, but I didn't recognize him. Moaning. Shivering. Sweating. Jonas came to me, and though it didn't look like him, it had to be. Who else could hear my thoughts? Who else always knew what I was thinking before I said it? Though I couldn't recognize him, I reached for him.

But his cologne was strong. It was not the smell of an American boy. It confused me to have this smell wrapping around me. I expected something else.

He wiped my head. He touched my hair. He could do anything to me now, and I would lie here in sweat. Then he left without turning off the light or closing the door. I opened my eyes and tried to focus. I knew I was not well. I pulled the blanket over my head to block the light. I could still smell Jonas's new scent.

Then the blanket was pulled from me. Had I dozed? The light was still on. It was Gaetano. He was the man with the cologne. But there was another stronger smell coming and I knew that smell was going to burn me all the way down my insides.

He put a glass with the smell on the nightstand, pulled me into a sitting position. I wouldn't stay up by myself, he leaned me against him. I was aware of how little I was wearing but too messed up to really care.

"*Sei dimagrita.*" I didn't understand what he was saying. I started to protest when I got another whiff of what he was holding out to me in the glass. But I was weak and he was fast. He pushed the glass into my mouth, so the liquid rushed onto my tongue. I drank it down quick, because I didn't want the strong bitter alcohol taste in my mouth for too long. He held me still for a minute, timing the minute even as I started to feel it come back. He whispered something to me about learning this in his country, *paese*, whatever. He said he would take me to see it one day when I felt better.

"*Allora,*" he said when the minute was up. Then he led me to the bathroom and waited outside, listening to me wretch.

"*Brava,*" he said. "*Stai meglio adesso.*"

I nodded, understanding. I would be better now. I was doing the right thing. I needed to purge the sickness from me, get everything out. I felt better already but weak. I climbed back into a bed. He pulled the blanket around me. I knew that I would at last be able to sleep. He kissed my forehead and turned off the light in the bedroom.

"*Grazie dottore,*" I said from my dreams.

"*Grazie a te.*"

I stayed in bed for another day and then spent a miserable day back at school, where everything remained cloudy. On the third day, I could hear better, my head felt lighter, and the fog on my brain seemed to lift.

The cough remained, though. I carried it with me for the next two months. And after a couple of weeks it sounded a lot worse than it felt. It remained beyond my control and came out at the worst times, drawing looks from the class and Signora Laza whenever I hacked.

I still didn't have much of an appetite. I forced down the canned soups from the supermarket. I lost weight from not eating for so long. I noticed my pants were falling off and my shirts were bigger, but I only realized how different I looked from Janine's daily sweep of me.

"You lost weight," she said. She and Michelle were flipping through fashion magazines in their room when I went through to take a shower in their bathroom. It wasn't a compliment or an expression of concern. It was like she was acknowledging a threat.

"I guess," I said. I hadn't been trying to and I didn't think the sickness was something positive.

"How did you do it?" Michelle asked seriously, almost admiring.

"It's called the get really sick and not be able to eat diet. Oh, and throw in a couple of pukes. It's great," I joked. Michelle nodded.

"That's Michelle's daily life," Janine said, smiling. I couldn't believe she was making a joke out of this. Neither could Michelle. She looked embarrassed. Janine backtracked. "Just kidding, Michelle."

I looked at Michelle who buried her face in pictures of skinny bodies that looked a lot like her. I wasn't sure what to say to that. "Well, I'm going to take a shower if you guys are done in the bathroom."

"Go ahead," Janine answered for both of them.

I went into the bathroom that smelled faintly of vomit and wished that I could take a shower without being scrutinized.

Olivia was waiting for me outside my apartment building one evening. It was a surprise. Her bright smile, her cold cheeks accepting my kiss.

"It's freezing out here. What are you doing?" I was already a thousand times happier from her presence.

"Your roommate Lisa didn't exactly look thrilled to see me. She was trying to study. I decided to wait for you out here. *Ecco*!" She handed me a bag of prosciutto bread from the pork store. I hadn't really figured out how to order from the *pescheria* and *macelleria* yet. The pigs hanging in the windows intimidated me, and I doubted I could afford meat or fish anyway. Occasionally I bought some cans of tuna at the supermarket.

"I saw Gaetano on my way up. He had come to see you, too. He said you were a *tesoro*, a treasure, that everyone waits for you. I think it definitely helped to sour Lisa's mood."

"Jeez! Well, come up. I'll make you some dinner. Then we'll go out."

Upstairs, I washed someone's leftover pots in the sink. I made *pici*, the long thick pasta of Siena, with a light tomato sauce and mushrooms. Olivia insisted on cutting up the mushrooms. All the while we snacked on the *pane prosciutto* that Olivia brought.

Olivia was happy to be cooking. She and Suzie were living with a family and didn't feel comfortable using the kitchen in their apartment. They also had a meal plan that covered lunch and dinner in a variety of restaurants around Firenze.

Lisa had her books spread out across the kitchen table and didn't offer to move them. So Olivia sat on the couch by the kitchen while the pasta cooked. We gossiped loudly about people in Olivia's group. Finally Lisa sighed dramatically and gathered her books.

"You're going to wash your dishes, right?" Lisa asked before she ran to hide in her room. "I want to make some pasta later, too."

"Yes, of course. I'm now accustomed to washing dishes before and after I eat." Lisa stomped to her room as I rolled my eyes at Olivia.

"Wow!"

"Yeah, that's what it's been like," I said, stirring the sauce. "We have stopped really trying to be nice to each other, any of us."

"Where are the other ones?"

"God knows, Michelle I bet is out for a run, and Janine is probably fucking some Italian zipper head. Roberto broke up with her, although she claims she broke up with him."

"I thought Michelle and Janine were best friends or something,"

"Somehow, I don't think they anticipated what it would be like to actually live together in a foreign country." I thought about mentioning what Janine said about Michelle puking and then, feeling embarrassed for Michelle, decided not to.

"Did any of us?'

"Absolutely not." We laughed. I offered Olivia a piece of pasta from the water. I learned that *pici* takes a long time to cook, but if you overcook, you can't go back. "What do you think?"

"Another minute."

"That's what I thought." I stirred the *pici* and succumbed to a coughing fit.

"Gaetano said you were *ammalata*. I didn't realize it was this sick."

"*Si*," I said laughing through my phlegm cough. "He really helped me out."

"Of course he did. You are his treasure, his *tesoro*." She ducked as I swatted her with the dishtowel.

"I think he understands now that we can just be friends. He accepts the fake boyfriend." Olivia raised her ever-arching eyebrow and nodded, pursing her lips.

"It's true." I said defiantly.

"Okay, okay. Drain the pasta."

"Okay."

As we ate, Olivia told me all about her life in Firenze. She said that she preferred Siena, that Florence was big and overwhelming in comparison. She wished that her family talked to her more, but she thought that they took her and Suzie in to make money.

"I guess it was silly to think I would learn anything from them. When are you going to come visit?" I hesitated. A week before I got sick, I planned to go up to see her. When I went to the kiosk in Piazza Gramschi to buy the tickets, the man behind the counter had chastised me. *Biglietto*, the word for ticket had a *g* in it that was sort of silent but not exactly. The *g* made the *l* sound different. When I asked for my ticket, the man said the word again.

"*Si*," I nodded, thinking that he was clarifying. It sounded exactly like what I just said. I held up one finger. "*Uno*."

"*No, biglietto*," he said moving his lips to enunciate. I understood that I was supposed to repeat.

"*Biglietto*," I said, I might have still had a smile on my face. I smiled constantly, hoping the people of Siena would take a little pity on me and forgive my awful accent.

"*No*," he said again, quickly. He held a hand up to his mouth. "*Biglietto*."

I repeated it again, concentrating on saying exactly what I thought he was. There was something subtle I was missing, because I had to repeat it again seven times. He moved his hand by his mouth so I could see how his tongue slid under his moustache into the *o*. At last he shrugged and relented, handing me a ticket. I knew I hadn't perfected the word, hadn't figured out the subtlety I was missing. I was a lost cause. I imagined a wall of sound I couldn't comprehend on the bus to Firenze. The idea of being trapped again in the language for the whole ride overwhelmed me. Instead of going to surprise Olivia as planned, I went back to my room and took a nap.

But I didn't tell Olivia any of that.

"I was going to come, I bought the ticket, but, you know, I just got sick."

I hesitated too long, and she looked at me, perhaps reading that something was wrong. She was debating whether or not to ask me, to go there. I got that look from Kaitlin many times. I looked down at my plate of *pici* and took another bite.

"Well, you can use that ticket if you want," she said at last. "You can meet up with me and Suzie and come with us to Milan and Switzerland the weekend after next."

I was so happy that she was asking me and excited about a weekend away. I agreed.

"Good, then let me show you the plan." She pulled a book out of her bag. The book was a bunch of train timetables for all of Europe. Olivia mapped out an entire plan for our trip. She was so positive and ready to take on everything.

"This is pretty cool, Olivia. *Brava*, as they say. Who is this Thomas Cook guy anyway?" I asked, reading the name on the train guide.

"Someone who is going to help me see this continent. And you too, *tesoro*."

"Great. Is Suzie coming?"

"I hope so."

"Is Kurt coming?"

"I doubt it. Can you take Friday off?"

"And miss an exciting educational and challenging lesson that will have me speaking this language like it was my mother tongue? Absolutely. I'll take you to the hot new bar Gaetano showed me now that we are just drinking buddies."

8.

I broke into my budget to buy a pair of short-heeled boots of brown leather from the store in the *campo*.

"*Mi piacciono queste scarpe italiane*," Gaetano said, nodding with approval over the shoes. He smirked and reminded me that this was one of the reasons that American women came to Italy. He liked proving his points.

Those shoes were slippery. I slid around some of the downhills in Siena. I didn't like walking with the clumsy steps. But I had to get used to walking in them.

I tried not to wear my sneakers anymore. I didn't want to be an obvious American. Michelle and Janine were constantly exercising, donning their sneakers and sweats and running through the streets with the Italians shouting, "*americane, americane.*"

I didn't run, didn't want to run. But one day, I wanted to explore the outskirts and head toward the red brick rooftops I saw from my window. I grabbed my Walkman, put on my sneakers that were almost dusty and borrowed one of Michelle's bulky sweats.

I didn't walk through the city. I didn't want to be seen or shouted at by Italians. I didn't want to be labeled for what I was. I walked out of my building, turning right down the street, past the few pizzerias where darker *stranieri* cooked in kitchens. There was a fish store I still hadn't been into. It was icy and I couldn't get any colder. I was beginning to identify the smells of the city, separate the *pizza al forno* from the *pane*. It was a small victory that I knew which windy cobblestone hill of a street bisected another.

I continued out of the walls through the Porta San Marco, traveling past the hotel that Olivia and Suzie used to live in and then into what wasn't exactly the countryside but more like the Sienese suburb. I passed houses with laundry hanging and the smell of delicious meat being cooked. I smelled the fresh fertile dirt in the ground.

When I walked for about twenty minutes and passed at most two people, I was far enough away from the center of Siena. I began to sing along with my tape. I hit all the high notes with the singer. I belted at the top of my lungs, singing along and also trying to will it in myself. "Change, change, change."

I was outside myself for a little while. I imagined one of those movies where they just start singing. I was finding that cinematic freedom and hoping that by the time the credits rolled I might have a happy ending.

One night, as I was finishing my *compito*, there was a knock at the door. It was Gaetano and a man with bright blue eyes named Duccio. Gaetano laughed as he introduced Duccio, because his name was *troppo sienese*.

In culture class, we read about a number of Tuscans named Duccio. I would be sure to tell Olivia about that name. Duccio playfully smacked the top of Gaetano's head and then they both laughed at my bare feet. This they said was *troppo americana*.

"So, *tesoro*, have you eaten? We'd like to take you to a *trattoria* outside the walls. Of course this means you must put on your shoes." I invited them in while I got shoes. Lisa pounced on the Italians and tested out the new words she learned. She wasn't flirting; she was showing off, hungry for praise. I quickly zipped my new boots and went out to the dining room to rescue them. Lisa excused herself. I was certain that if we didn't hurry she would return after boning up on another idiomatic phrase to impress them with.

"*Andiamo?*" I asked. I wanted to make a quick getaway while Lisa was in her room.

"Will your roommate come?" Duccio asked.

"Her?" I pointed toward Lisa's bedroom.

"No," he said, staring into the kitchen where Michelle had just begun to prepare a low-fat meal. "Ask the beautiful one in the kitchen. The one wearing the American pants."

The sneaker-clad Michelle had no idea she was being talked about. We *stranieri* had a tendency, maybe a gift, to tune out Italian when we weren't directly involved in a conversation or concentrating on our professors.

"Michelle," I said. I began speaking English fast in a way I knew the Italians couldn't understand. "Seems you got a little admirer. This dude wants to go to dinner with you. He wants you to come with us."

"What?" Michelle said, coming out the kitchen. She wiped her wet hands on her nylon running pants. She stopped when she saw Duccio and smiled. Something happened between them that I felt. I looked at Gaetano, who shrugged and introduced Duccio to Michelle.

Michelle was quite pretty, even with her hair hastily pulled back. Her eyes widened, and she extended her hand to Duccio. A color rose into her cheeks across the top of her neck. When she spoke, her accent was casual and perfect.

"*Piacere*," she said, taking his hand, as they were introduced. Then she turned to me and spoke fast, "Give me five, okay? And I'll come with. Tell them."

Since she hurried out of the room, neither of the guys understood that she was coming until I explained it. Duccio was so relieved that Gaetano offered him a cigarette. Gaetano got up to make us espresso, and while he was in the kitchen, I stole one of his cigarettes.

Gaetano and Duccio began to discuss their favorite soccer team, and I tuned out as Michelle had. What about Michelle made Duccio so smitten? I wished I could create that reaction to me even if I wasn't ready to deal with it. When I looked up at Gaetano's constant gray gaze, I realized. It wouldn't have really mattered if Duccio had liked me. I would always be off-limits to any friend of Gaetano's, no matter how cute they were.

After fifteen minutes, I went to Michelle's door to see what was taking so long. Michelle stood in her bra and a long tight skirt she must have been hiding, even from Janine.

"Shit, shit, shit," Michelle said. "I'm trying to hurry. I don't know what to wear. Come in."

Inside, just about every shirt Michelle and Janine owned was on the bed, having been tried on and discarded.

"Michelle, I was just going to wear this. Gaetano's in jeans, did you see?"

"I know, I know. I just, I don't know, I want to look good."

"I hate to say this, but you weren't exactly dressed to impress when you came out of the kitchen and obviously you had an affect."

"Well, I'm not going to wear my jogging pants, if that's what you mean." Michelle gave herself a look in the mirror, making a face she never made in life. "And I look like shit, fuck. Oh, hey, can I borrow your red cardigan?"

"Okay. Do you want the tank that goes underneath?"

"No, a little cleave will do me good. Don't you think?"

"Yeah, sure. I'll go get it." I started for the door and stopped. "I'm starving."

"Okay, okay, I'm hurrying."

I ran to my room to get the sweater, saying "*un attimo, un attimo*" to the guys as I ran back through the dining room. As I suspected, Lisa, textbooks open, was asking Duccio and Gaetano detailed question about *forma passiva*. It was a lesson she wouldn't have for another three weeks.

"So can I use it with all tenses or just third person?" she asked.

Michelle was putting on makeup when I got back to her room. I held out the sweater. "Now they are being attacked by Lisa and her thirst for knowledge."

"Okay, okay." Michelle grabbed the cardigan and put it on. She smiled at herself in the mirror, tugged the neckline down and then tugged it back up. She turned to me for an assessment, and I tugged it down, once again.

"I think you're ready," I said, and Michelle took another critical look in the mirror and applied more lipstick. I sighed.

"C'mon, G, you know it's less of a production with me than with Janine."

"That's not really too much of an accomplishment, now is it?"

At last we were on our way. Gaetano said "wow" when Michelle emerged from her room and I briefly considered changing my outfit into something nicer. No, who was I trying to impress?

We walked through the city to get to Duccio's car. Gaetano and I helped Duccio and Michelle communicate. It wasn't easy, Duccio's English was worse than Gaetano's.

I had no idea where they were bringing us, but at last we passed what looked like a small racetrack and went into a building. This was the *trattoria*. It had maybe fifteen square wooden tables with the straw-backed old-school chairs I had seen in a lot of in restaurants. Wine was on the table before I had a chance to think about it. Gaetano winked at me while explaining to Duccio how long our semester was.

We all got *cinghiale*, wild boar, except for Michelle, who didn't eat meat. It took a while to explain how and why Michelle didn't eat meat. Duccio was amazed by this fact about her, as all Italians were, but he was amazed by everything about her. She split the *primi* pasta with us and then asked for *fagioli all'uccelletto*, white beans with rosemary for her *secondo*. I noticed she pushed her food around a bit, but she ate more than usual.

After a decent amount of wine and almond *ricciarelli*, the official cookie of Siena, Duccio decided we should go to Monteriggioni. This was another fortressed town in Tuscany and a little drive. Duccio was excited to show Michelle a part of the area she hadn't seen. This time, Gaetano and I sat in the back seat together. Gaetano winked when Duccio took Michelle's hand.

"He good, even though *di Nord*," he whispered mixing English and Italian so Duccio couldn't understand. "He very pride to show dis Toscana to 'er."

Once we got to Monteriggioni, Gaetano and I hung back because Michelle and Duccio were able to manage on their own. We walked around the town, looking at the impressive fortress. I was enjoying this time with Gaetano. Now we only spoke Italian to each other. I was much more comfortable talking to him than the random people I ran into in town. But I was still surprised with every conversation I could carry.

Eventually Duccio had to get the car back or his mother would worry. This time in the car, Michelle leaned against Duccio's shoulder and he kissed the top of her head. This was moving fast. I was envious again. Not because I wanted Duccio, but because it was so simple. Boy and girl like each other. They can't speak the same language, but who really cares? I stared out the window, wishing everything could be so easy.

When we got to the piazza nearest Via Stalloreggi, we all got out of the car. I kissed Duccio and Gaetano on both cheeks. Duccio smiled at me. He spoke to me in English, "I very 'appy dis night, *bella*."

"Yes, I can see that," I smiled. "*Ci vediamo.*"

"*Ciao, bella.*" Duccio gave me a hug, and then I walked a little way up the street to let Michelle and Duccio have a proper goodbye. I couldn't resist a peak back to see the two in a passionate embrace. I laughed at Gaetano's mock shocked face from the front seat, and I turned away. At last, Michelle came behind me, grabbed my arm, laughed in my ear and swept me up in someone else's happiness.

"I can't believe it, G. I can't believe the way he kissed me. Did you smell him? Was it me or he did he smell better than anything?'

"He smelled pretty good."

"I can't believe this. I cannot believe this. I couldn't even understand half the shit he said, but I loved the way he said it."

"Are you in love?"

"Oh. My. God. No, I can't be. I just met the kid."

"Kid? I think we'd have to call that a man."

"A *uomo*. We should call him a *uomo*." We only had two bottles of wine, but Michelle was drunk from something else. She was shouting in the quiet streets. "*Uomo Italiano bellissimo.*"

"Jeez," I said, laughing as Michelle pulled me close and kissed my cheek. "Save it for the *uomo italiano*."

"He wants to see me this weekend. We're going to meet Friday night. Can you and Gaetano come? "

"I can't, Michelle. I'm going away with Olivia and Suzie. You'll be fine. You don't need us crowding you."

We went up into our apartment. It was dark. Michelle came into my room when she saw that Janine was already there, passed out in bed.

She washed her makeup off and pulled her hair back as it was when Duccio first saw her. She looked so young when she smiled at me and whispered, "Thanks, G, for everything."

"I did shit," I said. "You're the hottie who got the hottie."

"The *caldo* –ie," Michelle said, destroying the Italian word for hot. "Good night, girl."

"Good night. *Buona notte.*" Then Michelle left my room and I pulled off my socks and got quickly under the covers. But then I sat up in bed and listened. I wanted to see if Michelle stopped in the bathroom on our side, the one without the shower, to puke like she often did. But I didn't hear her. That night, she was going to let everything settle and just enjoy being herself.

9.

Olivia and Suzie were waiting for me at the station in Florence. Immediately, I noticed that the normal fun-loving Olivia had been replaced by someone who meant business. She informed me that we had about a half hour to our train. We grabbed an espresso from the bar in the station. We stood around the circular table with our backpacks between us and the table, so that we could protect them from the criminals we had been warned about. Our lives were in those backpacks. Not just clothes but passports, journals and money.

We compared the benefits of each of our backpacks and imagined the places we might go with them. Then we talked guidebooks. Suzie and I both had our own copies of Let's Go tucked in our bags. This was the requisite guide for finding the cheap and definitely discovered places to eat, sleep and see. Suzie also had the Berkley guide, which seemed to have nicer pictures and more expensive suggestions.

Olivia clapped her hands when it was time to head to the track for the train. I was giddy with the idea that we were on our way. We were on a weekend trip to a great city, and it was possible because we were here in Italy. Any trip was possible.

"She's been a little drill sergeant about this whole thing," Suzie stage whispered.

"Somebody has to be," Olivia said, matter-of-factly. She was the oldest of five, and it was in her nature to be the organizer. She made sure that each of us validated our tickets by stamping them in the little yellow machines at the head of each track.

We had our own compartment on the train. I left all the arrangements up to Olivia. She insisted that I could just show up at the designated time. She chose the slow *locale* train for us, so we flattened the seats and made them beds. This way we would arrive there in the morning, not the middle of the night. We wouldn't have to pay for an extra night in a hotel.

Olivia pulled some crackers and cheese out of her bag. She divvied out slices of the hard *pecorino toscano*, using my Swiss Army knife. The conductor came to check our tickets.

"*Attenta le borse*," he said, looking up at our bags on the racks. When the door slid closed, we climbed on the chairs and fastened our bags more securely to the racks.

"I wish we had something to tie the door with," Suzie said.

"I'll bring it next time." Olivia said, handing us baby wipes for our hands.

"I'm sure you will," I said, smiling at Suzie. Olivia set the alarm for 5:30, which was fifteen minutes before we were supposed to pull into the Stazione

Centrale in Milan, according to Olivia's new bible, Thomas Cook. Suzie shut the lights in our compartment and we said "*buona notte*" to each other in the darkness.

I slept poorly, aware of the lights from each of the stations we traveled through, but I liked the steady feel of the train beneath my body and the sound of Suzie's gentle snoring.

Our giant backpacks toppled us forward as we walk up Via Pergolesi to the hotel. Olivia (of course) found Albergho La Pace in the Let's Go. We left our bags at the hotel and explored Milano.

Gaetano told me not to expect too much from Milan, but I liked it a lot. Compared with Siena, the streets were wide and after a few hours, the morning rush began filling those streets with people with lives.

We went to the *duomo* because it was necessary to visit the cathedral in every city. We learned this from all of our culture classes. Going to each city's cathedral meant you would get an idea of the style. It was a free tourist attraction, which made it more attractive. We spend forty-five minutes or so studying the sculpture and paintings inside. The stained-glass windows were beautiful, unlike anything in Siena, and so were the freaky gargoyles that lined the walls looking at us.

Afterward we took pictures in front of the *duomo* surrounded by pigeons. Then we got an espresso. The popular Italian pastime was perfect for backpackers because it was cheap and ideal for people watching. One thing about Italy that rubbed off on me was the ability to just sit, to observe. Things weren't as rushed here. No one expected you to be on the move all the time. It was slow. It was walking around and looking, seeing. So I wouldn't be able to say I saw everything you were supposed to see in Milan. I was content with what I was getting, a stillness.

As I listened to Olivia read about the cathedral we just saw, I realized that I wasn't going to remember anything about the dates and artists represented. I was going to remember the old woman kneeling at the pew, next to the statuesque model type who sat with her hands in her lap and her eyes closed. They were both lost in prayer and would have made an excellent picture. Their *duomo* wasn't a tourist attraction; it was a cathedral that was part of their lives.

The painting of *The Last Supper* was undergoing some kind of construction so we couldn't see it. Olivia was bummed about this, but I didn't really mind. Maybe I took the art in this Italian city for granted, but it was the hustle and bustle, the cool and stylish people who hurried in and out of the café that really interested me. Suzie didn't seem to mind the missed opportunity either. There was more to traveling then checking off museums.

"I still haven't seen the David," Suzie said. "I just don't want to pay the admission."

Economics determined much of what we did. Our parents scrimped and saved to get us here, and now we did the same. And I was glad. I don't regret any of the things I didn't see. Instead, I remember those moments in piazzas, passing on the 10,000 lire admission fees and "splurging" on 2,000 lire gelato that tasted better than anything else.

After the *duomo*, we window shopped, stopping in front of many of the stores we would never be able to afford. The streets were alive. We bought some fresh bread and cheese and sat in a piazza. Among all the businesspeople, there were teen-agers gathered around a guitar singing "Imagine." Somehow they seemed so much more determined to imagine "all de peephal leevin in 'armoneeah" than I ever could be.

Olivia read us more on the city between chews of bread. There was a pastry shop in one of the guides. It said, "Splurge for sweets like you've never tasted in your life." Suzie, who had an incredible sweet tooth, insisted that we go.

"Ask the captain," I said, looking to Olivia.

"Okay, I just hope it's not too expensive."

We looked like what we were, grubby traveling students, when we were seated at the *pasticceria*. At another table was a group of Italian ladies who lunch with extremely long hair and extremely short skirts. The waiters were in tuxes. On the table, there was a white linen tablecloth and fine china.

"We should have known when it wasn't in Let's Go," I said.

"What should we do?" Suzie asked.

Then the waiter was there, asking us what we wanted in a formal way. We temporarily lost the ability to partially communicate in Italian at all. We smiled at each other, stupidly. *We can't leave*, our smiles said. Finally, Suzie said, "*dolce*" and I said "*the*" and the waiter hurried off.

"What are we going to do?" Olivia asked.

"Eat pastries, I guess," Suzie said hesitantly.

"And drink tea," I said, more sure.

"Okay," Olivia said, knowing, as we knew, that this would have worked out better if we stuck to the affordable suggestions in Let's Go.

The waiter returned with a delicate pot of tea, a beautiful plate of lemon and a china bowl full of sugar. Another waiter placed a plate full of mini pastries in front of us. I looked at Olivia and Suzie, who were as equally delighted and horrified as I was. There was an abundance of scrumptious pastries. We each managed a perfect *grazie*.

"What are we supposed to do with all of this?" Suzie whispered.

"I have no idea." Olivia said. "I count eighteen pastries."

"How expensive is this going to be?" I asked.

"Eighteen pastries that look like that? Pretty expensive." Olivia said.

"Plus tea," I added.

"Plus tea," Olivia said decisively so that we all laughed for a second and then got quiet, embarrassed. Perhaps it wasn't cool to laugh in a place this fancy. Better to fly under the radar. "Maybe they charge us by the pastry."

"Yeah, they can't expect us to eat all this," I looked around to see if anyone else was having this pastry predicament. "You think we just eat what we want and they reserve the rest? Is that what they do in Italy? Why isn't it in the guidebook?"

"If it isn't in the guidebook, I don't know what to do," Olivia said, feigning a quiet mental breakdown. We had to try hard not to laugh. I was feeling more delirious from the lack of sleep.

"But if they do charge us for all of them, I want to eat all of them." Suzie was certain of this.

"I guess I'm pretty hungry, too." I said.

"We've got a lot of time until dinner," Olivia said, eyeing one of the chocolate delights.

"How often are we going to be eating pastries in Milan?" I asked.

"Never again," said Suzie, grabbing hold of something covered in nuts. She plopped it into her mouth. She smiled like a satisfied cat. It was on.

"Well, I guess we have our answer," Olivia said, and we began to eat. Once we decided, we got quite gluttonous. Six pastries each is a lot. We barely had time for our tea. At first, each time the waiter passed by, we froze, trying to gauge whether or not we were doing the right thing. Finally we gave up and gave ourselves over to the yummy concoctions.

When we were done with the pastries, the tuxedoed waiters swooped around us, taking the plate, pouring the rest of the tea.

Now we felt a part of this cosmopolitan world. I pretended that tonight we would be dining in the finest restaurant and be able to spend as much as we wanted without regard for the budgets all our parents had imposed on us. I wished that it wasn't a hard, small bed I would sleep in but one made of feathers that I could fall into after a good hot shower.

I knew that all of those things were impossible, would be impossible for any of the traveling I could do as a student. And while I didn't have any five-star luxuries just then, at least I ate the right pastries.

When we called for *il conto*, we were charged for each individual pastry.

The next morning catching the train was not as easy as Thomas Cook or Olivia led me to believe. Still not sure of the layout of the city, we ate dinner close to the hotel, barely able to keep our eyes open. We were in bed by ten with our guidebooks and journals, promising to have more energy after a good night's sleep. I thought about rallying us out to some place in the nightclub section of Let's Go, but I realized that I wouldn't be doing it because I wanted to. I would be doing it because I wanted the story of a night in Milan.

But if we had gone out, perhaps we would be able to figure out where we were on the Let's Go map instead of making wrong turns back to the station in the morning. How had we navigated it so easily the day before with eyes crusty from train-sleep? We saw a bus coming and got on that, manipulating our giant precious backpacks through the sleepy commuters. We had to transfer. All of this was more confusing because each of us was translating the Italian directions we got differently. All our limited knowledge put together only frustrated us in figuring out what we were supposed to do. And because none of us knew each other well enough to admit that, we were annoyed with the other two.

With three minutes to spare, we got to the *ferovia*. We checked the *binario* on the big board, stamped our tickets and ran for it. The conductor saw us and waved his hand for us to hurry. The train pulled away five seconds after we were on it.

But we still weren't done. We hustled through the aisles and cars of the train with our big backpacks. We walked through first class. We walked past Italian *militario* who looked us over and whistled, making comments to each other in their dialects. There were no compartments on this train, but luckily we found one of the tables with four seats surrounding it.

I peeled off the sticky layers I was wearing and heaved my backpack on the rack next to the other two. The three of us sighed at the same time. And then we cracked up and slapped each other five. We made it!

"That was a bitter minute," Suzie said.

"I can't believe we made it," I said.

"I'm still in shock."

After our tickets were checked, Suzie brought us cappuccino from the dining car. She handed out packs of packaged breakfast sweets. "I'm somehow doubting these will be as good as yesterday."

After our quick snack, we played cards and then we started letter writing and journal entries. Eventually we stopped to stare out the window at the beginnings of Switzerland. I couldn't believe we made it, not only to the train but to the country.

In Lugano, they have a funicular. None of us knew what that was, but it was our first stop after changing money and checking our backpacks for the day in the station. We only planned for a day in Lugano and then to Luzerne in the late afternoon. Olivia got it all figured out, and Suzie and I gave the okay.

A funicular is almost like a train car that travels on a cable up a hill. And for Olivia, who was afraid of heights, it was a little scary when we took it up to the Piazza Cioccaro. We sat in the first car. Olivia squeezed Suzie's hand and my shoulder, while I took goofy pictures with the cheap camera my parents gave me for Christmas.

From the piazza we had to keep traveling up, exploring the city. It was a long, brisk, ascending walk to a restaurant that had a beautiful view of the mountain range. We drank hot cocoa. Olivia felt calmer. Chocolate made her phobias disappear.

We could kind of communicate with people because they spoke Italian. We might have been speaking better there than we did in Italy.

The mountain air was fresh. And in spite of the cold, we hung out at the table, high up but below the mountains, discussing what we expected from Switzerland. The money was strange. The francs came in paper and coin. Suzie held up one of the bigger coins.

"This is bizarre. It's worth like $20. I feel like I'm going to lose it."

"Don't lose it," said Olivia. "Should we walk down to the *ferrovia*? We've got like an hour

"And miss a ride on the funicular?" Suzie asked.

"It costs, though, and we might get a better view of the city," I said. I would have taken it again but suspected that Olivia didn't want to and wasn't going to admit it.

"That's true," Suzie agreed, quickly. She looked at the view and sighed. She was thinking of Kurt.

I wondered if Jonas would love it here. I closed my eyes for a second. Only a second.

"You're really into Kurt, huh?" I asked Suzie to distract myself.

"Yeah, it's so weird. I'm not usually like this. It's just like have you ever had someone who just kind of gets you? No matter what you look like or what you do." I thought without meaning to of my once-confident walk, my naked lips. Suzie looked at me and it made me scared to answer. But she continued. "He's so cool."

When we walked down toward the station, Olivia had the map accessible. We didn't really talk on the way down. Each of us was in our own thoughts. The air was pure and the cold didn't bother me. It was easy to get caught up in your head. I thought of Jonas, as usual. I wondered when I would become exhausted by the memory of him. Maybe that's how you got over someone, just plain fatigue.

When we passed the Piazza Ciocarro again, there was a large crowd. We stopped to peer in. There were signs up that said "Strudel 100 m."

"What the hell is this?" Suzie asked.

"It looks like a big strudel," I said pointing to the long strudel on a table that curved around. It was the biggest pastry I had ever seen.

"Delicious," Olivia said. I listened to the languages being spoken around me. At first I heard German, but then we heard someone explaining in Italian. It was a record-breaking strudel or at least that's how we translated it. Who knew there was such a thing? But from then on it would always be, in our heads, the record-breaking strudel.

"This is super surreal," Suzie said.

"No one is eating any," I noticed. There were people standing behind the strudel table. Each had a knife and a cash box in front of them. "Look, the record-breaking strudel is 5 francs a piece."

"I will never see another strudel without knowing that I have seen greatness," Olivia said.

"But can we eat greatness?" Suzie asked. She was a sucker for sweets.

Olivia asked one of the men if she might buy a piece of the record-breaking strudel. He told her that it would be cut at three. Then she looked at her watch. "It's quarter of 3. Train leaves at 3:35. What should we do?"

"We want to get to Lucerne tonight and this train is the only train to get us there in time to have one fun night out. Yet how can we pass up the record-breaking strudel?" I didn't want this decision to rest on me. We were talking about a record-breaker after all.

"I guess we might make it if we get the first pieces and run down to the station," Suzie said. One look in her eye and I knew she needed the strudel.

"It is down hill, but I don't know," I said. "We could eat it on the way."

"We have to," Suzie said. "Worst comes to worse, we take the funicular back down."

"But who knows how often it comes." Olivia said.

As we tried to figure it out, the crowd broke into song. They sang an Italian song that none of us understood, but we laughed. Any strudel of this magnitude deserved a song.

"I vote for staying," Suzie said.

"Me too," I said, nodding, looking over at Olivia.

"How can we pass this up?" Olivia said being jostled a little by one of the singers.

And after the song was over, they cut into the strudel and the crowd went nuts, cheering and hooting. I couldn't tell who was happier, Suzie, whose strudel dream was realized, or Olivia, who held up her watch and shouted over the crowd at us, gleefully, "They did it early. It's seven of three."

We collected our 15 Swiss francs, we grabbed our record-breaking strudels and then we walked swiftly down the hill. We all walked the same way–one arm swinging for more power and the other held up, holding our strudel, protecting it with our thumbs on top to prevent the precious victorious record-breaking strudel from being lost forever.

The train station was closer than we thought. We grabbed our bags and waited at the *binario* for the train to come. We still had four minutes to spare. The operation was tight.

When the train came, we hurried onto it, found a car and stacked up the bags on the rack above us. It was as if we were competing in some kind of event of our own. Finally, we flopped onto our seats and smiled at each other's efficiency. Then we began to eat our reward.

"I think *we* broke the record," Olivia said.

"I'm so glad that they cut it early," Suzie said.

"To think we might have never known record-breaking strudel joy," I said, chewing happily, licking my sticky fingers. In a way, it wouldn't have mattered if we didn't make the train. I believe we would have gone with it, rolled into whatever we had to do. But we did make it. And got the strudel too.

I looked out the window. I watched for hours the landscape of Switzerland. It was a beautiful countryside, and it changed from dark lush green to a pure white as we went, from being surrounded by forest to snowy peaks. The train trip lasted about three hours, but none of us were anxious enough to play cards. We were all content to stare out the window and doze a bit.

I was beginning to believe that we were having exceptionally good traveler's luck, that there was some force looking out for us. Some fate was willing us to be okay. I won't jinx it, I thought. I will just enjoy it.

10.

When we arrived in Lucerne, Olivia stopped in the travel agency and grabbed a map. She asked Suzie and me if we wanted to be in charge of it, but we knew it was just a formality and declined. She was meant to be the navigator; it was her gig. She already chose the accommodations from the list in Let's Go.

The woman in the travel agency spoke English and gave us directions to the hotel. We walked over a bridge to get there. There were paintings of goats on the bridge. I wondered if this was like the three billy goats fairy tale and if a troll was waiting on the other side. I didn't feel scared of anything, the way I did when I got to Siena. I felt ready for a troll, for whatever. But, instead of a troll, it was an amazing party.

We maneuvered our big backpacks through a crowd of dancing drunken people speaking German. The people were red-faced and energized. We weaved through the joyous gyrating bodies.

"Must be Carnevale. They must have that here, too," Olivia said. There was a smell of roasting chicken. I noticed a sign advertising cheap beer. We didn't need to know German to understand that. We fell in behind Olivia, who expertly navigated the people onto a side street. She held the open map out in front of her. Suzie and I relied on this, that she could find the way.

The one-star hotel had breakfast and was almost as cheap as hostels and more private. This room had two sets of bunk beds with white sheets folded over pitted woolen blankets. We threw our stuff down on the beds, washed our faces in the sink in the room and went back out to the square. There was no way we were missing out on the fun tonight.

On the street, everyone around us was drunk and yelling in German. A band was playing loud music with lots of horns. We studied our coins before handing some over for mugs of cheap dark beer. We sat at one of the tables surrounded by other travelers. One husky bearded man grabbed Olivia and twirled her around the square.

"Should we be worried?" Suzie asked.

"She's laughing," I said, shrugging.

"I think she's terrified."

"Oh, it's good for her," I said. When I was done with my beer, I got three more and a basket of roasted pieces of chicken. Olivia, back at the table and breathless, finished her beer and took great gulps of the new one I offered her.

"What I really need is water," she said.

"Bottled water is almost three times as much as beer," I said, biting into the delicious chicken. "Try this. It's yummy. So who was your boyfriend?"

"I don't know. He couldn't speak English or Italian. Just French and German. Just." She laughed at herself. "Anyway, I couldn't tell if he was giving me his name or dancing tips. I just kept repeating what I thought he was saying."

At that moment three of the dancers with linked arms and flailing legs crashed into our table knocking over the remains of the plastic cups of beer. The dancers were laughing and slightly stumbling but apparently apologizing.

"It's okay, it's okay," Suzie said and then tried again. "*Niente, e niente.*" But neither language was understood. The dancers stumbled back over with more cups of beer. The beers were filled to the top and spilled on my hand as I took them.

"*Grazie,*" I said out of habit, but then I remembered and tried, "*Danke.*"

The dancers returned to dancing. I wasn't sure if it was a specific dance because everyone was just moving happily, drunkenly, without any amount of inhibition.

"This is insane," I said. "These people are out of control."

"Germans." Olivia said. "They know how to drink."

"Swiss-Germans," Suzie corrected. She counted out some coins for more beer.

We drank the next round up, hoping the alcohol would warm us and bring us closer to the mood of the dancers. But the cups were cold in our hands and we blew our white breath at each other.

"It's freezing," I stated the obvious through chattering teeth.

"Maybe we should try to find a bar or a club," Suzie said.

"There was a bar in the book," Olivia said. She reached into her pocket for the ripped out Lucerne page from the guide. "It's called the American bar."

"Sounds like it could be the perfect place," Suzie said. "Or it could be really cheesy."

"Take us there, Olivia." I said, leaving my fate in her hands.

"Okay," Olivia said. She looked around, looked at the river and back at the map. She wasn't bossy about being in charge, but she definitely liked it and it was a relief for me to have her so confident. "Follow me, ladies."

Once again we maneuvered through the dancing masses. The streets were darker as we got further and further away from the music. None of us were afraid, perhaps because of the alcohol.

"*Cazzo*," Suzie said, jolting us out of our thoughts after about 15 minutes of walking.

"What?"

"I lost my glove. It must've fallen out of my pocket." We reversed directions and looked for the glove for a while. In spite of the cold, it was our mission to find it. We looked around until my own gloved hands felt like they were going to be permanently numb. It was only when we realized we had been up and down the same street three times and would most likely have to totally retrace our steps back to the hotel that we continued on to the oasis of a bar. Suzie kept her hands in her pockets.

At last, we found the bar. We opened the door and stepped in from the cold. The bar welcomed us with a roar and then returned to whatever was happening before we stepped inside.

I woke the next morning in the one-star hotel with the smelly bathroom down the hall. I was in a bunk beneath Olivia and looking over to my side I saw the back of Suzie's head in the other bed. The night in Lucerne appeared to me as a series of images that I strung together in my mind. This, I thought, is what it is to travel. The travel bug took a nice juicy bite of my flesh.

Inside the bar the music was loud and sounded like American, 80s pop. A Swiss-Italian was serving drinks. We learned somehow his name was Massimo. Oh, we learned from the mother of the British rugby player who was also there. His name was Chris, and he had just broken up with his girlfriend. This didn't explain why his shirt was off. The mother seemed to want to get with Massimo. Massimo kept giving us fruity frozen drinks.

Another Swiss-German was also serving drinks. He spoke English really well, but he spoke it with an Irish accent. He said he had lived in Dublin. He told us to call him Johnny, but we doubted that was his name.

And here, my memories began to have holes. The crowd was raucous; everyone was speaking English. There were Australians, there were Brazilians, there was a guy from Nigeria. I would never see these people again, but they were forever imprinted on my memory. It was like the whole world was represented in the bar.

The three of us waited until the bar closed. Then there was some deception so Massimo could escape while Chris brought his mother back to their hotel. Massimo was taking us to a disco. He was holding

Olivia's hand. She was giving him the okay to be the leader, to get us to the next place. She deserved a break.

My vision was hazy. Suzie and I were holding on to each other, trying to count the number of beverages we drank that night. I pointed to Massimo, who had stopped in the street to unwrap a piece of gum.

"That means he is going to kiss her," I whispered to Suzie. Then I realized he might have heard me and leaned closer. "Do you think he knows he is?"

"He can't understand us; you don't have to whisper," Suzie said, leaning into me to avoid falling. She shouted up ahead. "Hey, where are we going?"

"To dance," Olivia said. "I don't know where."

"Ooooh, she doesn't knooooow," I said to Suzie, who now had both of her hands on me to steady herself. We laughed. "Let's see what they're going to do."

We watched Olivia's profile, chin tipped up and waiting for the kiss. When it came, it was sloppy, but she smiled. She held on to Massimo and turned to us. I have never heard her voice get louder

"You guys just have to kiss this man. We cannot walk any further until you kiss him."

We were all drunk and laughing. Somehow Massimo understood why Olivia was nudging him to us. Suzie said no right away, but her hands on me gave me a push toward him.

"She loves Kurt," I said. "He's her one and only."

This was not an expression of mine and it made me giggle until I realized that I wasn't going to be able to kiss Massimo either. I wanted to tip my head up expectantly. I wanted to go with the night and charge into whatever it offered.

But I couldn't. I didn't want someone else's mouth on me. I wanted to want it, but it just wasn't right.

"All for you, Olivia," I said. They kissed some more, and Suzie and I held the wall for support as we laughed. I thought my laugh was beginning to sound hollow now. Once again, I had begun to question everything.

Chris caught up with us, and we went to the disco. I couldn't remember anything about it, except it was dark and everyone was wearing jackets, still cold from outside. We girls danced. Olivia stayed with us when Massimo tried to get her to sit on his lap at the table. Eventually, Chris and Massimo were gone. We kept dancing.

"They are probably fucking his mother," Olivia said. I nodded. I wasn't feeling the fun anymore. I kept thinking about how I couldn't kiss Massimo even though I wanted to, just to do it, to get kissing someone else over with. Maybe I would never kiss anyone again.

"Hey," Olivia said. I looked up at her. She took my hand and swung it to the time to the music. "It's no big deal. It was just a kiss. Just have fun."

I nodded again. I kept dancing even though I wasn't into it. Suzie was spinning, eyes closed, totally gone. I wanted to be there, but I wasn't. Then Olivia came closer to me. Her eyebrows knit together. When she spoke it was a command, almost a fact, like she was telling me to turn right based on looking at her map. "Just. Have. Fun"

And I did. I let go, because I had a friend who wanted me to. I reminded myself that I was young and traveling and away from everything and everyone.

Then the disco closed and Olivia tried to remember the way home. We hadn't been paying attention to where Massimo was leading us. So we were like Hansel and Gretel in Lucerne. We crossed the same bridge twice over the Ruess River, the paintings on the bridge eerier each time. We didn't have the patience to marvel at how old everything was. Olivia was getting frustrated. She peed on a side street and looked up at us with a strange expression. Her eyes, usually scouting for road signs, seemed to float around in her head. It made us laugh so hard we had to pee too. Then we found Suzie's lost glove on a street I thought we already went down. There it was, just sitting on the sidewalk waiting for us. It was a blessed sign. Fate, I believed, saving us once again.

Soon after that we found the hotel. We tried to be composed for the hostess who handed us our key. We took aspirin and gulped handfuls of water from the sink in our room. Olivia and I were too dizzy to brush our teeth. We took our jeans off, left our shirts on. Then we passed out. How Olivia made it to the top bunk, I can't remember. I closed my eyes as fast as I could to stop the spinning.

It finally stopped when I lay down on the thin mattress.

We slept through the continental breakfast hour at the hotel. Olivia found a cheap cafeteria in the Let's Go. The city was different in daylight, everything a little less spooky and wild. As chance or fate or whatever puppet master was pulling the strings of our trip would have it, Johnny, the bartender, worked at the cafeteria. He greeted us in his thick Irish accent.

"I have decided to offer you drinks," he said, awkwardly placing latte and orange juice before us. We saved several Swiss francs just paying for the chocolate pastry.

We had our meal and waved goodbye to him. Olivia hustled quickly out of the place.

"Slow down, O. I'm still hungover," Suzie said. "Actually, I got to use the *bagno*. Can you guys hang on?"

"We'll wait outside," said Olivia. She tugged my coat and said, "I need a cigarette."

"Since when do you smoke first thing in the morning? And not to mention when you're hungover. You are hungover, aren't you?" I asked.

"Yeah, I just wanted to get some air." Olivia took a deep breath, but didn't light up a cigarette.

"Yeah, I know what you mean. That latte did me good though. Woke me up a bit," I said. "It was nice of him to give us those. What's so funny?"

"Nothing," Olivia said. Her expression was mischievous.

"C'mon, what?" Olivia looked past me into the cafeteria.

"He should have given us the whole thing."

"I don't get it. "

"I kissed him on the way to the bathroom in the bar last night."

"You did? I didn't even know you liked him."

"I didn't either. It just kind of happened. I actually forgot about it until he winked at me when he gave me the latte."

"Shit," I said laughing and then remembered what we did after. "You hussy, you kissed the bartender, too. You're a kissing bandit, that's what you are."

"I know. I wanted to tell you. They were both fun. Here comes Suzie."

We saw the sights of Lucerne in the daytime. We got a chance to really study the eerie paintings of the Spreurbrucke bridge in daylight. We took a bus and two cable cars up to the breathtaking views of Mount Pilatus and hiked around, studying the landscapes from above.

For an early dinner, we ate fondues and salads and drank pints of German wheat beer. Our hangovers disappeared. We talked about all the traveling we wanted to do in the future. We vowed to each other that no matter what we did or where we worked, we would live for vacation days, always planning to get as far away as we can on the money and time that we have.

And then back on a train. Once again we were not sure we were on the right train. We asked the German-speaking conductor when we should change, and he told us to stay on. We weren't as preoccupied with a schedule now. Right or wrong, I believed we would get to where we were meant to be. Sure enough, the train split in two with some cars going in a different direction. Our part wound up headed to Firenze as we expected. A new Italian conductor came on to check our tickets. He smiled when he punched our tickets and called us "*ragazze*."

As I looked out into the darkness rushing by, I kept thinking of being called *ragazze*, girls. In the states, at our liberal arts college, we would all be called women, never girls. But here, I didn't mind being called *ragazze*. I felt, at that moment, that I wanted to be a *ragazza* for as long as I could.

MARZO

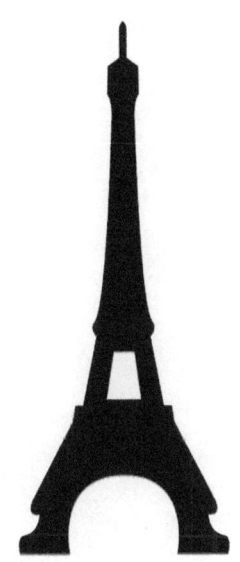

11.

Sometimes Gaetano waited for me outside the *università* on his *vespa*. He took me into the countryside, to the churches I hadn't yet seen or to a pizzeria that he discovered. He enjoyed showing these things to me.

Sitting behind Gaetano on the bike, I was often overcome. It wasn't the smell of his brown leather jacket and the strong wind in my face. But it was all the old stone buildings around me, the promise that the gray fields we passed would some day blossom to green. If there was promise under that cold dirt, there might be hope for me.

I was there, listening to him sing in dialect. The words I would never understand. I imagined they were songs he heard as a child from fishermen in the sleepy Southern Italian town that he considered a country.

I still wished I could have seen this all with Jonas or at least climbed into bed with him at the end of the day and described it, with our hands and bodies interlaced.

"You're crying?" Gaetano asked once after a ride, noticing my full eyes. But I blamed it on the wind–*il vento*, and he nodded, seemed to accept that, but still watched me closely.

Gaetano and I spent a lot of time together. Now that we spoke only Italian, he no longer tried to show off the bits of English he knew. He accepted my make-believe boyfriend and seemed to respect that we were only friends. He asked me about the boyfriend occasionally, and I made stuff up on the spot, hoping I wouldn't be caught in a lie.

Part of me wanted to like him. I knew he still wanted to be more than my friend in spite of what I said. It would have been easier in some ways if I could just let my guard down, but I didn't know if I ever was going to stop finding Jonas in my thoughts late in the evenings when everything else was gone.

Once we passed the monastery where he lived. Visitors were allowed into the church and on the grounds, but the dormitory was for monks and male students only. I teased him that he was like a little monk.

"If I am a monk, it's because of you." He knew how far to go with me. "You are a sly fox. *Quanto sei forba*."

Slowly, I relaxed around him. I relied on him for certain things and enjoyed the teasing between us, as long as he wanted nothing more, or if he wanted more he could contain it. We had gotten past the point of just hooking up, and I liked having him as a friend. I suspected that sometimes he took the hillier roads so I had to hold him tighter on the *vespa*.

But, I would not let myself expect to see him outside the *università*. If the class got out early, I went to Lucy's apartment or to buy lunch.

Wednesdays, when the stores were closed in the afternoon, I went to the outdoor market to browse the clothes and shoes I couldn't afford. Sometimes, when I didn't see Gaetano after class, I sensed that he was following me. But when I looked up, he wasn't there.

On the *festa della donna*, the feast day celebrating women, he brought me mimosa flowers and took me out for lunch at the Osteria la Chiacchiera, where I got *pici boscaiola*, the thick pasta of Siena in a rich creamy mushroom sauce. After lunch we walked *in giro* around the city. Every woman had a bunch of mimosa. I was happy to be one of them. For once I felt a part of Siena, a citizen.

Gaetano stopped at a *palazzo* and asked me to wait for him outside the building while he picked something up from a friend. I leaned against a wall, holding my spray of mimosa, staring up at the window he might be behind. It was cold and I wished he had asked me up.

I envisioned someone crashing through the glass, being thrown by him and then I knew what he was doing, why he didn't ask me up. I remembered when we first met what Dino said about him being a criminal. I thought of the fight the second time I saw him. When he came back down, I glanced at his jacket, suspecting it was fuller, that there was money in his pocket.

"What?" he asked. "How did you know where I was?"

"You saw me looking? I just guessed that was where you were. I expected someone to come flying out of one of the windows."

"Why would that happen?" he asked, playing dumb.

"Because you're like a bookie, aren't you? That's what it is." I nodded at his expression of surprise. He understood the English word *bookie*. I kept walking when he stopped. After a while he caught up to me.

"Gabi, I told you it's normal for many men of the south to do things that are a little illegal."

"A little illegal?" I turned to him and shook my head. "And you wonder why you have the bad reputation if Southerners do what is *a little illegal.*"

"*Gabi, aspetta,*" he stopped me on the street, to concentrate fully on the conversation. It was impossible for him to multitask. "I do this, so I will have more money. I need it. I don't have enough for what I need."

"Gaetano, I don't really care how you get money. It doesn't matter to me. I'm not your girlfriend. It doesn't bother me in the least. Do what you want."

He smiled at the way I said "*non mi frega niente*" about his activities with the passionate dispassion of a true Italian. There was nothing else for either of us to say about this revelation. We shrugged at each other and decided to get an espresso.

"Did you get mimosa?" I asked Olivia when she came to see me on Friday. We were sharing a loaf of *pane proscuitto* that I bought for her in the *macelleria* with the big pig out in front. I finally had the courage to go in. It was down the road from my apartment and every single tourist seemed to need a picture with the big pig. They made the best proscuitto bread, though, and Olivia was a fiend for it.

"I don't have a Gaetano, Gabriella. I'm not going to get mimosa from anyone."

"He was just doing it to be nice. He's not my boyfriend."

"But *you* are his *tesoro*," she teased.

"I really think he understands that there is not going to be anything between us. I think he knows that we are just friends." Olivia looked at me with an expression that was becoming quite familiar. She narrowed her eyes and tipped her chin in disbelief. "Okay, okay, well, I understand that there is going to be nothing between us. So there is going to be nothing between us. We won't even see him tonight, okay?"

"I like seeing him. I want to see him. He's funny. I don't get mimosa from him, but I still think he's cool. And he's cute too, those sexy eyes." Gaetano was endearing himself to her. I wondered if this was his evil plan. "Why don't you do something about it? Why don't you get with him? You don't really have anyone at home, do you?"

"No," I said. "I don't."

That was the sad truth. I didn't say anything else, and she let the subject drop.

I called the monastery, but I couldn't get in touch with Gaetano. Olivia and I drank a few glasses of wine with some pasta at my apartment. Then we went to Le Colonial.

"Look, your roommate is here," Olivia said. She was looking over to where Janine was holding court with two guys. She was wearing a low-cut black shirt. Her blonde hair was pulled dramatically off her face. Olivia turned to me. "She is able to get that look with the cheap blow dryers from the Upim?"

"She's a pro. Do you want to stay?" Olivia shrugged. It was stupid of me to not want to be where

Janine was, but I thought about avoiding her completely. Janine caught my eye and waved us over.

"Hey, Janine, what are you up to? You remember Olivia?"

"Hey," said Olivia. Janine gave her a big smile that didn't hide the fact that she was no longer happy with the boy-girl ratio. She introduced us to the guys, Luigi and Carlo. I gathered that she didn't know either one of them and that she was out alone, because Michelle was with Duccio.

Luigi couldn't speak English as well as Carlo, so it made it harder for him to speak with Janine. She focused on Carlo. But Luigi was beautiful. He smiled at me. We were communicating. He didn't understand me as well as Gaetano. I would be self-conscious of my accent if it weren't for the buzz.

I laughed at his hemmed jeans. Luigi told me I had a good liver—*un buon fegato*—and that's why I could drink so much. I was drinking glass after glass of *gintonnico*, saying *buon fegato* over and over again. I liked understanding new phrases right away and alcohol helped me do that. I leaned into Luigi. I wanted to be normal; I wanted to forget and get caught up in something like every other American girl in Italy. I didn't have anyone at home. It was true. I was free and I should act it. I wanted to kiss this Italian. I told Olivia so in fast English.

"Do you want me to go back to Firenze?" Olivia asked.

"No," I said, taking Luigi's hand in my lap. "I'm not going to do anything."

But that was a lie. It was not my intention. I wanted something. I wanted to get over this hump with this man.

Olivia started to say something, but then I saw Olivia looking up at Giovanni, Gaetano's friend. He caught me before I had done anything wrong. We waved to him, but he didn't come over. Luigi wanted to know who he was, if he should be worried.

"*Amico*," I said, assuring Luigi that he was a friend. My eyes were scanning for Gaetano. This wasn't going to help my fake boyfriend story. Everyone was finishing their drinks. They wanted to leave. Olivia asked me again if I wanted her to come home with me. Yes, I told her. Carlo and Janine were holding each other tight as we started to walk out. Luigi pulled me into his chest. Then I saw Gaetano with Paolo, saw that he already understood everything that was going on. His gray eyes were on fire. I was no better than any of the other American girls. And then I thought of his temper and that time I saw him fight.

"I'll be right out. I have to go to the bathroom," I said to Luigi. And to Olivia, "Come with me. It will look better."

"*Come va?*" I asked Gaetano. He smirked at me. I kissed him on both cheeks. He nodded his head.

"*Bene. Ciao, Olivia.*" We looked at each other until I felt Paolo, Giovanni and Olivia getting uncomfortable. I am not yours to be jealous of, I wanted to tell him. I am not anyone's. I am alone. Now there was a dark cloud on my good night.

Awkwardly, I told him that I got a good grade on the homework he helped me with. He shrugged. I kissed him again on both cheeks, twice. Four kisses.

"My friends are waiting for me," I said.

"Then of course you must go. *Ciao, Olivia.*"

"*Ciao*," Olivia said and kissed him goodbye.

Outside. Outside Carlo and Janine already started hooking up hard against the wall.

"Will you walk us home?" I asked Luigi.

"*Sì.*"

"I'll walk behind you." Olivia said.

"Don't be silly," I said. I felt grateful to her but also somewhat embarrassed for my behavior. I couldn't be as carefree as I wanted to be.

"C'mon, have your moment."

"Okay, here's my key. Walk ahead. Leave the *portone* open and the door to the apartment. You can take my bed."

"You got it."

We looked at the two still passionate against the wall. Then we started to walk. Olivia walked much faster until she was comfortably ahead of us. I shrugged at Luigi and tried to find that feeling again. He laughed and took my hand. His hands were warm. His eyes were blue and almost like Jonas's. It was not the first time I noticed that. Luigi asked me again about the boys I was talking to in the bar. I told him they were friends.

"You have a lot of friends."

I was charmed by the way he spoke, his Tuscan accent dropping the *c* when he asks about my *casa*. He walked me through the *campo*. I looked up at the tower. It grounded me. One thing solid and still in a swimming night. Our fingers were interlaced. I wanted to feel his warmth. He wrapped his arm around me.

At the *portone*, he told me he would call me. *But I don't have a phone. Well, he'll see me then.* We smiled. I wanted to kiss him, see those eyes close and open. I did. My hands reached up into his hair as he groaned in his throat. It was a good kiss but not the best I ever had. And while I was hoping my stomach would drop like it does when you kiss someone new, I felt a pang in my sternum. My heart hurt. It felt so different to me, bittersweet. This confirmed something I already knew. I smelled the bread starting to cook in the air. The baker was up, working. We hugged. We kissed again. This night should be wonderful even though it was the wrong boy

I didn't invite him up. We kissed again and he left. I didn't want to go into my apartment. I lingered in the hall until the electric light shut off. Then I went inside.

Olivia was passed out on the floor in spite of my offer. I almost tripped on her in the darkness. When I apologized, she said nothing and I whispered her name. Part of me wanted to get her up to talk. When she didn't wake up, I turned on the light. I wrote drunken scribbles in my journal. I had been trying not to write about Jonas. What more was there to say? But I wrote instead in a sloppy hand, "When will I be over this?"

"Promise me, you'll never start or end anything drunk." Where did that voice come from? Once it came from me. I said it to Jonas. We thought we had it under control. It didn't matter that we were sleeping in the same bed, for a while. We could do this.

I thought that Jonas was going to kiss me that night, but he didn't, he hugged me. His fingertips touching my back like eyes seeing. That was all he would do at that point. So many memories are about waiting. It was easier to remember the waiting than the way it was once I got what I wanted. It hurt less, physically.

And so I was getting sober, lying in a tiny bed in a faraway place. The kiss of a beautiful Italian boy reminding me of the words of a beautiful American. Why couldn't I shake it? When would I be over it?

Sober, no longer normal or carefree. Me once again. His.

12.

Of course, I didn't hear from Luigi. And I didn't really mind. I didn't know how I could have. I guessed an American girl who doesn't really put out isn't that interesting for a Tuscan man as cute as he was. It was for the best. I would always be expecting something more from his blue eyes.

I didn't call Gaetano for three days. I spent the weekend with Olivia. We took the bus to the town of San Gimignano and admired their towers. It was a quiet sleepy town, smaller than Siena.

Gaetano didn't come to the *unversità* that Monday, so I called him to see how he spent his *fine settimana*. He sounded sad when he spoke. But I tried to keep the conversation light. I told him that I spent the weekend with Olivia.

He asked me if I wanted to go to a Brazilian club in Florence.

"Sure, I'll call Olivia. Why don't you ask Dino?"

He hesitated. "You want them to come, too?"

"Of course," I said. "This way, Dino can drive. How else would we get there?"

That wasn't really it. I just didn't want to be alone with him. I didn't want to be held accountable. I had made my position clear. I just wanted to be friends. But I did feel like I had disappointed him. And I prayed that he just let it go. I wasn't going to see Luigi again, and I didn't want to explain to Gaetano why my fake boyfriend hadn't been an issue.

I called Olivia as soon as I hung up the phone with Gaetano and asked her to come along.

"Yep," she said. "By the way, tonight's the night."

Suzie was going to sleep with Kurt.

"Huge. Good thing he has his own apartment."

"Yeah, it would be impossible to sneak him into this fortress."

"Anyway, they want to go to a Brazilian dance club. Before that they want to go to the Mexican place you and Gaetano were talking about it. You know where it is?" I asked.

"Yeah, I pass it all the time."

"Does that sound *bene* to you?"

"*Benessimo*. It's a regular international evening with the international girls."

I met Gaetano and Dino in a piazza north of Via Stalloreggi. Dino had a bright yellow Alfa Romeo that he was very proud of. I heard that he liked to drive it fast, but neither he nor Gaetano wore their seat belts. They laughed when I asked for help buckling into the seat in the back. Dino was honestly puzzled trying to find the seat belt.

"I'm not sure there is one back here," Dino said to a convulsing Gaetano.

"There must be a buckle if there is this," I said, holding up the strap, making due with the limited language. Dino reached into the backseat, close to my butt.

"*Bravo!*" Gaetano said and winked at Dino like Dino was going to get lucky.

"Must everything be about sex with you?" I asked.

"Yes, everything." Then he changed to English to impress Dino and me. "Everything in my life–sex."

"*Bravo*," I said and rolled my eyes.

"*Faccia di cazzo*," Gaetano said. Translated this phrase seemed to mean "dickhead," but Gaetano convinced me it was a compliment.

"*Ecco*," said Dino, when he finally located the buckle. "*Andiamo.*"

Gaetano was being cool about everything. I thought that it might turn out to be a good night.

Dino's driving was worse than I expected. He tailgated every car in front of him. When the cars didn't move out of the lane, he high-beamed them. He zipped in and out of lanes in a way that would have infuriated my driver's ed teacher.

"Jesus," I said, clutching the side of my door. Gaetano relayed it to Dino, who turned while driving to look at my hands. They both laughed at me, exaggerating expressions of fear. It was a nightmare.

"Um, Dino, can you please watch the road," I said. They laughed even harder. There were several close calls where my stomach dipped up and down. I squinted to try to avoid all of our near misses. Gaetano turned in the seat every time. I heard his breathy laughter. With eyes closed, I shook my head at him and stuck out my tongue. He laughed even harder.

"Why are you sweating?" Olivia said when she came to the door.

"You should have seen the car ride. Is that restaurant far from here?"

"No, but I think the club is."

The Mexican place was pretty close to where Olivia lived. I suggested that we walk, but Dino wanted to impress Olivia with his car. Luckily, this ride was quick.

"You have hardly seen the worst of it," I said to Olivia.

The restaurant looked like every stereotypical Mexican restaurant in America. There were woven sombreros pinned to the walls and colorful tablecloths that looked like Mexican blankets. It was familiar to us, but the Italians thought this would be an authentic experience. For them, Mexican wasn't something they ordered in; it was exotic. The food was standard Mexican fare, but the cheese was different from cheddar or jack. When we tried to order Mexican beer, the *cameriere* didn't know what Corona was, so we drank Sol beer instead. It tasted almost the same.

At dinner Olivia remembered what day it was. The seventeenth of March. It was St. Patrick's Day. Olivia explained the significance of St. Patrick's Day in America, and I added, "It's another excuse to drink."

"Yeah," said Olivia. "On St. Patrick's Day, everyone is Irish."

"Today, we Italians will be Irish also," Dino said, smiling at Olivia. I wondered if there would be something between them more than the minor flirtation. Were all my friends destined to match up with Gaetano's? Was this another part of his evil plan?

I looked at him, narrowing my eyes. He was also looking at Olivia and Dino. Then he saw me looking at him.

"What a face!" He laughed. "What are you thinking with that face, *tesoro*?"

"Nothing. What are you thinking with *your* face?" He waited until Olivia and Dino looked at him to answer me. He did that a lot. When he thought he had something funny to say, he needed all eyes on him.

"*Senti*. We are Italians and Americans, who are Irish today in a Mexican restaurant. It's strange, you think?"

We toasted this with a chin-chin. It occurred to me that that was a Chinese expression taken by the Italians to make a toast.

On the way to the club, they insisted on showing us the transvestite prostitutes of Firenze. They were tall and blonde, striding around in stilettos and skimpy outfits. They all had fake breasts that they took out and jiggled at the passing cars. This made Dino and Gaetano howl. In the backseat, Olivia and I got impatient.

"Okay, are we going to the club?" I asked.

"You don't like the transvestites?" Dino asked.

"Are we supposed to like them?" Olivia asked back.

"It's not like we've never seen transvestites before," I said.

"I forgot you're *americane*," Gaetano said, mocking. There was the first hint of bitterness.

"Remember on St. Patrick's Day, we're supposed to drink," I said.

"Excuse me, Gabriella, I also forgot that you go into convulsions if you don't get a drink into your liver." This was one of the times he successfully waited for everyone to listen, because everyone laughed at me, including me.

"So can we go to the club?" Olivia asked the front seat.

"*Andiamo*." Gaetano said. He waved at the transvestites as we went by. They shook their bare fake chests in response.

The club was another giant warehouse but bigger than Tendenza, the club outside of Siena. There was a giant dance floor, a stage and several levels surrounding them with small tables. We climbed up a couple of levels. Dino and Gaetano wanted to get a table so they could have a good view of the Brazilian *spettacolo* that was set to come on at eleven. I liked that word, *spettacolo*. It seemed so much better than a show.

"You are beautiful tonight," Gaetano said so that only I could hear.

"But not as good as the transvestites, right?"

"*Stronza*. I'd do better with a transvestite."

"Probably," I said to make him laugh. He didn't.

We ordered Brazilian drinks–mojitos and cuba libres. We drank for a while.

Gaetano was being especially touchy-feely with me as Olivia and Dino flirted. I thought we already covered that. But maybe, now that he saw me with another Italian, he thought things had changed.

The *spettacolo* was a bit disappointing compared to what I had in mind. It wasn't really a show at all, just scantily clad dancers who came out shaking all the parts of their bodies and blowing whistles. The rhythmic Brazilian drum livened the place up. In their seats, Dino and Gaetano shook like the dancers. Behind them, Olivia and I smiled at each other.

"Why are you laughing?" Gaetano asked me.

"I'm laughing at your dance. You're dancing in the chair."

"Do you want to dance?" he asked me, already starting to get up. I shrugged. "C'mon, let's dance."

On the dance floor, he pulled me close, too close. I stepped away from him, as far as I could against the crowd. I raised my arms and moved my hips, trying to go with the beat. He was staring at me.

"The dancers are better than the transvestites, too, no?" I yelled over the drums and whistles. I wanted him to look at the dancers, at their hips, not mine. I looked back up at Olivia laughing at whatever Dino was saying. All the people on the dance floor were just letting go. I wanted Gaetano to look anywhere but at me. I would have danced by myself.

He smiled a little at me. He still wouldn't look away from me. He wouldn't even joke with me. It was just the same look. He was pushed toward me. It wasn't really him, it was the crowd, but he reached out to touch my waist. He grinded against me. I could feel him still staring at me. We could never be true friends. I was naive to think we could.

I stopped dancing.

"What's wrong?"

"I'm tired of dancing. Let's have a drink." He was still moving to the music, still looking at me the same way. I again tried to joke with him. "I am getting the shakes."

Now he stopped dancing. Bodies around us still moved, jostling against us, swinging, oblivious. He didn't smile at my joke. Instead, he reached out to me. He grabbed the top of my arm, so I had to look up at him. Then I looked away, beyond his hair. He pulled me closer, put his thumb to my lips and pressed hard.

"Gaetano," I said.

"I just want to look at you like this." He spoke quietly, but I heard him in spite of the music. There was desperation in his face. I realized I was wrong to even do this, to hang out with him, when I knew how he felt. None of this was fair to him. I liked having him as a friend, having someone to hang out with, but it wasn't going to work with the way he felt.

I finally looked back up at him.

"Gaetano." I tugged my arm away from him. "I am going back up."

I walked away from him on the dance floor, back up the steps to the little tables. Dino and Olivia were talking with their faces close together. I regretted that I may be busting up the vibe between them, but thankfully, Gaetano was right behind me.

"We can sit here," he said into my ear. There was a table not too close to Olivia and Dino.

"*Grazie.*" I don't know why I said it. He hated when I thanked him. The waitress came. I ordered more drinks. Still trying to keep things afloat, I smiled over at Olivia to try and change the subject.

"I think it's going well with Olivia and Dino." He nodded. I couldn't say more than I already had. I knew what it was to want someone and usually not much can dissuade it.

"I don't know what to say to you. I don't want to hurt you," I said, linking verbs as I had just been taught to do in class. I was struck by the fact that even my social life was a language lesson. I said it again. "*Non voglio farti male.*"

"It is me," he said. "I have been feeling strange lately. A little down."

"Because of me?"

"Partly because of you. Partly because of me."

"I'm sorry for my parts."

"I miss the sweetness."

"What sweetness?"

"Sometimes you are a bit cold to me."

"I know. It's true. I don't want to be. But sometimes I feel that I have to be or you will get the wrong idea."

"The idea that you don't have a boyfriend." He looked at me hard. I couldn't tell if he was trying to be cruel. Maybe I deserved it for letting him see me with Luigi.

"Is this about what happened at the Le Colonial? I'm sorry you were upset. It wasn't a big deal."

"But you didn't have a boyfriend then?"

"No, I wasn't really thinking about anything then." I felt all the mixed liquor but still wasn't sure I wanted to fess up about the imaginary boyfriend. "It's got nothing to do with my boyfriend, Gaetano. My boyfriend has nothing to do with us. You said you didn't care that I wanted to be your friend. You said you liked spending time with me."

"Would you be upset if I had a girlfriend?"

"Why do you ask me that? No, I wouldn't be upset."

"Why?" I inhaled before I answered. It was hard to know how to be delicate in Italian, if it was possible to say things better than I was able to say them.

"Because, Gaetano, I don't want to be with you."

He nodded, swallowing. I reached across the table to touch his hand. He pulled away, almost knocking his glass over, but he steadied it in time with his other hand.

"I don't want to be with anyone. Not the boy in Le Colonial. That was just dumb. No one. Not now." I wished I could make him understand. He didn't say anything for a long time. He looked down to the dance floor, not really seeing it.

"I must return home for a while. I'll go south in a couple of weeks." He nodded to himself. "I'll feel better. I will feel more up."

I sighed. It made me sad to think of him having to go home. I wondered if I would see him again when he returned. I wondered if he had gotten tired of me. I wouldn't blame him.

"I'm sorry," I said. Then he looked at me and smiled. The smile was startling. Perhaps he was better at changing the subject or mood than I was.

"You must never say sorry. You must never say thank you and never say sorry. Friends do not do this." I didn't detect irony in the word friends, *amici*, but perhaps in this language, I missed the subtlety.

"Okay," I said. I looked over at Olivia. Dino motioned for us to come over to their table.

Later, we danced again, all four of us. It was different. There were still a lot of people on the dance floor, but we allowed some space between each other somehow. I was expecting Olivia and Dino to be closer than they were.

"Did we ruin the mood?" I yelled in quick English to Olivia over the music. She shook her head.

"I'm not sure what he wants. He's confusing." She faced away from Dino when she said this. His English wasn't bad. "We'll talk about this later."

When the club closed, we piled back in the Alfa Romeo. This time Olivia got to sit in the front with Dino. She finally understood the terror that was Dino's driving. When she turned around to look at me, I warned her about getting whiplash.

Gaetano said little to me in the backseat. When we dropped Olivia off, he got into the front seat. I closed my eyes and dozed a bit, the jerky zigzags of Dino's *macchina* lulled me to sleep.

"*Bella,*" I heard Gaetano's voice from the front seat. He didn't touch me. "We're here."

They drove me to my door. Late at night, you could do this. You weren't supposed to drive cars into the streets of Siena past the walls, but you could sometimes. It was frowned upon but done anyway.

I leaned up in the seat to thank Dino. "Let me know if you want Olivia's number."

"I already have it. *Ciao bella.*"

Gaetano got out of the car to let me out of the back. He kept his arms on the door and the roof of the car, so I had to lean in to him to kiss him.

"So when will you go to the south?"

"In a few weeks." The way he said this, quick and dismissive, made me think he wanted me to just go away.

"Should I call you?"

"Do what you want, *tesoro.*" Still his treasure.

"Then I will call you."

"Okay. *Ciao bella.*"

"*Ciao, ciao, ciao.*"

Back in my room, I felt *un po' giu*, a little down, like Gaetano. Maybe I should have cut it off. Maybe I should just give in. He doesn't know what he would be getting into with me, I thought. He wouldn't want it. He cared too much. It's not good to care too much. Shit.

I remembered how one time back at school when the Stalker girl was waiting down the hall for the boy that was never coming out, Kaitlin shook her head.

"I know, it's ridiculous," I said when we were back in our room. I was, at the time, firmly in control of my emotions and relationships.

"She reminds me of someone who can't get out of her own way," Kaitlin said. I didn't really understand that expression then, but I got it now and I wished I knew how to say something like it in Italian to explain to Gaetano why I just couldn't get involved with him. I couldn't get out of my own way. And I didn't want to get in his.

"You aren't going to be able to just ignore me," Jonas said. He said this after I stepped through the distance of his dancing circle. It was before either of us understood the strength of my will or how deep my hurt could go. "You can't do this, not after all this."

"But you can go back to her?" I asked, my mouth a thin hard line. "You'll touch her like you touch me."

"I haven't decided yet."

"Right, *you* haven't. So I will. I'll make it easy."

"It's not easy."

"No, it isn't, but I'd like to be spared your little soap opera." It was hard to be that cold to him. I turned to the window and looked at his face in the glass, looked at him watching me so I wouldn't have to see what my words had done to his eyes.

Sometimes we looked at each other's reflections in windows or mirrors when we were smiling too much. We could never understand how well we got along.

My memory was not to be trusted. This was another rule I made. I must never trust my memory. It could not have been either as good or as bad as I remembered. It was impossible for me to remember it in pieces. If I could separate out the pieces I would be okay. I could do things to make me okay.

No, no I would never be okay. Even the pieces hurt.

I remembered sitting on the bus and making him laugh. I remembered his face exploding with a smile, body convulsing, rolling his head around in happiness. What did I say? Something stupid? Something wonderful? It didn't matter. I cannot imagine that I had the power to do that to him, to anyone. To have that power over someone else. Surely if I'd had it, we wouldn't be apart. None of that can be true.

But if I get his face smiling I have to see everything. I have to have it tinged with hurt. I did some bad things, too. I must not remember those.

I am not a violent person.

13.

Finals week for my first Italian semester came when I would be taking midterms at college in America. Afterward I had a whole week off to go visit Kaitlin in Paris. For the whole week, I studied hard for the final.

There would be multiple choice and written essay questions. There would the requisite Italian oral examination attended by both Signora Laza and another professor. The oral test would be given to two students at a time.

Normally, I would ask Gaetano to help me study. I counted on his help, but I called him only once since the night at the club. He made no attempt to see me.

Instead I spent a couple of afternoons studying with Lucy at her apartment outside the walls. Lucy was a far superior student. She had no fear about the language. She was willing to say things. She let herself make mistakes. She learned more that way.

At her house, she made us cups of espresso and in return I bought her packs of Dunhill Lights. Lucy was much more sedate than the rest of the girls on the program. She was almost twenty-eight and mature. I was flattered that someone like Lucy enjoyed my company. It was a bit of a privilege that I had another person to help me escape my apartment.

At Lucy's house we ate plates of fresh vegetables and the saltless Tuscan bread with tangy cheese made from sheep's milk. One afternoon Lucy whipped up a crepe. There was always wine. This was the special excess of living in Italy–that there was always wine.

Lucy hinted about her past wildness, but those days were over she told me. Lucy alluded to all this through a cloud of cigarette smoke, but never gave away too much. All I knew was that this was not her first time in Europe. I liked her mystery and felt flattered that I might be the one to someday figure it out.

On the Tuesday before the final, Signora Laza came up to me as I was getting ready to go for the *pausa*. Most of the class was already out the door. As always, I tensed up in her presence. I lived in constant fear that Signora Laza would tell me that I couldn't speak the language and never would be able to.

"Have you been studying for the final?"

"Yes," I said, hesitantly. I felt my underarms begin to sweat. "A lot."

"I suggest you study very hard."

"Okay," I said. My tongue was thick in my mouth.

"I'm not sure you are going to pass."

"Okay." What was I supposed to say to that? Signora Laza nodded and buttoned up her coat.

"I'll see you in the café."

"Okay," I said again. I pretended I still had to collect something before *pausa* so I would not have to walk out with Signora Laza and hear more about how I was going to fail the final. I never failed a class in my life. My parents were disappointed when I got a 3.0 in my first semester of college. Now Signora Laza thought I wasn't going to pass. *Way to inspire confidence, Signora Laza.*

Shit.

That afternoon, I didn't take a nap. After I made lunch, I began studying furiously. I managed to commandeer the dining room table, so that Lisa had to work around me. She finally gave up and went to sit at the desk in the foyer.

Michelle and Janine also had finals, but neither one of them were too nervous about it. Michelle was doing surprisingly well, just learning the basics from scratch and from Duccio. It was not in Janine's nature to care. Lisa, on the other hand, was holding out hope that she would be so fluent during her oral exam that they would automatically skip her a level.

When Michelle came home, she immediately burst into tears. I got up to meet her at the doorway of the dining room. We hugged.

"What's wrong? What happened? Is it Duccio?"

"No, it's my grandmother. She's been sick, you know." I didn't.

"Is she okay?" I asked.

"No, she doesn't have much time. If I want to see her again, it's now or never."

"Oh, I'm so sorry," I said. I squeezed her arm.

"I've been at the office at the *università* all afternoon trying to book a flight, so I can just go home since we already have a break. I got my *professore* to give me the exam early and I've got to take it tomorrow and then I catch a flight out of Pisa at four. Jesus, this is going to be a hell of a night."

"Oh, I'm so sorry to hear about your grandmother. I'm going to be up all night, too, if that's any consolation. My *professoressa* told me she doubts I'm going to pass." After I said it, I wondered if I should have. It wasn't at all comparable to Michelle's problem. But Michelle was smiling.

"Are you serious? Do you want to pull an old school all-nighter with me?"

"*Assolutamente, bella.*"

"Okay."

We stayed up the entire night studying. I made room for Michelle on the dining room table. I didn't give a shit what Lisa thought when she came in to forage for pastries on the shelf. *Non mi fregga niente.* Lisa looked over at us.

"What?" I asked.

"Can I have one of your biscotti?"

"Sure," I said. I wondered if Lisa was the food thief, if Lisa would take it whether we were there or not.

When Janine came home, Michelle told her the whole story of her grandmother, the final and how she had to go home.

"That sucks," said Janine tugging a strand of Michelle's hair. "When are you coming back?"

"Sometime after spring break."

"So does that mean everyone is leaving me for the break?" Janine said, her voice starting to grow to a whine.

"I'll be here for part of it," shouted Lisa from the hall.

"Great," Janine said, openly rude.

"I thought your friend from school was coming here for the week," I said.

"That fucking bitch, she can't be relied on for anything," Janine's eyes were narrowing. Her pretty face was becoming bitter. She added, "Just like Michelle."

"Um, I don't think I can really help it that my grandmother is going to die." Michelle caught a bit of an attitude herself.

"Yeah, I know, hon. I'm sorry." Janine also was taken aback by Michelle's snap. She smoothed Michelle's hair and then leaned over to give her a big hug. I looked back down at a list of verb tenses.

"Do you want to get a drink or something?" Janine asked in a poor attempt to be sincere. Again Michelle grew incredulous.

"J, I just told you I have to study all night because I'm taking the test tomorrow."

"Okay, fine, I was just asking." Janine turned her attention to me. "Why are you being such a nerd, Gab? You can always be counted on for a drink."

I swallowed before answering. "I'm just trying to get an early start on things. I want to pass."

"Isn't anyone any fun anymore?" Janine yelled this at the ceiling.

"I could get a drink," Lisa called from the foyer. The three of us stared at each other with wide eyes. It was unbelievable. Was Lisa really going to go out? On a school night?

"Thanks a lot, guys," Janine whispered. Then she said louder. "Let's go in, like, an hour, Lise."

Lise? They got ready to go. It was quite a scene. Lisa was following Janine around as Janine belittled her appearance with excuses of giving her a makeover. She lent "Lise" her perfume and clothes.

"Okay, you nerds, how do I look?" Janine stood before us in a midriff-baring halter and a tight short denim skirt, her stiletto boots adding a couple of inches to her height.

"I believe there's a word in Italian I just learned, let me see..." Michelle said flipping through the text. "Oh yes, here it is. *Putana*."

All three of us laughed. Janine pretended to kick her leg at Michelle, so we could see that she was not wearing any underwear. Then they were gone and Michelle and I got a lot of studying done.

When they returned, makeup faded, Lisa too drunk and looking bloated, Janine not as put together as she once was, Lisa passed out immediately, but Janine sat with us for a while, blowing puffs of cigarette smoke inconsiderately. I waved the smoke away with my hand, exaggerating. Janine scowled at me and didn't apologize. Smoking had, as is had for many of us, become her new habit. And she did it to the extreme, milking every puff for the dramatic look it gave her.

Finally, she went to bed and Michelle made instant coffee in the kitchen. Although I couldn't see her, I knew that Michelle was crying. When she returned to the table with a *cannella* laced cup for both of us, I smiled up at her, wrapping my hands around the warm cup.

"You okay, Michelle?"

"Yeah, hanging in. Just been feeling a bit homesick, you know. I think it's good that I'm going to go home."

"Yeah, but you'll come back right?"

Michelle waited a second before answering. She sipped from her cup and savored it. "Of course, I will. I can't leave you alone in the house with these two freaks."

We agreed to stay up until six. At five, we decided to go for a walk. The night we walked home from Tendenza, we smelled bread. We found the bakery again, we banged on the wooden door and tried to negotiate with the round Sienese man with a bushy beard.

He offered us a basket of steaming rolls. He refused payment. We took two rolls each and walked back to our apartment with the warm paper bags. We ate the first one quickly and the second one we relished, letting the bread practically dissolve in our mouths.

"I have to come back," Michelle said. "We don't have bread like this back home."

At the *pausa* the next day, I saw Michelle who winked. "I got a B on my final."

"They tell you right away?"

"Yep. And let me just say, it's a good thing you schooled me on those *passato prossimos*. It was in, like, every multiple choice."

"I didn't think they'd tell you right away."

"Why wait?" Michelle asked. She gave me a big hug. She was in a rush because she had to get to the airport in Pisa. "Listen, G, have a good time in Paris. And tell Janine I said bye, in case I don't see her. *Ciao, bella.*"

Then she was gone, leaving me in the café to look over at the terrifying Signora Laza. I was going to know in two days whether or not I passed this class. Grades had always come easy for me, but I had been studying harder than I ever had to do well in this class.

Shouldn't this language be innate in me? I was Italian-American. Didn't that count for anything?

I studied for five hours straight after class. I didn't even eat lunch, because I was going out for dinner with the class and Signora Laza at a pizzeria on the *campo*.

"Don't you think you are overdoing it a bit?" Lucy asked when we finally met up to walk over to the dinner.

"You're going to get an A. I'm the one *La Strega Laza* said had to study."

At the restaurant, it was just my luck to be sandwiched between Lucy and the opera singer, directly across from Signora Laza and the beautiful German, Brigitte, at dinner. I whispered in Lucy's ear that whatever happened, she couldn't leave me exposed to any kind of conversation with the *professoressa*.

Signora Laza literally let her hair down. She still wore her unstylish glasses, but she chain-smoked and she laughed. It was an actual sound coming out of her open mouth, not merely the strange tight smile she had when one of us *stranieri* said something stupid.

She ordered the meal for the group, dropping c's like a Tuscan and not using the perfect accent she did in class. We were served family-style. We started with the bruschetta and crostini with chicken liver. There was copious amounts of wine.

Then the food came in waves. All of the pasta was *fatta in casa,* homemade. There was the ubiquitous thick Sienese *pici* pasta served with peas; there were large ravioli served with some kind of sweet meat that tasted like duck. Then there were roughly cut pieces of pasta served in a rich glistening sauce and tossed with crispy pieces of sage.

The *secondi* were brought to us on deep blue beautiful china. There were thin slices of beef served with earthy mushrooms, grilled pork chops and the wild boar *cinghiale* that was a treat I only splurged on occasionally. I also sampled some roasted rabbit, which was tender and delicious, though I couldn't quite get over what it was.

Initially, I tried to avoid eye contact with Signora Laza, but unfortunately Lucy got caught up in a conversation with the Greek over my plate. They were scandalously speaking English. If I participated, Signora Laza would believe that I instigated the English, because I couldn't speak Italian.

The Greek woman and Lucy were arguing. Lucy accused Maria of being disruptive in class. I giggled when Lucy sincerely called the her a prima donna, but it wasn't a big deal, because Maria liked it.

"I'm an actress," she said again and again. "I'm an actress."

"And you, Gabriella," Signora Laza said. "What will you do for this break?"

"I will go to Paris to see my friend." My Italian was perfect. I pretended I was saying it to Gaetano. And because I drank too much delicious Chianti, I said it with the best accent I ever had, rolling my r's a bit too much, truth be told. "I need the rest after all of the studying."

In the light of the restaurant it was hard to be certain if behind Signora Laza's glasses she winked, but Brigitte, the German, laughed. I shrugged and smiled. Under the table, Lucy pinched my leg. Over the table, she poured me more wine.

The plates kept coming from the kitchen, bringing more and more until it was finally time for dessert and espresso. We ate *zuppa inglese* for dessert. It was a yummy sponge of orange, vanilla and liquor. We all shared it and when we thought the meal was over, Signora Laza insisted on ordering the Vin Santo and *cantucci* that completed every meal. I couldn't help thinking that she really was a *strega*, a witch, fattening me for the kill.

"Okay, *ragazzi*," the *professoressa* said, clapping her hands together as she did in class. "I would like us to go to the *campo* and get to know a little something about your culture."

We were confused, but everyone put their jackets on. When I stood up, I realized how incredibly full I was. It was rare for me to eat so much, but it was all on Signora Laza. I wondered if the school subsidized her or she was actually that generous.

When we got to the *campo*, it was strangely empty. We stood before the tower. I was scared of what came next. I was too drunk for any kind of weird language lesson she might have cooked up. I didn't trust this scheme of Laza's.

"Okay, who will be done with their studies after this final?" Signora Laza asked the group. Brigitte and two of the Koreans raised their hands. "Only you three may climb this tower. The rest of you must wait until you know that you are done with your studies here in Italy or you will have bad luck. Now I would like all of you to sing to us a song from your country. The national anthem or another song that you prefer."

Lucy immediately handed me a cigarette and said, "I'm not much for the 'Star Spangled Banner.'"

We smoked and watched as the groups of Japanese, German, Spanish and the Greek sang their songs. Maria, enjoyed this the most. She was a true ham, enjoying the solo, but she had a beautiful voice. It was the Americans turn, Lucy and I and Pete, from another program.

"*Boh*," Lucy said in the Italian way of confessing confusion. Then she looked at us, her two partners. "What should it be?"

"We could do 'American Girl.'" I suggested, shrugging once again.

"That's got that funny little break down," said Pete. "What about 'Born in the U.S.A?'"

"I could do the boss," Lucy said. "He represents."

"Okay," I said, "but I might forget the words."

So we sang and I hesitated a bit, but found I knew all the words. On the third chorus the rest of the group, including Signora Laza, sang along. The Japanese couple raised their hands in the air on each "born" and swayed from side to side. Afterward, everyone clapped, as much for themselves as for us.

Then it was the Koreans turn. Jung stood in the middle of the two Korean women. They sang a song with a title I would never know. But it sounded so sweet and they looked so sincere that I sighed. I understood why Signora Laza wanted to do this. The *università per stranieri* was more than a place to learn the language. I smiled at Signora Laza, not afraid for the moment to meet her eyes.

"Okay, *ragazzi*, now you must get some sleep. Remember, tomorrow is a study day for you, so I will see you Friday afternoon after your written exam. I suggest you all study very hard. And now I wish you luck the Italian way. Does anyone know what it is?" No one was sure.

"*In bocca al lupa*." The mouth of a wolf. I knew it and remembered how to answer.

"*Creppi.*"

We all wished each other luck the Italian way. I should have known that one way or another Signora Laza would manage to teach us a lesson.

On Thursday, I didn't pull an all-nighter but I did study during the day for eleven hours. I ate tuna packed in oil for protein. Lisa was overly confident about the test. She tried to engage me in Italian preparatory conversation. She claimed to want to practice, but I suspected she wanted to embarrass me. I would not give in. "I've got to study for the written part, Lisa."

Around nine, there was a knock at the door and I opened it to find Gaetano leaning against the door frame as if he was posing for a picture.

"Hi," I said in English, because I was surprised, then I remembered and switched to Italian after we kissed hello. "I'm happy to see you. I was just studying. Tomorrow, I have a final and then I leave for Parigi."

"Yes, I know, I wanted to see you before you left." He held out a bag. "Chicken, for you to eat."

"Thank you, do you want to come in?" He came inside, pointing and shaking his head at my bare feet. We sat at the little table in the hall.

"Do you want to get a drink later?" he asked.

"No, I can't. I have to study." What I really wanted to do is ask him to refresh me on definite rules for using *passato remoto*. I didn't do that, though. I had to get used to him not helping me. "Maybe we can get a drink another time, when I get back."

"Maybe," he said, glancing around my apartment as if he expected someone else to be there.

"Michelle has gone, you know. You heard about her grandmother?"

"Duccio told me." He was being matter-of-fact with me. He was providing answers to my questions, nothing more. There was no sparkle, no sweetness. I wasn't sure how to take him.

"So, did you go home? Did you go to the south?"

"No, not yet." So he just didn't keep in touch with me. I understood that. I didn't like it, but I understood. I changed the subject. I would be as charming and as social as possible.

"This chicken smells delicious. Do you want some?"

"No, *tesoro*, I got it for you. You enjoy it." I was still his treasure somehow.

"It was very nice to see you," I said. "Would you like me to make you lunch tomorrow? I don't have to leave until three."

"I may be busy studying, too."

"Okay," I said. I looked down at the chicken in my lap. The grease was seeping through the bag a bit. It was rare for me to get poultry here. I couldn't wait to eat it. I wished he would stay and eat with me. He reached over and rubbed my cheek, surprising me.

"I have to go, *bella*. Maybe I'll see you tomorrow." We stood up, leaving my books and my grammar questions behind. I opened the door for him.

"Thank you again for the chicken," He shook his head at my *grazie*. "I know, I know, but it was nice and I wanted to say thank you."

'Okay, *bella*," he kissed my cheeks. Then he wished me luck for the test tomorrow. "*In bocca al lupa, domani.*"

"*Creppi*," I said, pleased that I know how to answer, thanks to Signora Laza.

The chicken was delicious. The aroma filled the house. Both Lisa and Janine hovered around me until I offered them pieces. When I was finished, Lisa asked to eat my leftovers.

At midnight I went to bed. I was afraid to stop studying, but I knew I couldn't absorb any more. I crawled into my bed. It was still cold in my room but not cold enough for me to undress under the covers. I set the alarm for eight and checked it several times, neurotically.

I would not let myself think of anything, but verb conjugations and pronouns. As I reviewed them in my mind, I fell asleep.

14.

In the morning, I woke up feeling as if I had already taken my final but knowing that I had been dreaming about it all night. On the way to the bathroom, I passed Lisa sitting up in her bed. She was getting in one last final review. Lisa was more nervous about this test than she let on.

"*Hai parlato nel sogno,*" Lisa said. You talked in your sleep.

"In Italian?" I asked in English, not wanting to play her little games.

"*Sì,*" Lisa said.

"Because I'm obsessing," I said, going into the bathroom. I splashed cold water on my face and studied myself. You must do this, I whispered to myself. *Devi fare questo.*

Lisa was staring at the bathroom door when I came out. She had something to ask me. I could tell by the way she was quivering.

"What?"

She held out a worksheet. "Will you test me on *imperativo?*"

This is just an excuse I thought, for her to show off. Or maybe she was trying to psych me out like a boxer. Was she even that calculating? Maybe my accent was really good in my sleep.

"Please," she said.

"Fine," I said. "I don't have much time, though. I need to run an errand before school."

"Okay, I just need the irregulars."

"Okay and I'm going to do *sapere* and *volere*, too."

"You're right. Those are hard," she nodded, considering.

So I tested her, expecting that she would get them all right. And she missed some, too. It was good for me to review. It was impossible to prepare too much.

Then I dressed quickly and on my way back through her little room I said, "*In bocca al lupa*, Lisa."

"*Creppi,*" she said, smiling up from her book. Sometimes, she wasn't so bad. Or maybe sometimes I was just more patient.

I decided earlier in the week to go to the *duomo* for a last-minute prayer. I stepped into the cathedral and looked up at the paintings. I stifled an attack of the hacking cough that still stuck with me. And then I prayed to the severe-looking Mary in the golden dress. One Hail Mary. I wished I knew it in Italian. Hopefully, it would work.

Then I went to the *università*.

"*In bocca al lupa*," I whispered to Lucy who sat in a small desk a few rows up.

"*Studenti,*" the proctor said loudly. At nine, they handed out the tests.

I took a deep breath and closed my eyes. When I opened my eyes, Jung, the Korean man, was staring at me. I wasn't sure if the thumbs-up sign was universal so I just nodded. Then I began.

I read each question carefully. There was a lot of *articoli* and *congiuntivi*. None of it was as hard as I imagined. There was a mock conversation where I need to fill in the blank with an *imperativo* of *sapere*. My review with Lisa was worth it.

About an hour in, people started getting up to hand in their papers. We had an hour and a half, and I intended to use all of that time to make sure my essays were perfect. With ten minutes to spare, I looked it over as much as I possibly could. I got up and handed in my test.

"*Grazie*," I said stupidly to the proctor. I had two hours until the oral presentation. During that time the tests would be marked. Lucy was waiting for me outside, smoking.

"What did you think?" she asked.

"Not to bad. Can I bum a cigarette?"

'Of course. What should we do now?"

"Sweat the oral for a while," I said.

"C'mon it will be fine. Let's go to Osteria la Chiacchiera and get some *ribollita* for an early lunch. It will put hair on your chest."

"Just what I need."

Lucy prevented me from spending two hours biting my nails. The restaurant had delicious food served in communal-style tables. Gaetano loved it there, too. I looked around wondering, if he was there. He wasn't, and I considered calling him to tell him about the test. But then I doubted that he would care.

Back at school, Lucy and I were scheduled to go into our oral test together. We sat outside the classroom for a while before we went in. I coughed constantly.

"This is killing me," I said to Lucy. Then I translated, trying to make light of this whole thing. "*Mi fa morire*. What do you think of that, huh? Huh? Pretty good, right?"

"Save it for the *professori*." Finally, we got called in. I felt as though I was meeting a firing squad. It was just Signora Laza and Signore Pastorino. Lucy went first. She got a 30 on the written exam, pretty damn good. Thirty-two was the highest possible mark. They asked Lucy about a job she had in her country. Of course she did wonderfully. Her speech flowed, and her accent was perfect. I was envious of the way she held her mouth when she spoke.

Then it was my turn. I got my written exam back: 29. Not great, but pretty good. I knew that I would at least get a D, no matter how much I flunked the oral part.

"Okay, Gabriella," Signora Laza said, smiling. "In one of your papers you told us all about one of the holidays in your country, Thanksgiving. Tell us what you do on that day and why."

I began to talk about *La Festa di Ringraziamento*, Thanksgiving. My voice shook, but the words came out comfortably. I painted a picture of the ideal Thanksgiving. I was channeling Norman Rockwell. This was America. I only messed up once, when I described the turkey as a "*grande uccellino*" which meant "big little bird." Luckily, I caught myself and apologized. The professors laughed it off, helping my confidence. When my two minutes were up, I looked at Lucy, who smiled. I knew I did a good job.

"*Brave!*" Signore Pastorino said to both of us.

The *professori* talked quietly, not exactly hiding what they were saying. Lucy got an A- for the class, based on the conversion they had for Italian grades. The conversation got more heated for my grade. Based on my performance of the final, Signore Pastorino wanted to give me a higher mark. Signora Laza showed him my unimpressive grades from the semester. I realized they could still choose to have me repeat the course if I got a D. They were arguing between a C and a D. I cleared my throat, hoped that I wouldn't cough and looked into Signora Laza's eyes.

"*Per favore, professoressa, un C.*" Signora Laza smiled and shook her head, giving in. Perhaps it was my stirring rendition of "Born in the USA." I will always be grateful to Springsteen.

"Okay. *Non darmi una brutta figura, eh?*" Signora didn't want to look bad to her colleagues if she passed a girl who couldn't speak.

"*No, mai,*" I said, determined to never make her look bad. I wanted to lay out all the ways I would make her proud, but I didn't want to talk too much and have them revoke the grade.

"Okay, Gabriella," Signora Laza said. "C."

"*Grazie, grazie,*" I said. I got up and hugged Signora Laza. Lucy laughed loudly, then hugged me, too.

And it was over. I passed the final. Still in shock, I jumped up and down, holding on to Lucy's shoulders in the lobby.

"A C, I got a C," I screamed. "I can't believe it. I also can't believe I'm this excited about a C. It's the lowest grade I ever got in college, but I'm super psyched."

"Even with the *grande uccellino*," Lucy said, patting me on the shoulder.

"Even with the *grande uccelino*," I said, still disbelieving.

"We should get drunk," Lucy said.

"I'd love to, but I have to pack and take an overnight train to Paris."

"*Bienvenue*," Lucy said. "Have fun and call me when you get back."

I smiled through the *campo*. I ran into Lisa, who was flaunting her B+. She smirked about my C. She was back to her old self. It didn't bother me too much, though I was compelled to tell Lisa that Lucy got an A-.

Gaetano was at my apartment when I returned. He was sitting at the dining room table with Janine, who was wearing a tank top and cutoffs. It was too cold for the outfit, but Janine didn't care about comfort as long as she could show off her body.

Both Gaetano and Janine shared the same expression when I came in. They looked at me as though they would like to be caught doing something that they weren't doing. That we should all feel awkward even though nothing was really going on. *Non mi fregga niente.*

"*Com'è va?*" Gaetano asked, wanting to know how the test was.

"*Bene.*" I stepped into the kitchen and poured myself a glass of *acqua con gas* that seemed to be flat. There were dishes piled up in the sink.

"You packed?" Janine shouted from the dining room.

"Mostly, just need a couple more things." I was speaking English fast, not enunciating, not looking at Gaetano.

"Did you see those dishes?" she asked.

"Yeah, none of them are mine. I wash mine. I have a train to catch."

"I wasn't saying they were," Janine said, defensively. "I bet they are from Michelle. She's selfish. You in a bad mood today, G?"

Wouldn't you like me to be, I thought, but I smiled and said, "Not at all. How was your exam?"

"Fine, passed. Got a C."

"Hey, me too." We slapped each other five. Gaetano laughed, so Janine slapped him five to, but I didn't. Gaetano looked at me and spoke in Italian. This Janine couldn't really understand.

"I thought I would walk you to the bus station. Help with your bags."

"*Grazie*," I said on purpose. "I'll be ready soon."

"I can't believe everyone is leaving me," Janine whined in English.

"Lisa will be here until the middle of the week, right?" Janine just rolled her eyes.

"It's my birthday, you know. Thursday is my birthday."

"We'll celebrate when you I back," I offered. "It'll be something to look forward to. It's too bad your friend cancelled."

"Yeah, too bad," Janine said. She turned to Gaetano for sympathy. "*Il mio compleano*."

"*Quando?*"

He wanted to know when her birthday was, and she had to think about how to say Thursday for a second. Frustrated, I helped her and we answered together. "*Giovedi.*"

"Oh," said Gaetano with saccharine regret in his voice. He spoke English for Janine's sake. "We mus' maka party."

"There's no one to have a party with. Michelle *va via*. Gabriella *va via*." Janine pouted and flicked her hand in a going a way motion.

"*Facciamo un picnic,*" Gaetano said, ever helpful. I hated him at that moment. He was showing me that men were always disappointing no matter where they are from. And I was interchangeable. One American girl was good as the next, the sluttier the better. He was trying to test me. *Fine, fuck him.*

"A picnic would be great," Janine said. She would love that, to have her own little Italian friend just like Michelle and me. It would be better for Gaetano, too, I was certain of that. He could finally get laid.

"Janine, do you have that skirt I leant you the other night?"

"I think so," Janine said, still kind of smiling at Gaetano.

"Well, I need to pack it for Paris." Janine got up to get it, leaving Gaetano and me alone in the kitchen. He touched my arm.

"What's wrong, *tesoro?" Tesoro?*

"What do you think?" I said. As he was searching my face, Janine returned with this skirt. I pulled my arm free from Gaetano to take the skirt. I only wanted him to know I was annoyed and not give Janine any more satisfaction.

I went to my room to put the skirt in my backpack and packed up my toiletries. Gaetano followed me. My bed wasn't made, I never made it, but he pulled the blanket back to sit down. He whistled, when he saw the size of my backpack.

"Yeah, it's big," I said. "Now I'm sure that you won't want to carry it."

"So the test was okay?"

"Yeah, I passed. I did okay." I wanted to tell him about the "*grande uccellino*" but I didn't. He asked about my travel schedule, the train I'd be taking from Firenze. We were sticking to the specifics, exchanging information.

"You should be careful," he said with a fatherly concern that annoyed me. One minute he acted like he wanted to fuck me, then he ignored me and then he was bringing me chicken and trying to be protective.

"I'll be fine. I'm ready, if you still want to go."

"Yes, we could get an espresso if you want before ..."

I looked at my watch. "No, it's late. I need to get the bus."

"Okay," he said. I heaved my backpack on the edge of the bed and stuck my arms through, lifting it up onto my back, with a groan.

"*Madonna*!" Gaetano said. "That's a bag."

The bag made me hunch over a bit. I had to maneuver through the doors out into the kitchen, where Janine was sitting on the windowsill smoking a cigarette. I went through the motions of saying goodbye. I gave her a hug and told her to have a good time. I just wanted to go and be alone for the rest of the night. I wanted to get to it.

Gaetano and Janine kissed goodbye, too. I opened the door. Janine shouted at Gaetano in her stupid accent.

"*Chiamami.*" Call me? We didn't even have a phone.

"Okay," Gaetano said. He placed his hand on the back of my bag as we went down the stairs, trying to help.

"I'm fine," I said. I was walking as fast as usual, despite how heavy the bag was. I shouldn't have expected any more from him. It was wrong to be annoyed. He was, as he told me constantly, *un uomo italiano*. It was impossible for him to have a female friend. It wouldn't be any different with me. I should have understood that I was not in any way unique, but I wished his standards were higher than Janine.

"Do you want me to get you a drink to take with you on the train?"

"No," I said. "I can get one on the train."

At the bus station, he insisted on buying my ticket for me at the *biglietteria* so I wouldn't have to maneuver into the office with my bag. Though I didn't want to ask him for anything else, I was relieved not to deal with mispronouncing the word for *ticket* again. I had enough language fear for one day.

Once I had the ticket, I tried to say goodbye. He insisted on staying with me until the bus came. He helped me put the backpack under the bus, reminding me to stamp my ticket when I got on, as if I hadn't taken the bus dozens of times.

He kissed my cheeks. I didn't kiss him. I couldn't stop myself from being mad at him, even though he was being kind to me. I was just being bitter and blue.

"Have fun in Parigi, be careful," he said pulling away to look into my face.

"You, too." I got on the bus, stamped my ticket and waved at him. I sat across the aisle, so that he could no longer see me.

Somehow I knew that Gaetano was waiting on the curb. Even when I closed my eyes as the bus pulled away, I knew he was watching the bus until he couldn't see it anymore. In spite of how mean I was and how undeserving, he would stand there watching nothing until I was far away from Siena.

On the overnight train to Paris, I made friends with the conductor. My Italian was improving steadily so that I could express more of my character in the language. The conductor was an older man, who smiled at my open journal and told me that writing down my thoughts every day was a sound idea. When another man tried to sit in my couchette, the conductor called him out. And from there on in, he put only other women into my cabin, winking at me each time, telling the women to sit with his "*amica*."

At night, the three women and I pulled the bunks from the wall. We climbed into our beds, smiling at each other but not saying anything. How weird to sleep with strangers. But I was dead tired, so I was out when I hit the pillow.

When the train pulled into the station I still felt like I was in an Italian city, but of course everything was French. I looked around for Kaitlin, and then I saw her bright red hair. She ran toward me with open arms. I pulled her close, squeezed her tight.

"How are you? How was your trip?" Her voice made me feel peace at once.

"Good, good. I'm glad to be here." My friend regarded me carefully, looking me up and down. How could I have forgotten how I longed to be looked at with that quizzical gaze, those scrunched-up blue eyes? What a familiar comfort it was.

"You look different." It was almost accusing.

"Yeah, I guess, I've been letting my hair grow a bit."

"You sound different, too." Kaitlin looked like she might cry.

"Well, I'm not an imposter, K, you just haven't seen me in three months."

"You've changed; you're different." I shrugged and laughed a bit. Had I shaken some sadness she knew? Her suspicion was innate. It was one of her most lovable traits.

"Give me a chance, K, we've got a week, you can figure out if I'm for real." Kaitlin considered this for a few moments and then nodded her head begrudgingly.

"You see you've gone soft, Gabriella. You have changed." I couldn't have looked that different; it was just because she hadn't seen me in so long, after seeing me every day back at college.

"I'll be back to normal tomorrow. I'm just happy to see you today."

Kaitlin, still suspicious, seemed to accept this. And I hugged her again, confirming that I was softer.

"Enough," she said, pulling away. "Let's go. I have plans for us."

And then Paris. Paris was perfect. It was the end of March, but I kept singing "April in Paris" everywhere I went. This was a city. I loved Siena, but being in Paris made me realize what a sleepy town it was. Paris was where we ate Somali food one night and cheap upper-class French food the next. I spent the week going around Paris. Sometimes I went to class at the Sorbonne with Kaitlin. Sometimes Kaitlin had assignments in one of the many museums, so I managed to get in free with her class.

In the mornings, we woke up together in Kaitlin's big comfortable bed. We were awakened by the sound of pigeons, a low vibrating hum. They were nesting outside the window of Kaitlin's room. Every morning Kaitlin screamed, "Fucking pigeons," before I rolled over and cheerfully said, "*Bonjour.*" This routine was delightful. I never wanted to leave Paris. I never wanted to be unrecognizable to Kaitlin again.

One day when Kaitlin had exams, I slept later. I ate madeleines and drank *café au lait* with the ninety-year-old woman, Madame Marie, who Kaitlin lived with. I didn't speak French and Madame could not speak English, but although I couldn't answer the woman, I understood everything she said. Or rather, I understood what she was trying to communicate without knowing the words. My mind was opening to understand people. That day I used my weekly metro pass to get around the city. I went to the Rodin museum and got trapped there by a rainstorm. I never got to see the sculptures in the garden outside. But I saw enough of Rodin's white stone embracing bodies within the museum to be affected.

When the rain let up a bit I found a café. I ordered some water and soup. I said *carafe d'eaux* as Kaitlin taught me and pointed to the vat of liquid behind the counter, hoping it would be a type of soup I liked. I wrote in my journal, looking up at a poster of a large woman's butt.

I let Jonas come to me then. The letter *j* exists in the French alphabet unlike the Italian. I was using it a lot as I tried to communicate. Maybe it was Rodin's sexy frozen sculptures or that seeing Kaitlin reminded me of another time when I didn't feel so strong. But Jonas sat beside me at the window. I saw his reflection in the glass. I didn't question it for once. I let myself feel his presence beside me. On this rainy day, he could lie with me in Kaitlin's bed and listen to the pigeons. He followed me when I left the café, stopped with me in the film bookstore, pointing out a screenplay for me to buy. We walked around the city together, him just talking, finding words to explain it all, to make it okay.

I knew this was Crazy. A disguise of Crazy's, but it made me feel safer and less alone.

He left when I met up with Kaitlin. He had come and gone again so quickly. This time it was easier because I didn't fool myself that it could be permanent.

Kaitlin took me to the Jewish part of town. We bought the falafel, and then we went to a jazz club. It was a cliché that must be done, she said. I would have gone for anything.

We sat in the club, drinking wine, chain smoking, losing ourselves in the sounds of the band, in the French woman singing American standards. I had one more night in Paris and I didn't want to leave.

On the train back to her apartment, Kaitlin told me that she hated Paris, hated the French people, but she liked it better when I was there. She was having trouble with the language. Most of the Parisians pretended not to understand her. I told Kaitlin all about Siena, my roommates, school and Gaetano. With one night left together, we kept talking when we got back and into her bed. We whispered late into the darkness three months' worth of gossip until we were talking in our sleep.

My last day. We went to the Eiffel Tower. Kaitlin waited for me to do this. She didn't go when she had other opportunities. We were speaking with a kind of urgency. We were trying to update each other on everything we have been up to. It was so unusual for us not to have all the same references. We wouldn't be apart for much longer, in four weeks Kaitlin was coming to Italy for her spring break.

Then I did it, I could see Kaitlin measuring my face, but I did it. I would have regretted not doing it. I asked about Jonas. I kept my face still. If you took my pulse, you would see no change. I had to stay composed so she wouldn't worry.

Kaitlin took a minute before she answered me. No one mentioned him to me anymore, but I knew she still got letters from friends in the know. She took a deep breath, and I told myself that no matter what she said, I would stay stoic.

"I don't know, Gabriella. I hear they still fight about you," she said hesitantly. "But it doesn't matter now, does it?"

"No, of course not. I was just wondering."

I was happy she believed I was getting better, that I shut the door on Crazy. Maybe that was why she didn't recognize me at first. Maybe I was getting a little of myself back, standing taller. I was not so openly shaky and unsure. She wouldn't have indulged me with news of Jonas if she didn't think I could take it. I wondered if I was getter stronger or just faking it better.

I turned my attention back to the city. I didn't want Kaitlin to see the painful sick bit of hope she had given me. I didn't want her to regret it. We had walked around the city below together, Jonas and me. Paris was our city. I imagined that he still thought of me and that Kaitlin thought I was better. This was a victory. I knew that I couldn't react to it until later when I was on the train alone in my couchette. Instead, I pointed down to Paris and told her again how much I enjoyed the city and my time with her.

I swallowed Crazy down.

We went back to the Jewish section. I wanted another delicious falafel for the train trip. Kaitlin brought me to the train. We tried not to spend too much time saying goodbye. We hugged and I pressed my forehead against Kaitlin. Then I got on the train.

In the couchette, I ate the falafel quickly. Eggplant, chickpea, potato and pita blended together in my mouth. Oil dripped onto my jeans. The stain would never come out. When I got home to the states, it would be the souvenir of the long lonely trip away from Paris, away from Kaitlin. For as long as I kept those jeans, that oil stain made me think of making my way from the freedom of walking around with Jonas in my mind, the sick possibility that if he was fighting about me, if I was still an issue, that he missed me too.

But I didn't have much of a chance to revel in that because on this train there were no friendly conductors. I was alone in my couchette. I couldn't sleep. There were no other sweet tourists in my cabin. There were scary Italian *militario* passing by in fifteen-minute intervals, looking in at me, circling for an attack.

They shouted things in their rough dialects. I considered lugging my backpack to the bathroom and locking myself in for the entire ride, but I was scared to pass them in the corridor.

Everything changed so certainly from hugging my closest female friend goodbye to feeling like prey. I thought of Olivia and how she had sat on the train as we headed back from Switzerland, making a list of things that we needed for our next trip. How then I had seen traveling as full of promise and fun. It had been an adventure. Now I was alone and cornered. This was another side. I would have given anything to have a companion in my couchette, a friendly face to assuage my fears of the imposing men. But I remained alone.

And so I didn't shut the light. I didn't even feign sleep. I sat upright in my cabin alone. I undid the top bunk and waited. Threatened. Vulnerable. A woman. I kept my dull Swiss Army knife in my hand.

I traveled this way, learning there was always something to be afraid of. It was another one of the ways a woman travels. I was reminded of my breasts, reminded of the appealing dangerous parts between my legs all the way into the *ferrovia* of Firenze.

Then I caught the bus back to Siena. And then only when I saw Santa Caterina's church, the *duomo* in the distance, and the Torre del Mangia, I exhaled and let my shoulders widen, let my thighs loosen a bit. Only then, I relaxed. The city opened its arms without reproach for having left and having been slightly inebriated by someplace else.

And only then, inside the protection of the city's walls, when I sighed and appreciated my city's beauty, did Siena welcome me home.

APRILE

15.

The house smelled of sex when I got home. Someone was calling my name. I opened the door to Michelle and Janine's room and found Janine on her bed. She sat up and ran to me.

"I'm so glad you're back," she said hugging me. "Now you're my best friend."

"Really?" I asked. "Can I put my bag down first?"

"Let me help." Janine said. She was wearing a tank top and short shorts, her robe was tied around her waist, but she had pulled her arms out of it. Her hair was fastened back and her skin was glistening.

"I'm fine, Janine. I got it. I need to do some laundry."

"Let me come with you. Let me do it for you." Janine was scary with this intense desperation. There was a scratch in her veneer, a thumbprint through her foundation. "I've just been so lonely. Everyone left me."

"Didn't you and Gaetano have a picnic?"

"No, I spent my birthday by myself." I felt a wave of relief. I'd rather believe he was trying to hurt me than that I was so easily replaceable.

"Well, we'll take you out when everyone gets back. What did you do all week?"

"Not much. I wasn't going to go calling up any of those hos." All of the other girls on the program hated Janine with a smiling bitterness that never fully rose to the surface.

"Oh, and I brought a guy back here," she said, making a mock embarrassed face. That explained the smell.

"Where'd you find him?"

"The *campo*. He was older. Gave him the business all kinds of ways. He was in town for the weekend. From Rome."

"How fun." I said, willing to let it drop there.

"It was pretty crazy. We were all over the apartment. Stayed out of your room, though."

"Thanks," I said. I wasn't sure I wanted to venture into my room and speculate on whether she was telling the truth.

"I also did something stupid." Janine said this, too, like she didn't really believe she had a choice and was not responsible for the consequences.

"What's that?" I asked, because it was my cue.

"I called my old boyfriend from high school. I told him to come here, and he's coming later in the month."

"Is that bad?"

"I don't know," Janine said, shaking her head at her own unpreventable mistakes. "Let me just get dressed and I'll go to the Laundromat with you."

Janine suffocated me, sticking by as I pressed too many clothes into the washing machine. An episode of *Santa Barbara* was on the television in the Laundromat. It was a soap opera I watched as a kid. I wanted to watch it alone and try to translate the dub, but instead Janine just kept talking, trying to get me to commit to plans and comment on whether or not what she did made her a slut.

I hated this invasion. I wanted to be away from Janine, but I was scared for her. So I listened to her chatter on and on about the Italian she slept with. I wondered if she slept with him only for the story, and then I wondered if she slept with him at all or was telling me what she somehow thought I wanted to hear.

Janine was a demanding "new best friend." She wanted my opinion on every aspect of her life. She would drain all of my strength until the next best better friend came along. Eventually, she turned the conversation to Michelle, gossiping openly about her for the first time. She thought Michelle deserved these insults for abandoning her, for not keeping her company over spring break.

"You know it was her stealing the food, don't you? I caught her one time. And, I mean, why bother to steal it if you are just going to puke it all up later." She laughed at her joke. I kind of smiled. It was so wrong to joke about this. It might be true that Michelle was the food thief, but I knew that Janine was lying. Janine never caught her. She just wanted me on her side. She would have said anything.

"Really," I asked, not joining in but not defending Michelle. Part of me wanted to see how far she would take it, just let her go, let her spiral off into the sky.

"Yeah, and she's so selfish, you know. I knew she didn't speak Italian when we got here, that she was going to have to learn, but I thought she was going to, you know, be there for me. And she totally isn't."

"Right," I said.

"And I don't think she is coming back. I mean, she's much happier at home."

"You think so?'

"Of course, I do. I mean, what does she have here?"

"Well," I began, knowing it wasn't the answer Janine wanted, knowing Janine wanted her and their friendship to be the reason, but it wasn't. "There's Duccio."

Janine didn't say anything. She'd been jealous all along of this relationship, this special thing that Michelle had that she hadn't found. We all were.

When my laundry was dry, I snagged my exit. "Janine, I'm totally wiped out. I think I'm going to have to take a nap. I didn't sleep at all on the train."

"Okay," said Janine, considering the options, planning a new course of attack. "Maybe I'll go to Crai market and get some ingredients for a little *pranzo* for us."

She pronounced *pranzo* purposely wrong, dragging the *a* out in almost a Texas drawl.

"Let me get some sleep, and then we'll talk. Don't wait around on me for lunch."

"Okay," Janine said, relenting, looking defeated. "Okay."

It was true that I was tired, exhausted after a night worrying about the *militario*. But most of me just wanted to be free of Janine. In my bed, in a freshly cleaned tank top I thought that the worst and the best came out so far from home. The true you. Maybe we would have all been different if someone was keeping tabs on us. But no one was. We were free in a way we never had been in college. We could be anyone. It was liberating but also scary. I wondered if anyone could still recognize who they had become.

The apartment got quiet. While Janine was sleeping I snuck out across the street to the café that had a phone. I called the monastery. Another one of the faceless students answered the phone. I asked for Gaetano and heard the student calling down the hall. Gaetano's name echoed, but there was no answer.

"*Gaetano, non c'è*," said the student.

"*Okay, grazie.*" I bought a *ricciarelli* and ate the cookie standing at the counter. Then I went back to my room, back to bed. I thought of Gaetano's gray eyes in the dance club and wondered if I was ever going to see him again.

I woke up in the late afternoon to a knock. It was Michelle. "Wake up, sleepy G-dog."

"*Cazzo*," I said, running a hand through my hair. "You're back."

"Of course you believed the rumors. Brought some new clothes, too." Michelle jumped on my bed and hugged me.

"What's this? A new jacket?" I asked, rubbing the material. I could feel her bones through it. "Very *bella*."

"There's more where that came from." Michelle said, charged up, reenergized by her voyage.

"Are you okay?" I asked, wanting to know about her grandmother but not wanting to bust up the mood.

"Yeah, my grandmother passed right after I got there. I just made it, and I'm really glad I did. I got to say goodbye. It was good to be home. But also hard and weird." She looked out my window for a second. I held on to her arm. "You wanna get drunk tonight?""

"Yeah, did you see Janine?"

"No, she's not in our room."

"She's not," I said. So much for catering to my every need. "Did you call Duccio?"

"First thing I did when I got off the plane. Talked to Mama Duccio. She loves me."

"Oh, yeah?"

"Not really. Anyway, he is in Rome till tomorrow, the fucker. And I wanted to get me some sweet Italian *cazzo*."

"Girl, you dirty."

"Girl, you better *sveglia* or we ain't never gonna get all *ubriaca*," she said, grabbing my arm and pulling me out of bed.

We left Janine a note and went to the bar behind the *campo*, near Piazza del Mercato. The drinks were pricey, but Michelle got a whole bunch of cash from her relatives for leather goods. Now she was blowing the wad on Bloody Marys. With her new jacket off, I could see that she was skinnier than ever. I couldn't understand how her organs fit inside that slight frame. I almost asked her about it, but as usual, I stopped myself. I still didn't know her well enough to go there. And I wanted to keep up the mood.

"I'm glad you're back, Michelle," I kept saying instead, again and again.

"I had to finish it. And I missed you guys. I missed Duccio."

"Was it so weird to be home?"

"It's hard to explain. For a while, you're just kind of in awe. I mean, first everyone is really super excited to see you, asking all these questions, then you get a sec by yourself and you feel kind of out of it and then–," she looked around the bar "–you think of Italy and you try to remember and it's like you lose it all so fast, you know. I had to come back. I wasn't ready to lose it yet."

"Yeah," I nodded, looking around. I wanted to take it all. I was almost halfway done. I would be home in three months. How quick would I lose it?

"I don't know, I'm just glad to be back."

"I'm glad you're back, too," I said, surprised at how true it was.

We didn't stay out too late; we both had language class in the morning. When we got back to the apartment, Janine was waiting for us. She had a hug for Michelle and a little bit of an attitude for me. I had eluded her desperate grasp.

"We left you a note," I offered, shrugging.

"I'm just kidding, G," Janine said, using Michelle's nickname and flashing a toothy smile.

Michelle was oblivious to any tension or at least acted oblivious. She pulled out three boxes of Kraft macaroni and cheese, like she smuggled some precious jewels. "Not only this, *ragazze*, I got bagels through customs."

We made a big pot of mac and cheese, put the pot in the center of the dining room table and went at it with our forks. We ate much fresher, better foods on a daily basis, but we devoured this as if it were the finest plate of truffles. It was a taste of home far away.

Lucy was in my language class once again. She went hiking in Cinque Terre for the break. I respected that she went on her own. She was what I aspired to be. I wanted to ask her if she was ever scared to be a woman traveling on her own, but I was ashamed that I was.

"It was lonely at times," Lucy said. "It would have been nice to have someone to talk to, to share it all with, you know, but this way I got to do my own thing."

Our new language teacher was a spicy number, a far cry from Signora Laza. She waltzed into the class twenty minutes late in a green leather jacket and sunglasses, saying *allora*. She told us that she was into the culture part in many ways as much as the language. She believed in watching a lot of movies and taking field trips. Great, a slacker, I thought. But then she announced that we would also have to give a speech at some point throughout the class. I began to dread this immediately.

This new *professoressa*, Signora Filmona lectured the class for about a half hour, punctuating her sentences with a nasally questioning *bene*. After that, she released the class. I, who thought I was following along quite well for not having spoken Italian in a week and a half, was confused. I turned to Lucy.

"Is it time for *pausa*?" I asked.

"No, we're done for the day. That's it. I think this one is going to be very different from Laza."

I couldn't get in touch with Gaetano. He was never waiting for me outside the *università* on his *vespa*. I missed him. I didn't blame him. But I had grown used to him and now he was gone.

For the first week, my days in the second semester were busier. I not only had my language class and the second part of Arturo's class, but I also had to audit two classes in Italian, I picked a film class and a class on Italian cultural studies. There was no attendance taken in these classes; we were mixed with all the other *stranieri*. The general consensus of the group was that these classes weren't that important, and soon we all began cutting.

Finding me less than enthusiastic about becoming her best friend, Janine abruptly stopped following me around. Instead, she took up with the son of a Sienese restaurant owner named Andrea. He was even more attractive than she was, and together they were in constant competition for who could appear more posed.

"They look like a perfume ad," Michelle said to me.

Maybe Janine hoped that she could get her friendship with Michelle back somehow if they both had boyfriends. But unfortunately she didn't take into consideration that Andrea's neighborhood, *La Contrada della Torre* was an archrival of Duccio's *Onda,* so double dates weren't exactly in the plan.

There were a smattering of warm days. I pulled out the few summer dresses and skirts I had hidden in my closet. I began to shed layers and not see my breath in front of me. Everyone was getting spring fever. Lucy was infatuated with one of the butchers on her street and was constantly devising ways of talking to him. Her terrace faced the door of his *macelleria*, so it was pretty hard to get her to do anything but spy on him after class. I didn't mind sitting in the sun with her. I hiked the skirts above my knees and drank in the light.

Even Lisa was happy. She and her boyfriend–who I never got to meet but apparently existed–visited her friend in Barcelona over spring break and since she got back she kept managing to say the word *Barcelona* in the same lisping manner as the Spanish did. She scandalously skipped the first week of class. Even her skin was clearing up.

I went to Firenze to visit Olivia a couple of times. The guy who sold the bus tickets still corrected me. Apparently, I was pronouncing the silent *g* in *biglietto* right, but I still wasn't mastering the double *t*'s. I yearned for the day when I could ask for my ticket and have him simply nod and give it to me instead of openly correcting my pronunciation.

But still no Gaetano. Duccio said he hadn't seen him around either, that he might be busy studying for exams. I tried to gauge if he was telling the truth or not, but couldn't. Michelle promised to get the straight story, but all she could find out was what Duccio had said, that he hadn't seen Gaetano at all.

One day Lucy and I went to the botanical gardens and then to Lucy's for a *pranzo* of speck, hard cheese and bread. We were drinking *vino bianco* because it was lighter than the red wine we usually drank. Around us, grass was growing and a sweet smell was in the air. Everything was getting ready to come out and be reborn.

That day, Lucy was feeling particularly forthcoming. She let her skirt ride up so high I could see the dagger tattoo on her thigh, and she admitted to having four more, though she didn't tell me where. She told me about her past, almost testifying about her history of drugs and delinquency. That's why she was in college so late. She had even been married once.

"Do you ever miss him?" I asked about the husband. We were on her balcony overlooking the armed guards coming to get money from the bank next to the butcher shop across the street. All the guards had their machine guns out. The women looked tougher than the men.

"Sometimes," she said. "But it was never going to work. You're not meant to be with the person you love at nineteen or twenty."

She said this so easily, like it was something I should know, like only a fool wouldn't.

It brought me down, as Gaetano would say, "*Un po' giu.*"

16.

And then, at last, again, Gaetano was waiting for me.

It was unexpected. I was coming out of Arturo's culture class with Michelle. It was almost six, but still bright out, and there was Gaetano on his *vespa*, smiling, like I had just seen him. I looked at Michelle. She smirked and shrugged.

"Duccio said he'd been looking for you." She gave me a little push. "I'll see you later. I'm going to go see my *ragazzo*."

"Hi," I said in English, walking closer to the bike.

"Hi," he said, smiling, pronouncing the h like a harsh breath of air. And then in Italian. "Did you forget this language in Paris?"

"No." I was at the bike now, not sure where to go. He clucked his lips the way that I thought meant no in Italian. He got off the bike and opened his arms. Instead of kissing me on each cheek, he hugged me. It was almost American of him. I thought I could feel his heart pounding, but it might have been mine.

"I'm so happy to see you. I've been trying to find you." I said.

"I came by here a couple of times, but you weren't here. Don't you go to class?"

I explained to him that we got out of class early almost every day. I did an impression of Signora Filmona and the nasal way she said *bene* and then quacked like a duck and said *bene* like a quack. He laughed and called me *pazza*–crazy. He didn't take his hands off my arms. He was happy to see me, but he seemed different somehow.

"I thought you were mad at me."

"How could I be mad at you, *tesoro*. You are my dear friend. You changed my life." He said this with such certainty. It was partly Italian melodrama, but part of me believed it.

"Thank you. You have changed me, too. I missed you, when I thought you were mad..." I didn't realize how I felt until that minute. To see him, I realized how important his friendship was to me.

"It's okay, *bella*. I am not mad."

"I know. I know," I said, nodding. I kept looking him in the eye. His eyes sparkled against the tan he must have gotten down South. His skin was as dark as an Arab's.

"What are you doing tonight?" he asked.

"I don't know. We should do something." For once, I wasn't in the mood to drink. I kind of just wanted to hang out. I wanted to talk to him.

"Yes. I don't have much money. I should get some tomorrow." He paused for effect, because he knew I knew how he would get the money. I ignored it. "How about I cook dinner for you?"

"*Bene*," I said, impersonating the nasal Signora Filmona.

Together we walked across the glistening pink shell of the Piazza del Campo back toward my apartment. We passed my *fruttivendolo*.

"Do you want to stop?" I asked. He shook his head, clucked his tongue. "No vegetables?"

"I know Siena better than you, *americana*. I will show you an even better, even cheaper *fruttivendolo*."

That night we had the apartment to ourselves, but I didn't feel awkward or uncomfortable. I told him about Paris, about walking through the streets, the museums, how big it was. I told him everything except about Jonas's ghost.

"I feel like I know your friend Kaitlin, the way you talk about her."

"You would love her," I said. "She's wonderful."

"You are," he said smiling. "It sounds like you didn't miss Italy at all."

"No, I missed it. I missed you. I thought you were mad. I know, I know now you weren't but I thought you were. I had a good time, but I couldn't think about coming back without thinking it wouldn't be the same if you weren't here."

He made some decisions, he told me. He was going to get more serious about his studies. He said a lot of his feelings changed the night I was sick.

"I wanted to help you, but I couldn't do anything. I just used an old trick from my country, but I should have been able to treat you. You have helped me see." He kissed the top of my head and called me *bella*.

Later we made coffee and smoked cigarettes at the dining room table. I did all the dishes. Then I walked him downstairs and watched him start the *vespa*.

"Tomorrow, Olivia is coming. I think she wants to see you. Maybe we can all go out with Michelle and Duccio."

"*Bene*," he said with a nasal accent, smiling. Then he quacked like a duck, making my impression his own.

The next night when Gaetano came to see me, he looked significantly less happy. His face was cold when I kissed him. "What's up?"

"They stole my *vespa*."

"What? Who?" I asked.

"*Boh*!" It was the way Italians said they didn't know.

"Fuck," I said in English and so he switched, too.

"Yes, fuck. If I find, I keel." He was so dramatic in English that I laughed and he made a face at me. "*Stronza*."

"I'm sorry, I'm laughing. I wasn't laughing at your accent. I was laughing at your, your. . ." and I couldn't think of the word. "The way you are, like an actor. What will you do without the *vespa*? Can you call the police?"

He shook his head at the word *polizia*. He didn't want any dealings with them. A southern Italian man he told me didn't make trouble with police in the north. "No, it is gone. It was outside Siena. Dino has another one, I think. He'll lend it to me this weekend. Tonight I'll take the bus. Where is Olivia?'

"She is coming soon, I think."

We waited a while, assuming she missed the bus and would be up in an hour. We drank the red table wine Gaetano brought. After an hour and a half, Olivia still hadn't arrived. The candy store with the phone across the street was closed, so Gaetano and I walked down the street to the arcade alcove, where there was a phone and I called Olivia's house.

"Hey," Olivia said when she came to the phone. "I thought you would have called by now."

"I thought you would have been here by now."

"Yeah, can you come here instead?" Olivia asked. She lowered her voice. "Suzie is flipping out. Can you hear her?"

I heard something behind her, something muffled, but I couldn't make it out. "Not really. What's going on?"

"I can't really explain. Kurt turned out to be a...well, a dick. I don't want to leave her. I'm sorry, but there was no way to get in touch with you."

"Yeah, I know, shit." I said.

"Can you come here?" she asked.

"Do you think Suzie will want me around? I mean, maybe she wants to be alone."

"I know, but I don't think that's a good idea. I want you to come," she said.

"Okay, well, I can't come tonight. I sort of already told Michelle we'd hang out with her. I'm sorry. I'll take the 10 A.M. bus tomorrow, okay?"

"Cool, thanks."

I cursed and explained to Gaetano that Olivia wasn't coming because Kurt was a *stronzo*. He nodded. We went to 115 bar. It wasn't as popular as Barone Rosso, but it was dark and there were big wooden tables where you could sit with your cocktails for hours. Plus, they gave you nuts.

At the bar, we met Duccio and Michelle. Their faces were pressed close together. Gaetano and I slowly walked to the table, not wanting to interrupt. But, Michelle saw us and looked up smiling.

"Are you guys spying on us?" she teased.

"Yeah," I said, "*Siamo* spies." Then it took a while for us to explain what a spy was to Duccio and Gaetano so they could translate the word. The Italian word for *spy*, Gaetano said shrugging his shoulders was *spia*.

"Where is Olivia?" Michelle asked. "I thought she was coming for the weekend."

"I'm going there tomorrow. Suzie and Kurt broke up, and Olivia didn't want to leave." I explained.

"Shit. What happened?"

"She couldn't say, but I think Kurt was a dick."

"Dick?" Gaetano asked, questioning the word. "*Cazzo?*"

"*Si.*"

"*Stronzo,*" said Michelle and then we all switched to Italian, except for Michelle and I who spoke to each other in the weird Italian-English hybrid that had become our language.

"You thought Italian men couldn't be trusted," Gaetano said to me.

"Maybe all men can't be." I smiled, teasing him.

"Oh, Gabi," he said and rubbed my cheek. "*Tesoro.*"

As usual we drank a great deal of alcohol and I took too many of Gaetano's cigarettes. At midnight, Gaetano looked at his watch. "*Ohe,* Gabi, I have to go. The bus."

Duccio offered to give Gaetano a ride, but Gaetano declined. He never wanted to be a bother. I still wanted to hang out more, and Michelle and Duccio didn't want the night to end either. "Gaetano stay."

"I cannot, *bella.*"

"*Dai*," I said, "You can stay in Lisa's room."

Lisa was visiting a schoolmate in Bologna.

"Or you can stay in Gabriella's," Michelle said, laughing and winking up at Gaetano. Duccio cracked up too.

"Better in Gabriella's room," said Duccio.

"Or Lisa's if Lisa was there," teased Gaetano.

"I don't think so," I said.

"But you never know," said Michelle and in English, "That girl could be a frrrreeeeeeak."

For his comment, I refused to tell Gaetano what freak meant until he agreed to stay over in Lisa's room. He agreed. Then I told him. And we kept drinking.

And it was fun. They way they treated us. They listened and laughed at what we said, but there was something else. These men reminded you in their every action of sex. I felt this. It was everything about them, the way they smelled, the way they declared how they felt so strong and the way they looked at us. Always respectfully but acknowledging our bodies, too. I was aware of myself, of my shape, of things long dormant. I recognized what my body was made for. I was young and could feel my youth because of the wine and because of an arm around the back of my chair, brushing my shoulder. It's just Gaetano, I thought. We were clear on everything, but it was there.

I looked over at Michelle. She was still skinny, but she had put some weight back on since she got back. I was there when Duccio first saw her after she got back. He swept her into her arms, calling her *principessa* and telling her how beautiful she was. And then, he pulled back, looked her body up and down and said, "But too skinny, I must feed you."

And he must have been. Her body was in bloom. Michelle was happy. She caught me looking at her.

"What's up, G?"

"Just thinking."

"Always thinking." She looked at the boys and tried to translate. Pointing at me and her own head. "*Questa sempre pensa. Troppo.*"

"Yes, she thinks too much," Gaetano said. "She is very sly. *Mi raccomando, Michelle.*"

When we crept back into the apartment, all four of us were drunk. *Ubriaco.* We were trying to be quiet to not annoy any of our neighbors. We walked so slowly that the electric light turned off while we were on the second landing.

Janine wasn't home, so Michelle yelped like a cowgirl and slammed her door shut. Gaetano and I heard them laughing behind the door.

"Okay, we go to bed," I said. Then I saw Gaetano's smile. Did Italian men ever give up? "Not together."

"Okay," he said, "*pazza.*"

He climbed into Lisa's bed. One of her shirts was under the sheets and he made a big deal of sniffing it and pretending, for me, that he was overcome by the smell of her.

"*Stronzo,*" I said, grabbing the shirt. "But maybe when she comes home from her trip, you can stay over again. With her."

I bent to kiss him and pull the blanket around him as he laughed.

"Okay, *bella, buona notte.*"

"*Buona notte,*" I said. I went into my own room and bed.

I couldn't sleep right away. My room felt stuffy. I opened my window. I changed my T-shirt to a tank top and climbed back into bed. My legs felt hot. I tossed a bit in my sheets, I kicked off the blanket, then decided I wanted it around me.

In Michelle's room, Duccio and Michelle were having sex.

I had not felt this feeling in a while for anyone but Jonas. And I wasn't feeling it for Gaetano, necessarily, but I was feeling it. Restless. In heat. And it was Gaetano who just happened to be in the next room. The walls were thin. There was something happening inside me. A want I would like to satisfy. But I couldn't, not with Gaetano.

But what if I crept in there? What would his face look like when I pulled the sheet back? I wondered if his chest was as tan as his face. It could be so quick. We would both feel good.

But I couldn't do that. I couldn't do something like that and not experience the repercussions. I worked so hard to be his friend. I couldn't fuck it up. Not for stupid selfish reasons.

I forced myself to sleep.

When I woke in the morning, my thoughts surprised me. I was glad I didn't do anything but kept wondering why I wanted to in the first place.

Gaetano smoked three cigarettes and drank two espressos before he really opened his eyes. He got another espresso as we walked to his bus stop. He stuck one hand in his pocket and gestured dramatically with his cigarette. I knew that I made the right choice going to sleep. I couldn't deal with any awkwardness.

He kissed me goodbye at the bus stop and got on his bus. Then I got on mine to Florence.

When Olivia opened the door, her hair was a choppy mess. She had been letting it grow out of her bob, but now it was kind of long in some parts and short in others. There was no rhyme or reason to her hair. It was like someone just randomly clipped off sections.

"Don't say a word about it," she said, as I followed her back to her room. I couldn't stop looking at it. "I thought I was going to a salon, but it was apparently the butcher shop. I was saying the right words. *No* is pretty universal, but they did what they wanted. I believe it's anti-American sentiment."

"It's not too bad," I lied. "You should see what they did to Lucy's hair."

Lucy got her hair chopped at a beauty parlor in Siena. Like most of the girls in my group who got their hair cut, she was horrified and starting wearing a baseball cap. This made her stand out even more. A month earlier, I had let Michelle cautiously cut off about an inch of my hair.

"Let's never talk about it again, okay?" Olivia looked me in the eye. "And whatever you do, don't take any pictures."

"*Va bene.*"

The family that lived in the house was out, not that Suzie and Olivia really socialized with them that much. There was a tiny bathroom attached to their tiny bedroom so they were pretty self-sufficient. There was a whole side of the apartment that they had never seen.

"I thought we'd go to the Medici gardens," Olivia suggested.

"Great." I said. "I'm doing my oral report on the Medicis."

"So is everyone on my group," Olivia said.

"Really?"

"Yeah, it's that, Goitto or the Etruscans."

"I guess that makes sense. Where's Suzie?'

"In the shower," Olivia said looking at her watch. "She's been in there forever."

She was crying. I knew it. I pictured Suzie sitting naked on the tiny ledge of their skinny shower. Her open mouth turned up into the thin stream of water, so that Olivia wouldn't hear her sobbing through the wall.

"How is she?" I asked. I already knew the answer.

"Shitty." Olivia eyed the bathroom door and dropped her voice. "Did you ever meet that girl Jessica?"

Jessica? I remembered thick black eye-liner, husky voice, hippy shirts, and cigarettes. One of many faces I'd been introduced to. "Yeah."

"He was cheating with her. Jessica had her friend Deb tell Suzie. He didn't even deny it. It turns out everyone knew. The fucking assholes."

"Did you know?" I asked.

"I wish I did."

"It's better that you didn't," I said. I heard the shower stop in the bathroom. I whispered. "What could you have done? What would you have?"

"I know, but we always thought, you know–" She didn't finish because Suzie opened the bathroom door. She smiled at me. If you weren't looking for anything, you might not have noticed her red eyes and she would be as pretty as ever.

"Hey, Gabriella, sorry I'm taking so long. I'm a spaz today. I've still got to blow dry my hair."

"No problem, take your time." Suzie shut the door again. We heard the low hum of the blow dryer. Olivia looked at me and shook her head.

"Anyway, I'm sorry about last night," Olivia said, getting up to turn on the stereo. It was some San Remo mix with all the songs we heard the Italians singing in the bars. "I didn't mean to dis you."

"No problem. I wished I had a phone."

"I thought about calling Gaetano, but I figured he was already with you, his *tesoro*." I nodded and sort of smiled. Olivia wrinkled her brows. "What?"

"What?" I asked.

"Your face. You're making a weird face."

"Nothing, it's just, I was just thinking." I realized I was not going to get out of explaining this. "I felt kind of strange last night."

"Oh, my God, you didn't! Did you and Gaetano hook up?"

"No, no, no nothing like that. Shh," I looked toward the bathroom door. "I just felt kind of strange. He slept in Lisa's room. I guess I was just feeling kind of–"

"What?'

"But I didn't do anything." I protested.

"What?" Olivia was getting angry now.

"I felt kind of ... I don't know. I believe the word is horny."

"Oh, my God."

"Listen, I didn't do anything." But it was too late. Olivia was thrilled by this. She was dancing around the room. She pointed a little finger in the air and shook it at me. I picked up one of her pillows and swatted it at her. I yelled. "Nothing happened! *Niente.*"

Then Suzie opened the door and we stopped laughing. For some reason, we didn't want to be too happy. It might have hurt her. She looked good. She blew her curly hair out straight, which was quite a feat with the cheap, low power blow dryers we all bought at Upim department stores.

"So are we ready or what?" Her voice sounded different, deeper. Olivia and I jumped up and put on the lightweight denim jackets we bought at the *mercato*.

We stopped at an *alimentari* on the way to the garden to pick up bread, cheese and pesto for a picnic. I knew parts of Firenze; I had a general sense of direction even though I was usually following Olivia around. That afternoon, I knew enough to see that Olivia chose the long route to the garden. Her path was farthest away from where Kurt lived.

After we got back from the gardens and some shopping, Suzie decided that she didn't want to come out with us that night. We tried like hell to get her to come, but she wouldn't. And she yelled at us when we offered to stay with her.

"Look, I just want to be alone, okay. I don't need a babysitter. I'm just going to go to bed. I didn't sleep that well last night, you know."

And so Olivia and I reluctantly went back to the Mexican restaurant where we ate tacos with fontina cheese and listened to obnoxious Americans screaming over the music. Then we went to an Irish bar where we cursed all men over beer after beer.

I really wasn't supposed to stay on the floor of their tiny room, but Olivia snuck me in. We were quiet when we went into the room. We didn't turn on any lights. We slipped off our clothes in the darkness, and I wrapped Olivia's extra blanket around myself on the floor.

When I heard Suzie's uneven breath, I knew that we made the right choice not turning the lights on. In the darkness, Suzie was crying.

17.

Finally, winter completely broke in Siena. It was spring, not just a random warm day here and there. *Primavera*. I felt my body open a bit. I no longer had to brace myself and hunch over in the cold on the way to school. The first morning I felt this, I was surprised by it. Like a flower I thought, then translating, *come un fiore*. My posture improved; my shoulders became less stiff.

"You are taller," Gaetano said as we walked *in giro*.

With the new warmth, the town became full. Everywhere I turned there were groups of tourists filling the streets from every nation. Usually a woman holding an umbrella high above her head led them around.

"You're kind of like one of those umbrella women," I said to Olivia one afternoon as she led me around Firenze. I had blown off classes once again. The tourists had shown up in force there, too. I suspected spring was the time they were all over the country.

English was the common language spoken by all of these people. I felt cursed to speak such a cheap language. The most amazing part of the influx was that all of the shopkeepers in Siena, who looked at me with such awful puzzled expressions when I first arrived, now seemed to be able to communicate in English with the deep-pocketed tourists. Where was this knowledge when I stumbled over ordering bread?

I was offended when I went into a bar by the church of Santa Caterina one day and the man said "may I help you?" instead of "*dimmi.*" Granted, it wasn't a place I frequented, but I expected to be spoken to in Italian. I answered in the most formal Italian, enunciating everything I could as I ordered a cappuccino.

"If I wanted people to speak English to me, I would still be wearing my sneakers," I complained to Olivia who was, as usual, three paces ahead.

"Now you know what it's like here in Florence," Olivia said without much sympathy. "You're lucky they spoke Italian to you for this long."

The warm weather was coming just in time for Kaitlin on her spring break. She wanted to see Tuscany the way I saw Paris. I was hoping to introduce her to Olivia, but Olivia was also going on her spring break. Olivia and Suzie would travel down the east coast of Italy and catch a ferry to some Greek islands. It sounded like fun to me, and I almost wished that Kaitlin and I could go with them, but I also wanted to show Kaitlin Siena.

Olivia wasn't sure she wanted to go with Suzie. She helped Suzie plan this trip a couple of months earlier.

And even though she researched all the hostels and locations, she felt like what she was—a replacement.

"You could stay here and meet Kaitlin. I think you'd like her," I said. I wasn't sure if this was true one way or the other, but I wanted it to be.

"Or you guys could come with us. It would be better for me to have women who weren't depressive around." I smiled, happy to not be considered the depressive one for once.

"I'd love to go, but I promised to show Kaitlin Siena and besides, we're going to take a couple of days to go to the coastal towns, Cinque Terre. I'm not actually on my spring break, remember?"

Olivia nodded. It was half-hearted. We all sort of believed that school was important, but the traveling was even more educational. Even Arturo turned a blind eye to absences from his culture class when we could prove we had been exploring other cities and not just behaving like hungover Americans.

"Have you talked to Kaitlin yet?" Olivia asked. "About the summer?"

"No, but I will," I said. "I'll talk to her this week when she comes down."

From the time that Kaitlin decided she was going to Paris, she wanted to railroad and backpack around Europe after classes were done. When I chose Siena, we agreed that we would do it together. Suzie and Olivia developed a similar plan early in their roommate history, but since then Olivia feared that it wasn't going to happen. First she thought that Suzie would throw her over to travel with Kurt. Now she was pretty certain that Suzie was going to go home as soon as classes were done. I didn't want to leave her in a bind and was hoping that three of us could travel together. While Kaitlin and I hadn't made any concrete plans other than buying our Eurail pass, Olivia had specific ideas about what she wanted to see.

"You sure?" she asked, meeting my eye. "I don't want to create any drama."

"No drama," I said, trying to sound emphatic. I didn't expect there to be any, but the weird thing was the way my world was opening up. Once it had been as simple as making a loose plan with Kaitlin and now there were train schedules to other cities and friends I had made and probably some she had made who would want to meet up with us or travel with us. The summer still seemed far away, but it lay ahead and full of possibilities.

Janine's old boyfriend Adam came to see her. They lay around in her room because she didn't want to take him outside in case her Italian boyfriend, Andrea, was around. Somehow, she made excuses not to see Andrea for the week that Adam was there.

Adam planned his trip back when Janine needed him, but now she had Andrea. Now she had someone to pay her all the attention she craved. She looked at Adam with disgust; he was a pathetic reminder of her past.

He was good-looking in the way of the frat boy that likes alternative music, but Janine was afraid of what the rest of the roommates would think. He represented her somehow, and she didn't want to make us think that she overplayed something. She whispered to us when he was not exactly out of earshot, "He used to be much cuter."

I felt bad for him, stuck in the apartment. He was not getting to see much of Italy at all.

"Maybe you guys should go south or to Cinque Terre or something. They have great hiking over there and it's not too far," I suggested as I was eating lunch after my class one day.

"Now she's the travel agent," Janine said to Adam. Janine was never at ease with two other people. She always had to gang up with one against the other to prevent them from ganging up on her.

"It was just a suggestion," I said, looking at Adam. He seemed like he wanted to get out of there, too.

"You're the one that's always traipsing here and there with all your friends," Janine said. She turned back to Adam. "This one gets more mail than anyone. You should have written me more."

Janine disguised all her digs as complements unless she was certain that you were weaker than she was. I got up from the table they were commandeering, washed my dishes and went to meet Lucy.

"Ciao," Janine called to me on the way out. She wanted to prove her Italian savvy to Adam.

One afternoon, Janine didn't come home from class. She left Adam sleeping in her room and never returned. He looked up expectantly when I opened the apartment door. I gathered he had been pacing in the kitchen for hours. His face was disappointed. I apologized.

"No, I just thought you'd be Janine."

"Do you want to go out? I could give you my key. I have a paper to work on." I doubted Janine actually went to class.

"No, I should wait for her."

"You could wait all day." I regretted saying that as soon as I did. I felt bad for him. He came here expecting something and wasn't getting it. I listened to the mixtape he made Janine. She tossed it at me when I asked if she had any music to lend. I imagined it was a tape someone made for me. I held up my bag of groceries. "I went to Crai, the grocery store. Want some bread and cheese?"

"No, if Janine wants to eat..." he said, shrugging.

"Right."

I put my groceries away and brought my lunch into my room. I opened the window to let the breeze come through and distract me as I read about the Medicis. I bought this book about them in the English bookstore, but now I had to translate my facts into Italian. It seemed that pretty much everything in Tuscany from art to architecture had something to do with the rich fourteenth-century family and their patronage. After a couple of hours of trying to make sense of it all, I checked on Adam. He was lying on Janine's bed, staring up at the ceiling. He sat up when I knocked.

"You sure you don't want my key?" I asked. He was trapped.

He was wearing a black T-shirt and jeans, his feet in their socks. He didn't realize how foreign he looked in this country. He looked nothing like the American I left behind, yet there was something so similar. They would never have recognized it in each other, but they were a part of the same crew. Countrymen. His T-shirt fit his shoulders in that same angry way.

Somewhere, back home, there was probably some poor girl wishing that Adam wasn't so preoccupied with someone else.

That might be the secret to the American boy. Maybe it was the way they chose to be miserable when they didn't have to be, swinging between choices, refusing to make them. They made you want to save them. They made you their mother. They brought out the nurturer the way the Italians brought out the other stuff. Maybe it was the challenge, thinking you could gentle them and love them and make them turn out okay.

Adam shook his head and looked at the palms of his hands. I felt bad for him. I reached out to touch his shoulder when the front door opened, surprising us. I pulled my innocent hand away. It was Janine. She finally returned to find us in her room together, doing nothing, but still undeniably alone.

That night, Janine and Adam went to Venice.

18.

Kaitlin arrived on a Saturday morning. I offered to meet her in Florence, but she took the train straight into the Siena station, where I met her. I helped her with her giant backpack, and we rode together on the bus back to town. It was surreal to have her there. She marveled at the skinny streets as I had and asked me tons of questions that I mostly knew the answers to, thanks to all the walks Arturo took us on with the culture class.

After her giving her the initial tour of Siena and lunch of the hearty bread soup, *ribollita* at La Chiacchiera, Kaitlin and I sat in the *campo*. Olivia had rubbed off on me, and I had planned out pretty much every minute of Kaitlin's first day. Then I realized that what she really wanted to do was chill. The Piazza del Campo was filled to capacity and the place to get the best look at Sienese life. The sun shown down on the light pink brick of the piazza and, for once, the ground was warm beneath my butt.

"This is awesome," Kaitlin said, smiling and people watching. I was happy that this was enough to impress her. "I love the buildings here."

"Cool. Let me know when you want to move on," I said.

"I will," she said. She pulled her feet out of her sneakers and socks and lay back onto her sweatshirt and that was that.

I looked across the piazza and saw Michelle walking quickly, eating a giant cone of gelato. I called to her, anxious to introduce her to Kaitlin. She came over and offered us each a bite of her ice cream. Kaitlin loved it.

"I'm definitely getting one of those every day I'm here," she declared.

"Are you kidding? I eat like five of these a day," Michelle said. I laughed and looked at her. She wasn't acting like she was making a joke. In fact, she didn't seem herself at all. She was hyper.

"What's up?" I asked.

"Yeah, you guys can still have our room, but I'm probably going to stay in yours, G." With Janine gone and Michelle splitting her time with Duccio, I planned on Kaitlin and me staying in their room with the better bathroom.

"I thought you were going to stay with Duccio." He lived in his parents' house, but snuck Michelle in all the time.

"Yeah, he's pissing me off." She looked at Kaitlin to explain. "Italian boys–assholes."

"Really," Kaitlin smiled. She didn't notice that anything was wrong with Michelle. She gestured around the piazza. "They seem pretty cute to me."

"That's the problem. They're so cute, you forget yourself, and then it's like you try to fight with them and you don't even understand the language you're fighting in. Don't bother." Beneath her smiling warning to Kaitlin, Michelle was agitated about something.

"What happened?" I asked. "You guys always understood each other, I thought."

"Who knows? I couldn't even figure out what he was trying to say at lunch. They're so dramatic about everything. You know how it is." She shrugged as if it wasn't bothering her. She looked at Kaitlin. "Wait until you meet Gaetano."

"Do you want to sit down with us?" Kaitlin asked.

"No, I'm starving. I think I'm going to go get a *panino* or something. I'll see you guys later. *Ciao.*"

"Okay, *ciao*!" I said.

"Nice to meet you," Kaitlin said.

When she was gone, Kaitlin motioned over to a group of good-looking men. "I don't know about Michelle, but I think I could forgive those guys anything."

"Yeah, it's weird, she's not usually like that. I didn't think they fought ever. I wonder what it was about."

"She seemed pretty cool."

"Yeah, she's my favorite roommate," I said. I was glad that Kaitlin liked her, but something wasn't sitting right with me about our meeting.

"This one's really hot," Kaitlin said, looking past me. I turned to see Gaetano, smiling as he came closer.

"The American beauties are in town, at last," he said in Italian. I stood up to greet him with two kisses on the cheek. Kaitlin was at her feet, too.

"K, this is Gaetano. *Gaetano, ti presento, Kaitlin.*" I introduced them.

"Bella, come va?" Gaetano said.

"Hey there," Kaitlin said. "Can he understand me?"

"*Piacere*," he said. He took her extended hand and pulled her in to kiss both her cheeks.

"Oh, okay," Kaitlin said, giggling. She looked over his shoulder at me. "I like this."

"I look you from deh," Gaetano said in English, gesturing to the other side of the piazza. "I say you are Kaiti, de fren of dis beautiful. I look your," he pointed down to her bare feet " and know beautiful *americana.*"

"Cool," Kaitlin said, smiling. She looked at me. I was smiling at the way he said her name. "No idea what he just said, but I caught the beautiful part and I like it."

I laughed. It was weird to hear Gaetano speaking English. It had been a long time. He couldn't express exactly what he wanted. I wanted Kaitlin to understand how smart and funny he was and worried it wasn't going to translate.

"They think it's weird to go barefoot here."

"She doesn't understand my English?" he asked, almost hurt.

"It's not your words," I lied. "It's the, uh, accent."

"HHHHow de tren?" Gaetano asked, trying again. Did he really hear my h's that hard when I spoke English?

"The train?" Kaitlin said, looking at me to confirm. When I nodded, she answered, her voice louder than usual. "It was long."

"You slep?" Gaetano asked and this time held his hands up to the side of his face to convey sleep.

"No, I couldn't," she said, dramatizing her disappointment. "Too much–" She moved her hands like the motion of the train and Gaetano nodded.

"Where are you going to take her?" he asked me.

"You have to show her a good time. You should show her that Italy is beautiful. You should take her to my town, but Siena will have to do."

I laughed. "He's worried that you won't like Italy."

"No, I like it. I like it already," she said, nodding emphatically. She was talking so much louder and more exaggerated than she usually did. People were so funny in other languages.

"Okay," he said. He pointed to her face and used a word I didn't know. "I like."

"What did he say?" she asked. I shook my head, then I got it.

"Oh, freckles, he likes your freckles." He mentioned her red hair and I translated.

"Thank you."

He took her hand. "Very beautiful *Americana.*"

She was smitten. "I love it here. Are they all like this?"

I shrugged. It was good and bad.

"Where are you going? Do you want to hang out with us?" I asked him.

"No, I'm going to the library to study. What about tonight?"

"Dinner and then the bar. Don't worry yourself. That's all I have to show her to make her love Italy. Will you be at the Barone Rosso?"

"Yes, but you should see. She looks tired," he said, smiling at her. "She should sleep."

"She'll be okay. Tomorrow, we're going to Cinque Terre."

"*Brava,*" he said, approvingly. He lit a cigarette and put his sunglasses on. He offered us cigarettes that we took and smoked with him. Kaitlin was appreciating all of this. When he was done, he nodded and kissed

Kaitlin again. "Okay, bella. *Mi raccomando con questa pazza. Ci vediamo stasera.*"

"Whatever," Kaitlin said, smiling, accepting his kisses.

"He's warning you about hanging out with me, I think, and says that he'll see you tonight."

"Oh, okay, *ciao*," Kaitlin said.

"*Brava*, she spek Italian," Gaetano said in English so she would understand. He kissed me goodbye. And Kaitlin sat back down on the ground. He looked at me. "Have fun tonight. If you don't make it tonight, call me when you get back."

"*Okay, ciao.*"

I sat back down next to Kaitlin, and she looked at me.

"You didn't say how hot Gaetano is," Kaitlin said. I shrugged. She studied me. "You didn't even notice, did you? You never want what you can get."

I looked away. There was truth to what she said. And I wondered when I was going to stop wanting the things I couldn't have.

We went to my favorite *osteria* with the Etruscan ceilings. They sat us at my favorite table, which was like a little cave. We drank a lot of wine, and Kaitlin learned the heavenliness of the truffle. I laughed at her expression when she took the first bite.

I wanted to take Kaitlin to the Barone Rosso, but she was spent. After the overnight train, she was content to sit in the stone alcove with the complimentary *cantucci* and Vin Santo that came after the wonderful dessert of tiramisu. I taught Kaitlin how to dunk the small hard cookies into the pink dessert wine.

"Are you sure you don't care if we pass? Is Gaetano going to be waiting?"

"No, it's no big deal. We can go when we come back from the coast. We left it open. It's funny, he knew you were going to be tired."

"I like him. You should hop on that. Have you hooked up with anyone?" I shook my head and held my *cantucci* in the Vin Santo.

"No, not really."

She nodded. We didn't say anything for a minute.

"Thank you," I said. It was so many things, just making sure I was okay every day and being there to listen to me. She was such a friend.

"For what? We're going Dutch," Kaitlin said, winking.

"For last year." Kaitlin nodded, knowing exactly what I meant but still uncomfortable talking about it for too long. I gripped the *cantucci* a little tighter.

"You'd have done the same for me."

"I know, but I didn't have to."

"I know," she hesitated. "Do you feel better? You seem to."

"I do. I really do. How could I not?" I looked around the room.

"Well, I mean, you can always feel bad even surrounded by this. Do you still think about him at all?"

"Yeah, sometimes. It's on and off, you know. It's better than before, though. I really think it is," I said, aware that I was trying to convince both of us. "You know, I really really cared about him, I did."

"I know." Kaitlin touched my hand across the table. "For what it's worth, I think he cared about you too."

"In his way, maybe," I said, feeling something dark

begin to pull back my covers. "Maybe."

"We don't have to talk about this anymore."

"Okay," I said, nodding, knowing that it was best not to. I finally took a bite of my *cantucci*. It was soft from all the time dunked in the wine.

I was feeling good as we came back into the apartment, but my mood soured immediately when I saw Lisa in the dining room. In front of her on the table were wrappers from candy bars and the kinds of packaged breakfast sweets that they sold in the coffee bars. It was a mess worse than any we had so far.

"What the hell is this?" I asked.

"*Non sta bene*," she said. I kind of laughed, thinking that she was at it again, trying to outdo everyone with her language skills. I didn't get why she would be showing off in front of Kaitlin, but then I realized that she had looked past me toward the front bedroom when she said "is not well" in Italian. Michelle. I looked on the table and understood. The gelato, the *panino* she had so close to lunch. Didn't I know when I saw her that something was a little off? But instead of asking, I thought I could just ignore it and enjoy my day.

"K, just hang out, okay? This is Lisa. Kaitlin." I introduced them as I went back into the bedroom that I had planned to sleep in that night. I banged on the door.

"Just a minute," I heard Michelle say when it had already been that long. I pushed the door open. My senses were assaulted.

"Nice to wait," Michelle said. She was going to try to make a joke of it, but she saw my sickened expression.

Across both beds were empty bags of potato chips, more chocolate wrappers and the thin oily pieces of cardboard that came under take-away pizza. And the smell was of human waste. I could see vomit in the trash can she had pulled out of the kitchen. I knew what I would find in the shower, toilet and bidet if I went into the bathroom. But I wasn't going to go in there. The thought of it made me want to gag.

I looked at Michelle, pale with reddened eyes. She was in baggy sweat pants and a tank top. Her chest glistened with sweat. For the first time in my life, I thought I saw Crazy reflected in someone else's eyes.

"What are you doing?" I asked. Part of me hoped there would be some other explanation.

"Nothing. Stop freaking out. I just had a snack and then I felt sick. Must have been the *panino*." She went over to the trash can and started to tie up the bag. "I just wanted to clean up, but you burst in. That's pretty rude."

"Is this because of Duccio?"

"What? Is what because of Duccio?" Her eyes narrowed, defensively. "I'm feeling better, thanks for asking."

I was shaking. I didn't know what to do. I wanted to help, but I didn't have the words. I tried. "Michelle, you can't do this."

"What?" She tried the smile again, as if I was being out of line.

"This. You're hurting yourself. You can't–" I stopped, speechless. She didn't say anything. She looked down at her legs. I wanted to hug her, but I didn't, my stomach was still churning. I was scared to be near her. Scared to smell her and get too close to Crazy. I will always regret that about myself. I will always be ashamed of being such a selfish coward.

"But it makes me feel so much better," she said, her voice far away and breaking a little. And still, I stood there frozen in shock. She was almost in a trance, but then she seemed to remember herself. "I'll just clean up and you guys can sleep in here."

"I'm not ever going to sleep in here," I said quietly. I wasn't being intentionally hurtful, but at that moment, I never wanted to be in that room again. Michelle shook her head.

"Fine," she said through gritted teeth. "Then get the fuck out."

I did. Back in the hallway, I took a deep breath and shuddered. In the dining room, Lisa was sitting, looking stupidly at all the wrappers. She told me that Kaitlin had gone to bed.

"What did she say?" Lisa asked. At last she was speaking English.

"Nothing."

"Nothing?"

"*Niente*," I said. "Is that better?"

"We have to do something?"

"We? You haven't even cleaned all this shit up." I started to gather up the wrappers. The residual scent of chocolate and sweet nauseated me. I realized that there was nowhere to throw them away. The trash bucket was still with Michelle. I wanted to throw them out the window, but I went into the kitchen to where we kept the garbage bags. Lisa followed me.

"But is she okay?"

"I don't know, Lisa," I snapped. She was an easy target. "You could have gone in there instead of waiting for me."

"No I couldn't. I couldn't." Lisa said, shaking her

head. She was almost in tears. And it made me feel better to be angry with her than really think about what I saw in that room.

"You're not going away tomorrow. You can't."
"I am," I said. "I want out of this shithole. She doesn't want my help."

Then I went to my room. Kaitlin was lying on top of the bed I had made that morning. I wanted Kaitlin to be sleeping, but she opened her eyes when I came in.

"Sorry, I was just exhausted. Are we changing rooms?"

"No. Change of plans. We're sleeping in here. I'll take the floor. Just go to bed. I'll wake you up when it's time to go."

Kaitlin closed her eyes and I heard her steady sleeping breath, but the time I lay down on one of the blankets on the floor.

I thought of how Lisa spoke Italian so Kaitlin wouldn't understand. She knew enough to protect Michelle from letting anyone else know. It was so shameful to both of us. And still we didn't know how to help her. We were too scared. Every bit of our behavior was worse than the smell of that room.

19.

There are five coastal cities of Tuscany that are linked by train and mountainous roads. Within Cinque Terre there was no specific tourist attractions to see, no churches or art that you had to check off a list. Everything there was to see was not made by man, unless you counted the pastel-colored houses that ascended the hills. What there was to see was beautiful beaches and hills.

I breathed the clean sea air deep as Kaitlin and I sat on the side of the road, taking a rest from some of our strenuous daily hikes. We enjoyed watching eighty-year-old village women speed by us. In spite of the physical activity, I felt restful. We filled those days with kayaking, hiking and meals of fresh fish caught five kilometers from where we ate it. It was still too cold on the coast for most tourists, and after dinner and a short walk *in giro*, we turned in early and I slept well.

I wasn't stressed about speaking Italian either. It

was okay being the translator for Kaitlin, and I rose to the occasion. It was starting not to matter so much if I messed up words, to me or to anyone. And I realized that the more I relaxed, the fewer mistakes I made.

It was peaceful. Kaitlin was excited about traveling in the summer, and she welcomed the idea of going with Olivia. There hadn't been a reason to worry about it at all.

When my mind wandered on some of those hikes it wasn't to Jonas, it was to Michelle and Lisa and the way I had acted. I felt guilty for leaving and still, relieved that I was away.

We spent four nights in Cinque Terre. And then we returned to Siena.

Lisa and Janine were home when we got back. Michelle, the person that I wanted to see most, was not. But then I was scared to see her also, so it was easier. I watched Janine give Kaitlin the once-over when I introduced them, but she had no idea where Michelle was. I studied her face to see if she knew anything, but it revealed nothing. I didn't bother to ask her how she enjoyed her time in Venice with Adam.

I tiptoed around Lisa for a little while and then when Kaitlin was in the shower, I went into her room. I had to walk through it anyway to get to mine, but for once I knocked. She was studying as usual, and she looked up at me, surprised.

"You can come through," she said, looking back down at her book.

"No, I'm not trying to pass, I wanted to talk to you."

She shrugged, and I took that as a sign that I could lean against her bureau and apologize for the way I spoke to her the night before I left. She nodded and accepted my words coolly. I hadn't known what to expect, but I didn't get the big scene where we hugged and realized that we really were more the same than different. We were different and I wasn't ever going to be her buddy, but I was going to respect her from now on. And I was going to be a little more patient with her.

For two days, Kaitlin slept in while I went to class. Afterward, I took her to my favorite places and met Gaetano for lunch in the piazza. Somehow, they communicated with Kaitlin picking up snippets of Italian and Gaetano sounding vaguely like a Japanese man when he spoke English.

On Friday we took off after school and I showed her Florence, but not before I asked for and received two tickets from the man in the *biglietteria* without correction.

"*Brava,*" he said when I thanked him for the tickets, still kind of stunned at how smooth the transaction went. I could almost detect a smile beneath the bushy mustache.

"What? Do you have a crush on that guy or something?" Kaitlin asked as we walked to the bus station. "You're grinning like a fool."

"No, I just...you wouldn't understand. I finally asked the right way." Kaitlin nodded, not really getting it, but I was so insanely proud of myself for mastering the not-so-silent *g*, the sound of the *t*'s and the long *o*. It was like getting an A+ on all my exams.

I wanted to introduce Olivia and Kaitlin, but Olivia was still on her spring break, so I did my best to maneuver around the crowded streets of Florence. There were tourists everywhere and people outside hawking leather goods. It was a zoo.

I forked over the admission fee at the Uffizi, so Kaitlin could see the David. That and the Ponte Vecchio were the only things about Florence that she really liked. Everywhere we went we heard English and saw overweight tourists in sneakers and ill-fitting shorts. Someone even stopped Kaitlin for directions in English.

"It's like Disney World," she said over dinner at a place that Olivia told me about. Here we could order different small plates of homemade pasta with different sauces so we could try them all.

Over thick curled ribbons of pesto, she said, "I thought it was supposed to be so beautiful. It's a tourist trap. I heard more English than Italian."

"There are nicer parts than what we saw, but I think what people are looking to find in Florence is actually in Siena tenfold."

"I can't believe tomorrow is my last day," she said sampling another type of pasta, this one with tiny shrimp and parsley.

"But you're coming back. Look how quick the time passed since our last visit."

"Yeah, it's only a month till I'm back in Siena and then the summer." She looked at me and pointed her fork. "You know, you got to do something about Gaetano by then."

"Whatever do you mean?"

"C'mon, if you don't I will," she teased.

"I don't know if he likes redheads," I said, laughing.

"What he likes is Gabriellas. And they should like him. They should get out of this funk and get on that."

"Okay, you're dirty. You happy? You went there. Do you hear yourself?"

"Yep," she said and sucked on the last ribbon of pasta so it squiggled in her mouth.

The morning of Kaitlin's last day I called Gaetano. He was going to be playing soccer all day, but promised to make it over to the Barone Rosso by ten to say goodbye to Kaitlin, his new favorite *americana*.

"Good news," I told her. "We'll see Gaetano, later and there's a big chance that he will bring his hot soccer buddies.

"That is great news," she said. "I just might get a little something before I'm gone. A souvenir of Italy, if you will."

"Oh, I will," I said.

"*You* should," she said.

We spent the day in the piazza with a bottle of red wine that I bought at the Coop supermarket. We got some gelato. Then when the sun and the wine seemed to do us in, we hit one of the pizzerias that I'd been to with Gaetano. We were already buzzing and the thin-crust pizza hit the spot.

"Are you sure you want to go to Barone Rosso?" I asked when I noticed Kaitlin sway a little as she stood.

"Uh, yeah."

When we got to the crowded bar, we didn't see Gaetano, but someone called my name and it was Duccio. He pulled me over to where Michelle was. He didn't seem to know about our fight, because immediately he saw someone else and left us alone.

"Hey," Michelle said to me, her smile was small and shy. The color had returned to her face and she looked healthier. She asked Kaitlin. "How's your trip been so far?"

"Awesome, I'm sorry I have to leave."

"But you'll be back, right?" Michelle asked. "I mean Gabriella says she'll come back for the Palio."

"Yeah, I hope." Kaitlin said.

Michelle looked around for a minute, her smile was bigger now, but she looked like she was holding her breath. "Listen, sorry about the other night." I felt a pang in my chest when she said that. I hadn't gotten into details with Kaitlin, and I hoped that Michelle wasn't feeling embarrassed.

"No worries," Kaitlin said. "Hey, anybody need a drink?"

"I'll take a gin and tonic," Michelle said.

"I'll have one of those big beers. A *birra alla spina*," I said. "Do you want me to come with you to translate?"

"No, I think I can make myself understood. It's alcohol, that's what I know," Kaitlin said, smiling. She put her hand up and gave me a little nod so I would know that she thought I should stay and take advantage of the moment.

Michelle and I looked at each other for a second. In spite of my buzz, there was tension.

"So, um," I gestured over toward Duccio. "Everything going okay with the boy?"

"Yep, all is forgiven," she nodded.

I hesitated and then said. "Here, too, I hope."

She nodded and the tightness left her body. "Most definitely."

Then we hugged each other and I was grateful for what I had to drink for making it easier to be okay with each other like I wanted to be.

"Gaetano will come soon," Duccio said when he came back. He kissed Michelle. I smiled at them. He was in love with her. It was obvious, though I thought someone looked at me like that one time, too, and it hadn't meant anything.

Stop.

"You're warm," he once said, rolling over the length of my body. "How can you be so warm? How can you warm me up so much?"

Don't.

I felt a cold glass on my neck. It was Gaetano coming to rescue me from my thoughts. His team won the soccer game and everyone was pumped. He gave Kaitlin a big hug as if it had been longer than two days since they saw each other. Over his shoulder, Kaitlin winked at me, reminding me of what she said the previous night. She was too late. I was thinking of someone else.

It was like any other night at the Barone Rosso, the women in short skirts passing with trays of drinks held high, the crowd singing and swaying. I was comfortable with my friends. All of this should have been familiar. And then someone put a song on. It was an Italian song called "*Ricordati di me.*" Remember me. I had heard it before. I didn't want to hear that song right now. I did not know how to get Jonas out of my head. I could not stop myself. I had to know if he really existed. How could he have? How could any real person made of flesh have affected me so much?

I began to feel like two separate people. One was enjoying that night like any other in the bar, but the other was somewhere else. I knew Crazy was waiting for me as she often did, waiting to get me alone. I had been doing too well and now it was time for a little visit.

Kaitlin's eyes were beginning to cross; she was swaying a little, far too drunk to be responsible. I wasn't drunk enough. I was not too drunk to take advantage, to confirm that he existed, that we did in fact know each other, that someone felt that way about me. Once.

I asked her if she remembered a time long ago when she called the room we shared and I asked her not to come back.

"I was with Jonas. He said he didn't want to let me go."

His name was foreign on my tongue after so long. It escaped me like a hiccup. Kaitlin wasn't sure why I was telling her this. She nodded. She was too drunk to worry about me. I had been doing so well. Maybe she wouldn't remember in the morning. But I was happy that she remembered. One of my memories was almost confirmed.

"Do you feel okay?" I asked, guilty for having taken advantage.

"Yeah, you know, I just have to spit."

"What? Are you okay? Spit?"

"Yeah, I'm going to go outside. My mouth is dry. All the wine today. I'll be right back."

"Are you sure?" Kaitlin nodded. It made sense to me. I wanted it to so that I could be alone. I needed to be alone. It was a compulsion. I watched Kaitlin make her way out of the bar.

Then I was in the bathroom, with all my disparate thoughts. I locked the door. Like I used to do so many nights back at school. When it got bad, I could be counted on to go into the bathroom and shoot the shit with Crazy. But I had not done this yet in Italy. I hadn't left a place to do this. I had stopped myself, squelched it, stuffed it down, forced myself to believe I could forget him if I kept myself from these kinds of Crazy. Tonight, something set me off. The look Duccio gave Michelle, the song, just being around Kaitlin, the foolish confidence that I was actually okay. Whatever it was, I couldn't help myself. This is what it must feel like to make yourself puke. Free and scary all at once.

And there Crazy was in the mirror. She looked a lot like me. Sometimes, in the past, her eyes burned with scheming delight, but now they were black.

No one told you to come here. No one told you to lose control. You were doing so well. You were fitting in, getting better. Isn't that the point? Have you looked at where you are? Do you appreciate any of it? You think this is a real problem? You don't know pain. People suffer and die all the time. And you, surrounded by beauty, you cling to this belief that you are hurting.

This was a trick of Crazy's to play devil's advocate. To taunt you so you wind up arguing her case. To mock you for your emotions. I knew this all too well. And still I played my part.

"I'm losing him. I'm losing him." I was growing frantic, whispering a yell into the mirror. It's how she drew me to her.

Let him go. You lost him already.

"I can't. I haven't. I don't want to. He misses me. He has to miss me."

If he missed you he would be here. He would have found a way to tell you himself.

"No." I grabbed at my chest where it began to hurt and I continued to be cruel to myself. But it was not me. I wouldn't be fooled. It was Crazy waiting to bring me back.

Fuck! I banged the mirror. I put my hand up in my hair and tugged, gritted my teeth. I began to remember what I didn't want to, what Crazy was leading me to all along. How I made the choice that he didn't want to that last night we were together.

A thumb is traveling, zigzagging down my bare chest. Jonas is above, smiling. He doesn't know me as well as I know him. He doesn't believe me when I tell him he needs to choose.

He's laughing at my eyes as the thumb moves down, teasing me. His pretty eyes are tired. We have not been sleeping, only dozing, wrapped in each other, waking to breathe each other again, keeping each other afloat with words.

"I'm remembering, I'm remembering," his voice a singsong joke. A long summer apart is coming. He still thinks he won't have to remember that I will always be what he wants, where he wants. Too many women have given him their flowers to hang up and dry. He expects this from me.

When his thumb is below my navel, I take him by surprise. I place the palm of my hand onto his beautiful sleepy eye, with my other hand grab his wayward fingers, unbalancing him onto me. I dig into his eye until he takes me seriously. I put my mouth against his ear. I speak from a place the thumb hadn't yet found.

"Go back to her. I'm deciding. Not you. It's my choice, you fucking coward, but know that I have bruised my name across your body," I say with a hesitant confidence. "And I will walk my walk across your daydreams. You are too weak not to go back to her, but when you do..." I pause, steel myself to continue, find the courage that is just a show–"she will sleep beside you and you, you will reach out and up into the night, hoping to find my hair. I will not be there. You will never be done with me."

I cursed myself to nothing. This was the price because I was scared to hold on, scared to leave it up to him. Because I knew all along that I should have worried. No matter what he said, I knew that I shouldn't have trusted him with my heart. But still I did.

Crazy wore me down with memories that were clearer than ever. I could feel the thumb on my skin, the way it made me tremble. But Crazy always finished by reminding me that in spite of all of it I was alone.

He was done with me.

And then there was the choice, give in to the black that she offered. Let go. Go off the edge. If I did it right, it would release me. The only other option was to live with the truth.

He wouldn't ever be mine again. I wouldn't know him anymore. He was just a part of my mind now, a symptom of Crazy. He would always disappoint me. He would never say what I needed to hear.

That I knew.

Sometimes it's better to hope than to know.

I didn't want to know.

I looked up at Crazy, her eyes were warm now; she opened her arms to let me in. To comfort me from what I knew, what was too hard, too unbelievable. Too true.

But then. Then. Someone banged on the door. I heard an Italian yelling, annoyed. An impatient Italian saved me from her embrace. I stopped talking to the mirror. To myself. I was in Italy, not in some single dorm room bed half a world away with him.

I was sane. I could delude myself a little longer.

Maybe he was still thinking about me. Maybe. I could still hope. Not done. Never done. But I was free for a time.

Fuck you, Crazy.

Back in the bar, I saw Gaetano. He was standing with the others. He was holding tight to the bar. When he saw me, he smiled at me. There was no sign of Kaitlin.

"*Dove sta Kaitlin?*" I asked. He shrugged. I had to find Kaitlin. "*Aspetta qui, okay?*"

He nodded, willing to wait. I made my way through the crowded bar, saying "*permesso*" as I passed, like one of the barmaids. On the street, there was no sign of her. I panicked for a second and then I turned right up the street. I turned again and then I saw Kaitlin, crouching in a doorway, throwing up. Her body looked small. Kaitlin saw me.

"Gabriella." Her voice was so tiny. I ran to her and put my hand on her back.

"This is some spitting you're doing." There's way too much puke in my life these days, I thought. I put one of Kaitlin's arms around my shoulders and pulled her up.

"Wipe your mouth. Hold on to me." We walked awkwardly down Via di Citta. I was holding her tightly. Now I had a purpose. We got to the apartment on Via Stalloreggi. We made it up into the elevator because I figured it would be easier than the stairs. When we got to the floor, Kaitlin paused, gagging. Of course the automatic electric light in the hall went out. I scrambled my hand along the wall, hoping that Kaitlin wouldn't puke in the darkness. I found the light switch in time and got Kaitlin into the apartment. I had just put the garbage pail under Kaitlin when she got sick. It was close to dry heaves now. I brought her some water.

I led Kaitlin into my bedroom. I peeled off the vomit-stained dress I lent her earlier. I threw it in the bidet in my bathroom, let some water run over it. In the end I would throw it away. I brought back some aspirin and tucked her into bed. When Kaitlin's breath steadied in sleep, I went back to find Gaetano, leaving the trash pail next to my bed.

I passed Michelle and Duccio on the street on the way back. I told them that Kaitlin was there, and I asked Michelle to look in on her.

Gaetano was drunker when I returned. The crowd had thinned, but those who remained were all singing. He didn't see me as I approached. Then he did and I liked the way his face changed when he turned to me.

"*Ohe, Gabi.*" He greeted me like one of his soccer bodies, but he looked at me like I was a woman.

"*Sei ubriaco,*" I said.

"*Tu sei bella.*" Only in Italy was it appropriate to answer a woman's accusation of drunkenness by telling her she was beautiful. He was still celebrating the victory, shouting bits of the game in dialect to his friends. He insisted I have another cocktail with him, saying we were "drinking like Americans." I ordered a tequila sunrise I wouldn't be able to finish. His friends were smiling at us. I drank and laughed at the passion of the Italians as they sang Nirvana, fucking up the words. I tried to let Gaetano's happiness spill onto me.

Finally, I told him I had to get back. I needed to see Kaitlin and I couldn't drink any more. I was past the point of really being drunk now. I was just full, and my head was starting to pound.

Gaetano led the way out, staggering slightly. He

was not used to drinking as much, as hard like we Americans did, just for the sake of drinking. Outside the bar, there was a crowd. It was a fight. Gaetano put his arm around me and guided me away, but we heard the man with the Tuscan accent.

"*Okio, stai a Siena*," the voice said.

I didn't understand the slang at first, I didn't quite hear it right. Gaetano explained to me that they were telling some kid, a southerner most likely, to watch out because he was in Siena.

"*Stronzo*," said Gaetano and then in dialect, "*Pesce della mamita*." I knew if he were alone he would fight for having heard that. At first he had his arm around me to protect me as we left, but then he was leaning against me, like Kaitlin. He was drunk. I understood that he planned on driving the borrowed *vespa* home, and I made a decision not to let that happen.

"You can't go home," I said as I walked him up the stairs of my apartment building. He was laughing and protesting; his smile was unguarded. He was following me, though. And again the lights went out. I took the opportunity to get close to him, to reach into his pocket and find the keys. He was too slow to stop me, testament to how drunk he was.

"*Che fai?*" he asked, following me into the apartment. I sat him on the comfy chair in the dining room. People fucked there; it was good enough to sleep on. I got one of the other chairs and put his feet up. I took off his black leather shoes. He was still protesting jumbled words. Tomorrow he had another soccer match early. He said he could drive. He was accusing me of being too American. It was something he heard about, taking the keys, but he didn't quite understand it and he was so far drunk it wouldn't make sense anyway. I waved my hand at him and stood before him, shaking my head.

"*Senti*, Gaetano, if you leave, I will never speak to you again. Do you understand? Never." He nodded. He understood. I may not have said it right, but I knew he understood my tone.

"The way you Americans drink," he said, slurring a bit. "It's too much."

I nodded. I found him a blanket; I took one that Kaitlin kicked off the bed. She was sleeping peacefully in my house full of drunks. When I returned to put the blanket on Gaetano, he was out. I kissed his forehead.

Back in my room there was the slight smell of sickness. I didn't have the energy to wash up. There was another blanket on the floor, I spread this out and bunched some dirty laundry under my head. I hid the keys to the *vespa* beneath it.

I woke to Gaetano kneeling above me saying my name. I sat up. It was late morning, he missed the beginning of his game. He had to hurry. I searched for the keys beneath the laundry pile. He looked exhausted but laughed anyway at my resourcefulness. He bent to kiss my cheek and whispered beautiful Italian in my ear.

"Last night you saved my life, *tesoro*."

I woke up again hours later with a hangover, a deep pain behind my eyes. Kaitlin lay helplessly dehydrated in my bed.

Gaetano rang the doorbell. He dropped off pastries and a package of espresso. He didn't stay, leaving me with two kisses on each cheek and best wishes for Kaitlin's trip back to Paris.

I got Kaitlin more water and made the espresso. I bit a piece off each delicious pastry, but that was all I could stomach. I put them in the fridge.

And later, when I got back from bringing Kaitlin to the bus station, I was hungry. Of course those pastries were gone save for a bite of one that mocked me. The out-of-control food thief struck again.

Cazzo!

I stood in my kitchen, hungry and livid. But I was alone in the apartment; there was no one to complain to or yell at. I stood there, listening to the stillness and looking out the window. I was alone, but for a change it didn't make me anxious. It was peaceful. My anger left me.

I thought of how it had been so long since I'd seen Kaitlin that drunk. Maybe she hadn't let herself go in months because she always had to keep track of me, but last night, finally, she thought she could relax.

What if I wasn't fooling her about getting better? What if I was actually starting to do okay?

And Gaetano was the one that I always leaned on, but last night he let himself lean on me. I thought about how we "Americans drink." Not all of us drank like that, but I did. Sometimes it was too much. I needed to get to a place where it was just enough but not too much.

My stomach nagged me again. I looked for the loaf of bread I split with Kaitlin before I took her to the station. That bread was gone, too. Oh, the fucking food thief. I was trying not to let it get to me, but I needed to eat.

I found three eggs in the fridge next to a brown bag of hardened rolls. I took them all, becoming a food thief myself. I entertained the notion that maybe the whole "food thief" thing was just a series of misunderstandings and desperate hunger and I laughed. How I wished that were true.

I wet the rolls with some water so they softened and I cut them in half. I cracked the eggs into a bowl, but I couldn't bring myself to whisk them just then. I admired them, in spite of my hunger. These were eggs from the Crai supermarket but the yolks were a bright yellow, unlike any I had ever seen at home. I wanted to talk to Gaetano sometime about the "Italian way" of eating and all he probably took for granted.

I added olive oil to the skillet and scrambled the eggs right in the pan. I dried the halves of the bread and drizzled them with more olive oil. I found a clove of garlic and ran it along the open tops of rolls. I put the bread down on the skillet around the eggs. It was starting to smell good. I added some pepper and some *pepperoncino* for color and heat. What I really needed was *prezzemolo*. I cut a bunch, and as I finished cutting the parsley, my eggs were done.

I considered eating it right there by the stove, but this simple meal deserved a little more. So did I. I put everything on a plate and added a few more splashes of olive oil, the rest of the parsley and a pinch more of the red pepper. I poured myself some almost flat *acqua con gas* that also belonged to someone else.

I ate that meal, looking out the window at the countryside. I was okay being alone. Being alone didn't mean I had to let my mind go anywhere I didn't want it to go. When I was finished, I smiled at the meal I made for myself, enjoying the feeling of perfect satiation in my body. I decided to give the whole kitchen a thorough cleaning. I paused before I brought my plate to the sink, still smiling.

"*Biglietto*," I said quietly to no one, to myself.

"*Biglietto*," I said again louder, listening, understanding how subtle and important that *g* was to the word. How the two *t*'s created a different sound from just one. They all worked together. Without each letter making each sound, you might have a different word in a different language. Without them, maybe you wouldn't deserve a ticket to go anywhere.

"*Biglietto*," I said again, now shouting out over those red-tiled roofs beyond my window.

There was no one around to hear me. But I heard. And I knew that my accent was perfect.

MAGGIO

20.

One Friday when Signora Filmona released us early Gaetano was there. I hadn't seen him too much in the past two weeks because he had to study for exams. He gave me the thumbs-up sign so I knew that he passed all his tests. He held up a plastic bag. Inside it was bread and cheese and pesto.

"I thought we could have a picnic and I could help you with your speech," he said. "Now that I passed my exams, you need to pass yours."

I planned on going to the film class. I had only been to the class twice. Part of my grade would be based on a paper I wrote about Italian film. I couldn't understand the teacher, who spoke fast despite the class being made up entirely of *stranieri*. Really, it was pointless. Arturo was going to grade my paper, anyway. The *università* was only responsible for our language grades.

I didn't know how to say, "Don't twist my arm" in Italian so I got behind him on the bike.

We went to the grounds of the monastery. It was nice there, with a lush green square next to the old stone church. We sat on the hill that led down to the field and ate our fine feast. We talked about my travel plans. In four weeks, I would leave.

I told Gaetano about all the cities we might go to. Lately, every time I saw Olivia, she had a new plan for us to attack the entire continent of Europe and perhaps a little of North Africa. I was budgeting only a month of travel and coming back to Siena for the July Palio, which was the horse race that took place in the Piazza del Campo. This was when most tourists came to Siena. It was supposed to be amazing, with all the neighborhoods, dressing up in medieval garb, partying and scheming to beat each other. It was the big showdown. I wasn't sure where we were going to stay. Hotels were supposed to be so expensive, but there was no way I was going to miss it.

Lately, I had been toying with the idea of traveling more after the July Palio and then coming back again for the August Palio. I had no idea how I was going to afford that or what I was going to say to my parents to make them agree.

"I can't believe it. I can't believe I've been here for four months already," I said to Gaetano as he handed me a plastic cup of cheap red wine.

"You have learned a lot. You have had a good professor," he said, laughing. He considered himself my best teacher. "You are lucky, you Americans. You get to see so much."

"Yeah, but it isn't enough. There's so much more I still want to do."

"You can. You aren't leaving tomorrow."

"I know," I said. "The weather is just starting to get nice. It's so strange how people are already starting to get their tickets to go back home. I feel like it's ending. If I left when some people are leaving, I would have been here for only five months." I stopped and smiled at him. "Did you hear that?"

"What?"

"I said, 'I would have been here.' Future perfect, right? Can you believe it?"

He laughed. "Gabi, I've long since stopped being surprised by how well you speak Italian."

"Well, I'm surprised."

"I can see that," he said

"You know I only talk this well with you."

"I don't think that's true anymore. At first you were most confident with me, but I have heard you speak many times. You speak well."

"And now I'm going to lose it all." He sucked his teeth and shook his head. His hands reached out to pinch a little of my cheek. Then he kissed his hand. It was all southern Italian mumbo jumbo that I had come to slightly understand like the future perfect.

"Don't worry so much. Worry about me for when you are gone." I pouted at him. He swatted at me and then grabbed my notebook with the speech. He handed it to me. "*Allora*."

The speech was mostly written. I read it to him, and he occasionally corrected my pronunciation or told me how to rephrase something so it flowed better. When I was done, we smoked a couple of cigarettes and finished up the wine.

Some of his fellow dormers called him from the field below. They were kicking around a soccer ball. He shook his head and shouted to them in dialect.

"Why not play?" I asked. "You should go. I'll work on my speech more. Go ahead. I never see you play."

"Okay," he said. He stood up, dusted off his pants and cursed over an imperceptible stain. Italians were vain about their clothes. I threw on anything, but they wouldn't dream of wearing something that was stained or ripped.

I watched them play for a while. Gaetano knew how to play the game he called *calcio*. I clapped when he did this funny dribble with his legs. He moved the ball with both legs, almost like an airborne Road Runner. I laughed. I didn't know anything about soccer, but this game meant so much to him. He spent so much time doing it, and I'd never seen it before. It was a change to be watching him without having him look at me.

Then instead of working on my speech, I wrote in my journal. For the first time ever, I wrote the whole entry in Italian. Finally, I felt I could express myself better in that language.

Gaetano came back up the hill, wiping his brow with a handkerchief. He shook his finger at me. "I thought you were going to watch me."

"I was watching you. I saw what you did." I moved my hands up and down fast in front of me like he had done with his legs. Once again, I didn't know the words.

"You saw that," he asked, pleased.

"Yes, Renaldo, I did." Renaldo was his favorite Italian soccer player. I knew nothing about this guy, but Gaetano's eyes got a faraway look whenever he talked about Renaldo. I had no idea what the player even looked like, but it didn't matter to Gaetano. He smiled at me for invoking the sacred name.

Gaetano took me back to my apartment. He was meeting some of his classmates for dinner to celebrate the end of their exams. He said that he probably wasn't going to be able to make the party that Janine decided to have, but he would try to come later.

"Don't get as drunk as you were last time if you plan to ride this *vespa*."

"Yes, Gabi," he said and saluted.

As we were standing at the door, Michelle came out.

"Where you going?" I asked.

"Duccio's parents are going to visit his aunt. I'm going over there."

"You're not going to Janine's *festa*?"

"*Mi piace sexa piu di festa*," Michelle said murdering the language for the humor and the rhyme.

"Shit," I said.

Gaetano repeated, laughing, "Shit."

"What? I thought Olivia was coming," Michelle said.

"No, Olivia's semester is done for the most part, but she has to finish a paper by Monday. I think Suzie's coming, but I wish you were going to be there. I hate those guys Andrea hangs out with. They're so arrogant." I was speaking fast, so Gaetano wouldn't understand. I didn't like the way they looked at the American girls, but I didn't want Gaetano to know that.

"Yeah, well, Duccio's no fan either. That's why we aren't going. It'll be fine though. Listen, do you guys want to come to the stable with us on Sunday? Duccio's friend has horses."

"I will, but Gaetano has *calcio*."

"Right," Michelle said. "*Senti*, I'm sorry you are stuck here tonight. Just drink wine."

I nodded. "Of course, isn't that the Italian solution?"

"Ciao, guys," Michelle said waving goodbye to us.

"Please try to come tonight," I said to Gaetano.

"Okay, Gabi, I'll try, but we may go to Arezzo." He squinted at me and pinched my arm. "*Tesoro*, I'll try."

I took a nap before the party, sleepy from the wine and the sun, and when I woke up, it had already started. There were girls from the group and wine bottles everywhere. It was going to be a night of "American drinking." I wanted to bail on the whole thing and see if Lucy was around, but I had already, stupidly, invited Suzie so I had to stay. I prepared for a long night.

When Suzie arrived, Janine looked her up and down. Then Janine shot me a look for inviting a girl who might have been competition for her. Suzie seemed less of herself, edgy and on the verge of tears. Somehow, it made her even more attractive and even more of a rival for Janine.

Suzie dressed for the night, dressed for eyes of Italian men. Her arrival meant that I was going to have to be at the party and not retreat to my room. She was smoking like a fiend, which she never used to do. She brought two bottles of wine, and she opened one for us, offering it to the girls. Janine took a glass and continued to size her up but smiled the whole time.

Then Andrea arrived with his friends. In their black leather jackets and hemmed jeans, they took over the apartment. Suzie and I polished off one of her bottles of wine then another. If I have wine in my mouth, maybe I won't have to talk to any of these guys, I thought.

I yearned for Olivia, Gaetano, Michelle or even Duccio. Someone who was real to me. No one in the apartment was saying or doing anything they really felt. Everyone must have had a script they were going by, but no one had given me my lines. I was sure they were acting, certain that every single person in the room was a fake. And to what end? I wasn't sure.

I hoped Gaetano was on his way. Alone. I worried about how he would get along with the men here. They were all local, Sienese, northerners. Duccio and Dino never made any regional distinctions that I could perceive. For them the issues of north and south were always made into a joke.

These boys were different. They were passionate about their city like all Italians, but they were the bad eggs. They were the ones who started fights outside Il Barone Rosso. Southerners, *stranieri*, even the rest of Tuscany, they felt were beneath them. They managed to put their feelings of superiority aside for the soul purpose of fucking American girls and the American girls at the party didn't mind.

I wasn't sure I could deal with it. I tried to remember the me of that afternoon. Now everything around me was false; Janine's laughter, Pam's intentional American accent, and the shadow on Suzie's eyes. It was so wrong to me. This was not the Italy I wanted to see. This was created by us, by American women who thought it was what we wanted, thought we could control it. But it was empty and I was being filled up with emptiness.

I thought about Jonas. If he were here, there would not be a script. We might sit in a corner with one of the bottles of wine and talk and laugh and not give a shit what anyone was saying. But he wasn't here and I wasn't sure I could do it alone anymore. Any of it.

Then Lorenzo, urged on by the girls, took out his guitar. He toyed with them for a while, strumming bits of Nirvana and the Beatles. He laughed, showing white perfect northern teeth. Finally, he settled on a song. He started to play "Wish You Were Here." The opening chords pulled me back to my dorm room.

"How does it sound?" Jonas asked so long ago, when it was just us, before she got well and came back.

"It's good."

"You like it?"

"Of course." He put the guitar on the floor by my small bed. He was smiling. I crossed the room and sat on the bed. We kissed long into the night. He touched me. I held him and looked at him. I believed that he was mine. Never took it for granted, not ever. But believed.

But what happened next? Did we go to the greenhouse the next day or was that the day we spread a blanket out on the hill? Which was it? Yesterday I remembered it too clearly as if it was happening at that moment, but now...

The girls were singing the words they weren't sure of, the Italians sang hesitantly, not wanting to look foolish in front of their future conquests. They didn't understand what a sure thing it would be. I closed my eyes. This was wrong. I was not where I should be. Where was he? Where was my American boy right now? Was he thinking of me? He must be. Wasn't he tired of this, too? Hadn't he had his fill yet of being away from me?

Why can't I go home?

I decided to call him. I could say his name to him and he would hear it and it wouldn't be like whispering into the darkness anymore. I remembered that I had two 5,000 lire phone cards. That was enough to call the U.S. I could figure out what else to say on the way. No, I wouldn't think. Just speak what came to my head.

I went to my room, searched through my clothes, looking in pockets of pants and jeans. Where were the damned cards? *Cazzo.* I hadn't used them up. Where were they? I emptied out my school backpack; I looked in the big travel backpack. They would not be in there, but I looked anyway. I looked in all my pockets again. Frantic. I looked everywhere.

I couldn't find the cards, but I had to call him. I was back at the party. Lorenzo was playing another song. I asked each of the American girls for a card. No one had one. None of them cared about me or what I needed. Only Suzie asked me if I was okay. What could I say to Suzie?

I asked the Italians. They made a joke out of my request. They offered me coins, *spiccioli.* Lorenzo got upset about the commotion.

"*Che cazzo vuoi?*" he asked, stopping his song to everyone's dismay. What the hell did I want? None of this mattered to me. My purpose was clear. I put on a sweater and ran out of the building onto the dark street.

The bits and pieces of my plan came quickly to me. The store across the street was closed. I could go down to the game alcove, but there was no way to get a phone card from there. All of the stores were closed. I crossed the piazza and went over to area just before one of the doors to the city where there was a piazza filled with phones. Maybe I could find a phone card there. I was desperate. I had two calling cards. How could I lose those cards? I bought them to call Kaitlin in Paris. I used a little bit of one to call Gaetano a few times, so I bought the other. They would have been enough to call the U.S. How could I lose them?

I would find something. I had to reach him. I had gotten too far away from him, from his memory. I thought of what I would say when I heard his voice.

I'm coming home. If you will have me, I will leave when my semester is done. I will forget about traveling. It will be done soon. I will come back. I miss you. I believe you miss me, too. I am starting to lose sight of you. All the wrongs we can right. We can be together for as long as we want. We can exhaust ourselves on each other. We can stay together till we don't want each other anymore. You can decide. You can do anything. I'm tired of fighting this. I want to come back.

There was a man by the phones. He finished his call. Perhaps he could help me. I was desperate but polite.

"Scusa. Ho perso la mia carta. Per cortesia, lei ha una carta. Posso pagare," I begged in the formal Italian.

The man smiled at me. He wanted to show off his English. "I no 'ave dis, but you very beautiful. Why no we go dance?"

Madonna! I didn't want to be stopped. I shouldn't have asked him. *"No, grazie."*

I walked away. I could try to find a Tabac. But I knew that none were open. It was late. It was too late for me. I had the cards. I lost them. I had lost everything. Perhaps it was meant to be. Perhaps he was not alone. Perhaps he was with his Mono Girl, touching her body, touching her hair making her believe him, without saying a word of truth.

Doubt crept carefully into my mind. I could not say

the things I thought I could. The card had been lost for a reason. I didn't want to go home to Via Stalloreggi or to the states. I could not go to him. Never again.

There was no place for me. There was not an us. I couldn't go any further. That was the truth. I longed for Crazy. All the time I fought her, she was just trying to make everything okay for me. She was a friend who would protect me from the blackness I felt now. Crazy was my crutch. Anything was better than this, the truth was so painful and far from what I wanted. The truth I had to accept. It hurt my heart. Crazy would have taken that away, but for once she was nowhere to be found. I was on my own with this. At last feeling it all.

I thought of going to the Piazza Tolomei to see the statue of the wolf, *la lupa*. What I wouldn't give to switch places with that wolf. I could howl for her if she would turn me to stone.

I walked by the bench in front of the Academy of Music. It was a gray stone slab. I didn't sit on the bench. I crouched next to it and leaned my hands on it. There was no one *in giro*. The streets of Siena were empty.

Siena was mine. He was not.

It hurt so much.

I didn't believe I would wake up in the morning.

But if I did...I could not live like this anymore. It was over. I had to say enough was enough. *Basta*. It was done. It had to be.

And I cried for him, knowing I was going to abandon him and that special way I was when I was with him. How could he have not held on to that? How could I have not? There were no answers. It just was.

We didn't hold on to it. We let it go. It must never have been what I thought.

If we were to meet again, we could never be the same. It was my fault as much as his. I could never get that back again. It was lost. Always.

Basta was the word you used when you had enough. Someone pouring wine in your glass, filling it up more than you wanted, you said *basta. Basta così.* This is enough.

I shouldn't have been satisfied so soon by one boy. You weren't meant to be with the person you love at nineteen or twenty. But maybe I would never be satisfied again. *Non mi basta mai.*

But how I missed him. It was so strong. He always used to know what I was thinking. Could he now?

All the way across an ocean, American boy, can you feel how much I miss you?

I waited and there was nothing. No him. No us. Only me. Only black.

I walked back up the street to my apartment. I didn't bother to turn on the electric light in the stairwell. I heard the party still going on. There was no more guitar music. Maybe people were getting ready to hook up. I hoped I could push my way through and back to my room and my bed. I opened the door, taking my usual deep breath.

But there was Gaetano.

He was sitting at the table, talking to Andrea. It was calm. There was no reason to worry. He could handle himself among these people. When he looked up at me, I felt my face almost crumble. I sat beside him. He kissed me on both cheeks. He looked into my eyes, confused. They were certainly still red.

"*Che c'è?*" I shook my head. I said nothing. I didn't want him to hear my voice. He watched me for a second and picked up a bottle of wine. "*Vino?*"

I nodded and accepted the glass of wine. Andrea beckoned him back to their conversation, and Gaetano went but he kept turning to me, searching for clues. I wanted go to bed, but I couldn't move. I needed to feel kindness. Gaetano was not a part of this fake play. He was real. As if he could read my thoughts, he rubbed my leg gently under the table. He wasn't coming onto me for once; it was a connection. He might have rubbed the life back into me with those hands. They were hands that could hold the weight of my heart if only I would let them.

Eventually, Janine sat on Andrea's lap. She began to kiss his neck in front of us. I looked away to where Lorenzo still occasionally strummed his guitar. Some of the girls hummed along. Gaetano reached up to my neck.

"You seem so sad tonight, *tesoro*. What is it? What happened today since I saw you?" I shook my head. I still didn't want to talk. He pulled my head onto his shoulder. He kissed the top of my head like a brother. He cared for me so much. I thought I was alone in this world until I saw him.

I sighed against his shoulder. Then without thinking, I tipped my head up to him, closed my eyes. He kissed my lips, hesitantly. I let my lips stay against his. On my leg, his hand tightened. But I didn't want any of the others to see, so I pulled away.

I finished my glass of wine and poured myself another. All the while, he watched me. I looked around the room. My heart was still beating. I could breathe. His hand was still on my leg, less certain.

I didn't want to think about this, I didn't want to see the projection of where this night was going. I didn't want to wonder if it was a good idea. I had already thought too much.

"You are strange tonight," he said in my ear. I shrugged. "What is it?"

I shrugged again. When I turned to him, I felt the *vino* replacing some of the sadness. I felt heavy. I shook my head.

"Okay, *tesoro*, I am going to go."

I nodded. Maybe this was really best. I told him I would see him out. We walked through the hall, where Pam and some drunk Italian were lying on the floor, cuddling, starting to make out. They didn't stop when I opened the door. Gaetano stared at me.

"Do you want me to go?" I shrugged again. He looked past me to where Pam and the guy were now listening to us. He took my hand and pulled me out into the hallway, turning on the electric timer light.

"Come here, come talk to me here. Tell me what it is."

I stared at the floor. If I looked up at him, I might start crying again. He put his hands on my shoulders. He crouched down and tried to place his face under mine to look into my eyes. The moment I looked at him the lights in the hall went out.

Then I surprised both of us.

I felt the sob about to come, so I pulled him to me and kissed him. My mouth opened to his. He led me into the alcove in the hallway. He did not stop kissing. He was afraid that I would change my mind. His hands moved quickly and with a certain desperation onto my stomach. He found the button of my jeans and unzipped them. There was no second base in Italy.

His fingers found me. He took a chance and moved his mouth down my neck, holding his breath until he realized that he was not going to be stopped. I began to tremble against him.

"Gabriella? Gabriella?" Suzie's voice came out in the hall as a door opening. Gaetano and I froze where we were.

He moved his other hand to bang the wall behind me, pissed we had been interrupted. He cursed in dialect. "*Pesce della mamita.*"

"Gabriella?' Thankfully, she didn't turn the light on.

"Yeah."

"I'm going to go to bed, okay? Can I sleep in your room?"

"Is it just you?" I was confused. I thought that Suzie would wind up with someone.

"Yeah," Suzie said. And I wasn't sure if I heard regret or confusion. "Just me."

"Okay, I'll be in it a bit." To Gaetano I said, "It's okay."

I stopped kissing him. Other people came through the hall, newly formed couples leaving for the night. I hugged Gaetano to me in case they turned the light on. I wrapped both my arms around him, pulling him close. He whispered in my ear.

"Come home with me, Gabriella. Come back. You can brush your teeth, and in the morning we can get you a nice breakfast." I laughed hard into his shoulder. He believed he was saying the words an American would want to hear. *Dentifricio* and *prima colazione* became words of seduction. It was that simple for him. Problem solved with breakfast and toothpaste.

He couldn't understand why I was laughing so

hard. He moved away from me, shaking his head. He reached for the light muttering "*pazza.*" *Pazza* and *crazy* mean the same thing, but for me they were slightly different. I was *pazza,* but not Crazy. I zipped up my jeans, suddenly sober, suddenly modest and now feeling almost giddy.

"*Perché ridi?*" He questioned my laughter. But at that point I had forgotten why. I couldn't stop so I kept laughing. "*Madonna.*"

"*Mi dispiace,*" I apologized. I hugged him. "I have to go to sleep."

"*Sei veramente pazza.*" I *was* truly *pazza* but not Crazy. He wasn't mad at me. He was just confused. I stopped laughing but couldn't stop smiling at him. He was dear to me and I couldn't help but say the word he hated to hear. I said it better now than when I first arrived.

"*Grazie.*"

"*Pazza,*" he said again, shaking his head. We kissed on both cheeks. And then he was on his way, leaving me to creep back through my apartment. Pam and her boy were under a blanket in the hall. Janine and Andrea were in her room. Another couple was on the chair where Gaetano slept.

In my room the lights were off. Suzie was on the floor. I whispered again, although I knew that Suzie wasn't sleeping. "You could have taken the bed, Suze."

"I'm okay," Suzie said.

I hesitated before asking, "Are you sure?"

"Yeah. Are you okay?" she asked. I waited again, thinking about the ups and downs of the night.

"Yeah."

21.

In the morning, I woke up. I slept hard and well. I crept through Lisa's room. Pam was now in Lisa's room with her Italian. The dining room was smoky, littered with bottles and cigarette butts put out in glasses. Lisa was on the floor wrapped in her winter coat.

"Hey," I said jostling her awake. "Go sleep in my bed. I'm up."

I opened the window in the dining room. I made myself coffee, a good strong espresso on the stove, not the instant stuff.

I stared out the window, over the red and brown rooftops. This view never disappointed me. I would be leaving soon but not yet. This country I loved. This city.

Suzie came out into the dining room. Her eyes were red. I poured her a glass of water and the rest of the espresso. We stood together, looking out the window.

"I feel like I'm never going to get over this," Suzie said. "I feel like I don't even know myself anymore."

I didn't know what to say. Some day it would get better but when?

"This doesn't even make me happy," Suzie said, pointing out toward the countryside. "I want to go home. I want to see things that are familiar, you know?"

I nodded.

"Part of me thought I should travel with you all this summer, but I don't think I can. I'm going to go home next week. I'm going to leave, and I hope that makes me feel better. I feel like such a fool. I don't understand why."

I didn't know what to say. I put my arm around Suzie and I kissed her cheek.

We dressed and walked to the bus station. Suzie bought a pack of cigarettes and we smoked one before the bus.

"Ciao," Suzie said before she got on the bus. We hugged goodbye.

"*Ciao, bella, ciao presto. Ciao,*" I shouted, waving, as she walked down the aisle to her seat. I watched her through the window and kept waving.

I wouldn't see Suzie again and neither would Olivia. Suzie would go home and return to her college and be the beautiful popular co-ed she was before. She could smile fondly when she was asked about Italy, but she would never return. She would forget and for her it was better that way.

When I returned to the apartment, no one was there except Lisa. She looked up at me with the report. "Everybody's gone out."

"Good," I said.

I made tea for both of us. We sat together at the table, not saying much. I worked on research for my papers. Then, when the outside light started to fade, I called Gaetano from the gaming alcove. I only needed change for that call. He was there when his dorm mate called down the hall for him. I heard his footsteps coming down the floor.

"*Ciao, bella,*" he said, exhaling smoke. "What are you doing?"

"I was studying. Do you want to go out tonight? Do you want to get dinner?"

"Of course, I will be there in an hour."

As I waited for him, I tried to piece together the night in my journal at the dining room table. I wondered if it would be strange to see him. Just when things had gotten so normal between us, I had to go and fuck it up. *Che pazzia.*

Then he was at my door. I opened it and smiled. We kissed two kisses on the cheek. I was anxious to move through the hallway, the scene of the crime.

We went to a *trattoria* that I had passed many times on the way to Lucy's. There was a large family there celebrating something.

"It's the family of the proprietor," Gaetano said.

"Well, can we sit?"

"*Prego,*" said the proprietor, putting his napkin on the table. Another woman in the family brought us bread. Gaetano ordered the wine. I got my default–the pasta with truffle sauce. It came wrapped in foil. I opened it up and inhaled. I smiled over at the proprietor's family.

"Your favorite," Gaetano said, gesturing with the

fork in his left hand down to my dish.

"I think so. Well, one of them."

Our conversation was easy. We avoided talking about the night before. I didn't feel uncomfortable, but I kept wondering if I should bring it up. I wasn't sure if now, we were supposed to get together. The events of the night before had been so strange.

Gaetano invited me, Michelle and Duccio to see his game on Sunday. "You must see me play with the right shoes."

"Okay, if Duccio will drive."

"He will drive if it is what Michelle wants."

"You're right."

"Just as I'll do whatever it is you want." I nodded, studying him to decide what to say. He changed the subject. "There is a bar near where I have my game. We can go there after."

"You think all I do is drink."

"Well, you do. I don't know how you can stand to just have espresso. Should we order some Vin Santo so you can avoid the tremors?" I laughed.

"No, let's go get some gelato."

"Ah," he said, "the other American addiction."

When I left the restaurant, I waved to the family at the table and said *grazie* and *ciao*. Gaetano was laughing when we came out onto the street.

"Why are you laughing?"

"Is he your uncle? Is he a friend of your family?"

"What? No? What do you mean?"

And Gaetano rubbed my face in the way he did when he thoroughly enjoyed watching me do something foolish.

"I shouldn't have said that?" I had no idea what I did wrong.

"No, it was too familiar."

"*Ciao*? Oh, God, I'm so stupid."

"You aren't. It was just funny. You're so funny. *Allora, tesoro*." He held out his arm to me. "Come, let us get you your gelato."

"Before I get the shakes." And we walked *in giro* around the streets of Siena with out *gelati*. We walked through the *campo* and said hi to Dino and Paolo who were smoking at the fountain. It was so easy

I was waiting to have to explain my actions to Gaetano, but he never asked for anything. We were just hanging out, as usual, having fun.

We grabbed a beer with Dino and Paolo. Then Gaetano needed to get back because of his game in the morning. Even our goodbye wasn't awkward. He took me to my door and kissed me on the cheek. His voice was soft in my ear, "*Buona notte, tesoro*."

In my bed, I could smell his cologne on me. I liked that he didn't try to kiss me. He had changed. He changed me. If I let myself have fun, maybe I really could.

"G, get up. Gabriella." It was Michelle standing above me in some outfit, tapping me lightly with what looked like a whip. She was laughing. Duccio was standing in the doorway of my room, smiling nervously. He wouldn't come in. For him, it would be impolite.

"What are you doing?"

"I'm waking you up to go *fare al cavallo*. And Duccio's freaking out because he had to walk through Lisa's stinky room. *Che schiffo*."

I sat up in bed and rubbed my eyes. I smiled at Duccio. His expression was so sweet. He shook his head.

"*Che pazzia*. I go on table out."

"*Si, vai a* table." Michelle said in their funny mixed up language.

"What should I wear?" I asked. Maybe I hadn't thought riding a horse through.

"Something, you can squat in." Michelle jumped up onto my bed, straddling me and hitting me with the crop. "Giddyup, G-dog. *Vai. Dai. Dai. Andiamo.*"

I covered my face with my hands. My laughter and Michelle's jumping were shaking the tiny bed. I thought we might crash through it onto the floor. Duccio called Michelle from the dining room. "Yes, go to him. Get out, you *pazza americana*. Save these moves for him."

"Oh, I do, I do." Michelle said, wiggling her hips provocatively. "I give it to my *uomo ogni notte*."

"Michelle, *vieni*." We heard from the dining room.

"You better go before Lisa gets up."

"You better hurry and get ready before Duccio does."

One of my most favorite places in Italy was driving in an Italian's car. I loved the feeling of being taking somewhere, the idea that my fate lay in the hands of a friend in the know. That day I wished that we would never get there, that I could always be anticipating what was to come.

Duccio smoked and sang along with the radio. "*È bella, no?*" he asked about every song. Michelle rested her hand on his thigh, her other hand was out the window, making waves in the wind.

We drove out into the countryside to where Allesandro, Duccio's friend, was waiting for us.

"Could he be any hotter?" Michelle said. "You should hook it up, jump on *that* horse, G-dog."

I shook my head. I couldn't think about any more Italian men.

Everyone had ridden horses before except me. There was a giant white monster of a horse waiting for me to mount him.

"No way," I said. I look at Duccio and Allesandro. "*Non posso. Mi dispiace.*"

"He good," Allesandro said, trying to calm me with broken English. "He no jump."

"He is too big," I said in Italian. "And I don't want to die today."

Allesandro cocked his head at me. Then he bent to offer me his hand to put my foot on. I didn't want to go, but Michelle and Duccio were encouraging me with shouts of *dai*. This was my fate. I put my foot on his hand and got on top of the horse in the most ungraceful way possible.

"*Brava,*" shouted Duccio, stubbing out his cigarette and hopping on the horse, like it was his *vespa*.

When everyone was saddled up, Allesandro and Duccio galloped into the trees, racing each other. I looked at Michelle, horrified.

"We'll just go for like a trail ride, G. It'll be okay. Just give him a little kick."

"A little kick? Why? So when he throws me off, he can give me a little kick?"

"C'mon, just a little one," Michelle gave her horse a kick, and she was beside me immediately. "Hold the reins like this. C'mon. We'll just walk."

She moved her horse in front of me on my white monster. Michelle whistled at the white monster and I touched it a little with my foot. Surprisingly, it began to move. I was holding my breath. My hands were tight on the reigns.

"Relax, relax, you're doing great," Michelle kept saying. She was glancing back at me and smiling encouragingly. Finally, I started to relax a little. I kept my back as straight as I could; I relaxed my grip on the reigns and followed Michelle. Michelle kept chatting away. She was trying to calm me down, and I appreciated the effort.

"So when are you guys going on your trip?"

"In a few weeks. After the picking of the *contrade* for the Palio." We were sticking around until the neighborhoods that would run in the race were decided.

"That's soon."

"Tell me about it. Did you book your flight home yet," I asked.

"Um, no."

"Are you gonna?'

"I'm staying the summer. I'm renting an apartment in Lucy's building. I'm not ready to go yet."

"Wow!" I said. I was really envious.

"I know, pretty crazy, huh? I just think it's something I want to do."

"It's something we all want to do."

"Well, why don't you stay, too?" she asked.

"I barely have enough money for how long I'm staying."

"Do you guys want to stay with me for the Palio?"

"Michelle, that would be fucking awesome," I said, smiling. Staying with Michelle was the perfect plan. I couldn't wait to tell Olivia. That would mean I might have more money for traveling later.

"That would be cool."

"I know. I hook you up. C'mon let's trot." She gave her horse a kick, and then she and her horse were off. My white beast took off, too. We went through the green trees along the dirt path. I let out a surprised scream. I was scared but somehow laughing. I was high off the ground on an animal, a so-called domesticated animal, but an animal nonetheless. Suddenly, the horse stopped trotting. I didn't want to kick it again; I wanted to let it be. It walked along the path. I was glad Michelle has gotten far ahead of me. I realized I was smiling, slightly terrified with my body tensed, but smiling. I felt silly bouncing up and down on this horse with a stupid grin on my face.

There were birds chirping and the air smelled clean. It was spring in the air and summer on the way. I had my whole life ahead of me. More specifically, I had a European tour and all the unknowns that would happen on the trip. But now I knew no matter what, I could return to the city for the Palio.

I didn't feel lonely anymore. I felt completely opposite from the way I did before. Not alone but surrounded by the possibility of the world.

"Gabriella," Michelle called from somewhere beyond. "*Vieni.*"

"*Arrivo!*" I gave the horse a gentle nudge with my feet, and he complied, taking me off to meet my friends, to where they were waiting for me in a place I could not yet see.

Gaetano's game just finished when we arrived at the stadium. His team won. He and Duccio kissed each other hello. Gaetano spoke in rapid Italian about his game strategy. He was breathing deeply. He looked at me and winked.

"*Mi segui?*" he asked, wondering if I could follow his speedy descriptions, and I nodded, smiling. "*Brava.*"

Gaetano had to shower, and Duccio went back to the locker room with him, to talk to some of the other guys on the team. Michelle and I plopped down on the grass and waited for them.

"You're going to have a great summer," I said. My palms and elbows were on the ground, head back in the breeze, face turned to the sun. "You can feel it already."

"I know. I can't wait to move into the new place. I'm going to do it sooner rather than later. As soon as I get my papers and speech done." She was lying on her side, with her cheek in her hand.

"Have you told Janine yet?"

"No."

"You gonna?" I pulled my neck up to look at her while she answered.

"Guess I have to."

"I thought you guys were best friends," I said after a time.

"It's funny, I thought I knew her pretty well, but I didn't. I mean, maybe she thought she knew me, but I changed, you know."

"I think we all have," I said.

"I got caught up in her excitement about this trip. And I'll never regret that. If I wasn't here I wouldn't know Duccio. I wouldn't know you or Gaetano. You know I wouldn't be able to speak a whole other language. But I feel like she is so different from who I thought she was."

"Yeah, she's lost her glow or something. I think I'd have liked her better if I didn't have to live with her. If I didn't have to see all the cracks."

"There are a lot of cracks." She laughed and waited a minute before adding, "We all got these microscopic views of each other."

"Yeah, and some of us have been improved by it and some of us haven't." I took a breath. There was something I wanted to know. It was now or never. "Were you the food thief?"

Michelle shook her head and held up her hand, like a witness on the stand. "I swear I only binged on my own foods."

I laughed a bit uncomfortably. I wasn't going to ask her about it, but if she wanted to tell me I would listen. She laid her arm flat on the grass and put her face on it. "It's okay. I know it's a problem. I thought I had it under control. I'm trying. I'm trying to find a different way."

"Aren't we all?" I asked

"What's your different way, G-dog?"

"I don't know," I laughed. "I guess there are a lot of ways to torment yourself."

Michelle laughed. "Sometimes I think you think too much. There's something you don't say that keeps you down."

"I think you're right. I should be more sensuous." I slid the word *sensuous* around my mouth in an Italian accent that made Michelle hoot with laughter. Maybe I had deflected talking about my shit and her shit once again, but it felt good to not be so heavy for once.

Later, we met a bunch of Gaetano's teammates at a bar nearby. We all sat at a big table outside. Gaetano's teammates teased that they wanted to sit between Michelle and me, but I wound up between Michelle and Gaetano. Gaetano ordered a *birroza*, a giant beer. I never heard that word before, but I liked it. I was still learning, only just getting the hang of it.

At the table, I got lost in the conversations and realized I hadn't been paying attention to Gaetano. He was talking to his friend across the table. I overheard the friend's question.

"Is that your girl?"

"Yeah." He glanced at me. I met his eyes, and he didn't look away.

"What did he say?" I asked when the friend wasn't paying attention. He shrugged, and we smiled at each other.

I was still wasn't sure about anything, but that day it didn't feel like I had to be.

22.

Michelle and I pulled another all-nighter to work on our papers. These were the papers that were about the subjects we were supposed to be taking classes for. Luckily, one of the classes was Italian culture and that was a broad topic. We had no real guidelines for these papers. I thought that Arturo was just testing us to see what we could come up with.

We were both using English books about Italy and paraphrasing shamelessly. Michelle was doing her paper on the Palio and was doing elaborate drawings of all of the neighborhood flags. Duccio was trying to convince her to make the flag of his *contrado*, the biggest. She did take extra care over that one.

"So are you and Gaetano hitting it yet?" Michelle asked out of the blue on the way back from the bakery at 4 A.M.

"You're getting punchy, missy."

"It just seems like you guys are a little bit different lately."

"Remember, I'm trying not to think so much. Honestly, I don't know. We kind of kissed last week at the party." I hadn't admitted that to anyone.

"Oh, really." Michelle said, cocking her eyebrow.

"Yeah, it's weird. Well actually it *was* weird and now it hasn't been weird. I thought he would be, like, all over me. I thought I totally fucked up the friendship I was working toward, but you know, he hasn't tried anything. He's been the same. It's like he's giving me time to figure it out."

"He's awesome. He's so in love with you."

"I know. I mean, I feel like he really cares for me. He gives me space, though. It's so nice."

"Nice, Gabriella. Because he's pretty effing hot."

"Yeah, I don't know where it's going. I'm just going to let it go."

"Nice, Gabriella," Michelle said and held out the bag for me to rip off another piece of bread.

The next night, Gaetano came over after a soccer game. This time I was working on my speech, so I didn't really look at him when I let him in. I was planning to read it to him one more time. He stopped in the middle of the dining room.

"Gabi," he said. I finally looked at him. His lip was completely swollen.

"Oh, shit," I said in English. "What happened?"

He told me a long and detailed story of the other team's unsportsmanlike conduct and how it warranted several members of his team getting rough on the field. He got an elbow to the lip in all the confusion.

"I can't believe this," I said. I sat him on the arm of the chair in the dining room, the chair he slept in. Of course we didn't have an icemaker because it seemed that no one in Italy used ice, but I found a bottle of white wine in the fridge, which I held against his face. "You are crazy."

"Do you know what the worst part is?" he asked.

"What?"

"When I saw that it was bleeding I thought, If Gabriella decides to kiss me again, I won't be able to."

I pulled the bottle of wine away from his face and looked at him. "If?"

"It's whatever you want, *bella*, however you want. I'm not asking for anything. But you know that I love you."

I walked over to the dining room door and locked it. I started to kiss him, being careful not to press too hard against his mouth. His hands move around on me, finding the places I wanted him to find. Second base at last. He wasn't as persistent as the last time. I had the feeling that I was in control. He began to speak as I unbuttoned his shirt, teaching me again. This time I learned words I didn't know.

"*Si, si,*" he said. "*Spolgia mi.*"

And we were on the floor, on his black jacket. My legs were bare against the silken inside of it, the smell of leather mixing with his strong cologne. He used his hands where he couldn't use his mouth.

But before things really progressed, we heard something. It was Michelle trying to get in. We saw her through the frosty glass of the dining room door.

"Hey," she said, surprised, not getting it at first, but then when she heard my voice, she said, "Oh."

"It's okay," I said, arranging my clothes and checking to see that Gaetano was okay before I opened the door. "We shouldn't be doing this here, anyway."

"I'm sorry, G, I just wanted water."

"Get it. I'm done slutting it up. I should go somewhere else."

"Look at him," Michelle said, gesturing to Gaetano. "He's ready to kill me. *Mi dispiace,* Gaetano. Shit, what happened to his face? Forget it. Tell me later. I'll get out of your way."

"It's okay," he said. "It's your house."

Michelle quickly got a glass of water, muttering sorrys and *mi dispiaces* as she left. I walked back over to him and scratched the back of his hair. He closed his eyes, enjoying it.

"I'm sorry that happened," I said. "We could go to my room."

"So then when Lisa hears us, she can decide she wants to look out your window."

"She probably would."

"Come back with me."

"To the monastery?"

"Yes, we'll sneak you in. All of them on the bottom floor will be asleep."

"You mean the monks? All of the monks will be asleep?"

"Yes, *faccia di cazzo.* It will be fine. We will be quiet." He whispered in my ear. "At least when we are on the first floor and later..."

I smiled up at him, "Later I'll brush my teeth and have a great breakfast."

He stopped the *vespa* just outside the gate. I had only been on the grounds that one time during the day, so I held his hand tight. We walked the bike over to the rack.

"Are you nervous?" he asked, seeming a bit nervous himself.

"Yes, are you?"

"A little."

"Have you done this before?"

"Never." He moved his face close to mine so I could see him in the moonlight. "Really, never. I never wanted to risk this before."

"What will happen if we are caught?" I whispered.

"*Tutto* finish," he said, mixing our two languages so I took him seriously. I took a deep breath.

A long hall, a long dark hall. It does feel like a monster. There are doors on all sides. He will not turn the light on. Before he opened the giant wood *portone*, he knelt before me and slipped off my shoes. I balanced on one foot, bending to hold his shoulders for support. He squeezed my leg.

I follow his instructions. I run quickly down the long hall. There are a few windows, where the full moon shines in so I can see the doors on all sides. It is a straight hall, but without the moon I couldn't find my way. He is still at the other end, watching me run through the moonlight. Waiting to make sure.

My heart is beating fast as I make it to the first step. When he sees that I make it, he turns the light on. I am at the landing when the light comes on–before me, an illuminated giant statue of a saint. I am not expecting it, I squeal

Then I get scared that one of the sleeping monks will hear me and *tutto* will be finished. I run quickly down his floor to the end of the hall as he'd told me. I've heard him running down this hall to get my phone calls many times, but he never ran as fast as I am running.

His room is the last one on the left. I open his door

and go in, relieved. Safe at last, at least until a few hours from now, when I have to do this again. I hear him coming, laughing all the way down the corridor. I am ready when he opens the door.

I watch his face change as I turn to him. This is his gift. It is mine. Soon I will be going away.

I undress him, moving around his body as if it were my own. He lets me. We stand looking at each other and then laugh at the strangeness of finally seeing each other like this. I like what the sight of my body is doing to his. My body changed since I've been here. The hills of Siena have made my legs stronger. The fresh food has done my body good.

"You are beautiful," he says. I step closer to him. I reach across to touch him. Without clothes, he seems different, less himself. I take his hand and bring him to the bed.

What we do is new for us, and yet it feels familiar. He looks at me for a while and rubs his hands against me. I began to touch him, too. We kiss. I am careful of his lip. Hands on skin explore. He speaks to me, saying things that would embarrass me in my own language. They come to my mind in a musical string.

"*Mi fai morire. Quanto sei bella. Si. Si. Voglio fare amore con te. Mi piace quando mi tocci. Quanto mi piaci. Bella. Bella. Sei bella, tu sai. Mi fai morire.*"

We take turns, looking up at each other to see what makes the other's eyes close. We grow more confident. The room fills with us.

"*Gira ti,*" he says, turning me over on the bed, running his face down the length of my back. I cannot see him. I can only hear, feel and smell. The word for all of those is sometimes the same in Italian, *sentire*, to feel, and now I understand why. All of the senses are a part of what we do. My body rises up to meet his.

Turning me again, he buries his face into me. I am no longer the girl on the plane. I am a woman now. Our bodies move together. I hear the sounds we make and worry briefly about the monks sleeping below, but it floats out of my mind when everything else does.

And then I can't think anymore.

23.

My final weeks in Siena were a blur. I kept catching myself trying to mark time, trying to hold it up, but it all happened so quickly.

Gaetano and I alternated between sneaking into the monastery and staying in my tiny bed. He distracted me from my final papers, because he could, because he knew that he would spend a solid hour helping me work on them, so that I would do okay.

I gave my speech on the Medici. Signora Laza complimented my pronunciation and research.

Duccio and Michelle were thrilled about Gaetano and me. Duccio drove us to the restaurant where we went the first night together as a foursome. He gave a toast about how happy he was to have met these *ragazze americane*, he said. It wasn't like him to be emotional, but that night, holding on tight to Michelle, he was.

The next morning Michelle knocked on my door. I got up quietly to not disturb Gaetano. We crept through

Lisa's room and into the dining room, where I gathered Michelle was on her second cup of instant coffee. She was pale and antsy. I got nervous.

"Are you okay?"

"Duccio's mom finally wants to meet me."

"Cool," I said. "Right? Cool?"

"I guess. They have a country house, which I don't understand because we've driven to the grounds and it's only, like, 20 minutes away from here, but his parents spend the summer there. They want me to come for *cena* tonight. They're 'opening up' the house or something. His aunt is going to be there and his sisters and brothers. And their spouses. And his aunt's kids. The whole fucking family."

"Michelle, that sounds awesome. Right? What's wrong?"

"I don't know. I'm just nervous. I think she's been suspicious of me this whole time and now I'm suspicious."

"Maybe she is just accepting you're Duccio's *ragazza* and she wants to know you."

"Can you and Gaetano come?"

"I guess," I said. "Sure. If it makes you feel better. Now let's make some real coffee. We've got a big day, and those boys are never going to go for this instant stuff."

In a car again. And though I did love it, the one thing I didn't love was the way the Italians took the curves. I was safely buckled in and clutching Gaetano's hand, but Duccio was a speed demon.

"*Duccio, piano, piano, per favore,*" Michelle implored every few minutes. It didn't help. The men were laughing at us and calling us *americane*.

"*Si, siamo americane*," Michelle said, finally. "Now slow the fuck down."

"*Cosa?*" Duccio asked to our laughter. "*Cosa hai detto?*"

"Fuck sumding fuck," Gaetano said in English, unsure.

"Fuck something fuck," Michelle and I said in unison and then cracked up, turning the tables. Michelle had been so on edge the whole morning. It was good to hear her laugh.

And then we were there.

"*Allora, americane*," Duccio said pulling up the driveway to the large brown home. "*Ci siamo. Pronte?*"

Gaetano whistled his approval. He had never been here either.

"It's so big and *bella*," Michelle said.

"It's like the brochure," I said, getting out of the car.

"*Cosa ha detto?*" Duccio asked Gaetano. And then to us, "*Vi piace?*"

"Yes," I said. "I like it."

Duccio nodded, smiling. I realized he was nervous too.

There was something new and sweet in the air.

"What's that?" I asked Gaetano. "The smell."

"Aghh, lavender. See it starting to come up."

Duccio's mother came out, clasping her hands to the sides of her face. She looked like so many of the Sienese women we saw around. Her pumpkin-colored silk blouse tucked into a well-cut skirt and good pumps. She shone with bright chunky gold jewelry. The women around the town were always so cold to us, but Duccio's mother, Bruna, exuded warmth. She welcomed us all to her home with kisses on the cheeks.

Bruna ushered us through the house, which was beautiful and simple out through the back doors onto their patio. Under a pergola, a table was set, but for the time, Duccio's family was milling about with glasses of prosecco. He had an older and younger brother, Nicola and Andrea, and one sister named Lucia. His father was Piero and there was an aunt named Gianna. Gianna was dressed almost identically to Bruna, but her smart silk blouse was a shade of silver.

I was trying to keeping track of all the names for Olivia, who still loved noting Italian names. I couldn't quite catch the names of all the cousins or the spouses of Duccio's older siblings. I completely lost the names of the gaggle of children except for little fat Pino, who kept getting reprimanded and Alessia, a smart four-year-old who questioned why Michelle and I spoke funny.

As usual, the Italians tripped over Michelle's name, repeating it wrongly and asking her to spell it before finally deciding to call her Michele like the Italian boy name. I noticed only Duccio's mom made the attempt each time to pronounce it properly. I considered this her blessing.

My name got a typical reply, too. "*Aghh, Gabriella, italiano, semplice.*"

There was something roasting in an outdoor oven and that wood burn scent that I once associated with the cold winter streets of Siena was now mixed with this new perfect lavender scent to create something unique and ecstatic in my brain.

We sat for dinner, or early lunch, or midday meal, under the pergola looking out over the countryside. Lately, the shops around Siena had begun putting posters outside their stores for the tourists to buy. It was this kind of scene that they were selling. This was the picture of Tuscany everyone wanted to experience.

I didn't know if this was a typical weekend meal for Duccio's family, but the food kept coming. Starting with crostini and a plate of cheese and wild boar sausage. Then Bruna passed a cut pasta served with lemon and peas.

"*Fatta in casa*," Gaetano said to me in case I couldn't tell it was homemade. He complimented the hostess, and Michelle and I followed suit, nodding and agreeing that we loved all the pasta in Italy, but this was the best we had.

We took our time between courses. The wine flowed. Everyone was talking in little groups, and I realized that I couldn't just turn the noise of Italian out anymore like I once had. I heard it and I understood. Still, I wished Gaetano and I had our own dialect that we could speak. I wanted to tell him how awesome it was to be around women. Real Italian women. Save for the women who worked in stores and café and the ones who carried trays high above the crowd at Barone Rosso, I didn't get to interact with them. Now I was here at a table with them, talking about things like school and travel and family.

The *secondo* was *cinghiale,* and it was served with tiny potatoes, mushrooms and herbs in a light sauce. I could taste the fire in it. I looked across to Michelle and smiled. She was eating the meat even though she was a vegetarian. I raised my eyebrows. She shrugged.

It was Bruna and Gianna's show. They refused help clearing the table, returning with a light *rucula* salad with pepper, lemon and oil. And then there was the requisite break for cigarette smoking. At once, everyone pulled out their respective packs. I grinned across the table at Michelle.

"*Perché ridi?*" Gaetano asked.

"I'm not laughing, but it is funny," I said, quietly again wishing I spoke his dialect. "You almost think the kids are going to pull out cigarettes. Everyone is smoking."

"*Sì.*" He nodded, noticing. "But these are good vices."

I took one of his cigarettes and shook my head.

Then dessert: Bruna had made a *torta della nonna*. And there were little cookies and chocolates for the children that the adults ate, too. The cake was delicious. It was ubiquitous in Tuscany and always slightly different, but here under the pergola with the sun just a red puddle over the countryside, no other cake really stood a chance.

I found myself in a conversation about bare feet with some of Duccio's female relatives. As usual, they were fascinated by the way we walked around our houses with no shoes.

"It's just more comfortable," I said. And the women nodded, slightly disturbed. I had this feeling that they were curious about all the *americane* that came through their country, but just didn't ever have the opportunity to talk to them. Somehow the fact that we were there as someone's *ragazza* made us easier to communicate with.

There was more cheese and meat and wine. And then just as everyone's conversations were becoming more elastic *espresso* was served. But shortly after that when it was really dark, the grappa came out.

"Oh, demon liquid," I said in English.

"*Ti piace,*" asked Duccio's sister, Lucia.

"You know I like to drink," I said, finding myself happy to be kidding around with this Sienese woman.

"But this stuff, it burns."

"This one is a good one," Gaetano said.

"Try it," Bruna said across the table. "It will help you digest."

I looked across at Michelle, who shrugged again.

"I ate the meat," she said in fast English through gritted teeth. It was like we had our own dialect.

The whole table was watching me. I could already smell it. I held the glass up in a mock toast to the crowd. There were laughs and a couple of *dai*'s. I giggled before I could get the glass to my lips. I hated being on display. I took a sip. I swallowed. It did burn, but it wasn't as bad as when we did shots of it. It was meant to be sipped. The truth was when you didn't gulp it down it helped your stomach settle everything out.

"*Brava*," said Bruna and a few of Duccio's male relatives clapped. Gaetano put his arm around the back of my chair. I stood and did a little unsteady bow. And thankfully the table went back to the conversations and cigarettes they were already involved in.

And then the dinner was over. All of Duccio's relatives started to leave, kissing us goodbye and leaving us to sit with Duccio's parents and younger teenaged brother under the pergola, finishing one last bottle of wine.

"Did you girls eat enough?" Bruna asked us. "*Basta*?"

"Yes, it was delicious," Michelle said in perfectly accented Italian.

"It was," I agreed. "I feel full and perfect."

Bruna smiled broadly and did one of those funny Italian hand motions, pressing her pointer finger and thumb together in a circle, to indicate that all was right with the world. And it certainly seemed to me like it was.

Gaetano was smiling at me.

"*Che c'e?*" I asked.

"Full and perfect, eh. You are perfect," he said. "*Sei favolosa.*"

"*Favolosa?*" That was a new one for me. I searched for the translation. "Fabulous? Fantastic?"

He shrugged. "*Piu o meno.*"

"*Sei favolosa,*" he said again later when we were in Duccio's family room watching the dubbed version of *Pulp Fiction.*

He mouthed it to me when Duccio's parents were saying good night to us and having a conversation with Duccio that seemed like a formality about where we would all sleep.

"*Sei favolosa,*" he whispered into my skin later when we were alone in the room where Michelle and I were assigned to sleep. Again and again as if the words could penetrate my body and he could make me believe it.

Later, mouth dry, I crept out through the darkened house to the kitchen for some water. I was only in Gaetano's T-shirt, hoping I didn't run into Duccio's mom. I was more concerned that she would see my bare feet than realize I had been up to no good.

I was startled to find Michelle alone at the kitchen island, standing in her tank top and nylon *americana* running pants staring at the fridge.

"Hi," I said. She gave a little gasp, surprised. "Sorry. I was just getting some water."

She nodded and didn't say anything. I began to worry.

"Were you going for a midnight jog?"

"No." Her voice was quiet. I noticed her hands were clasped together.

I went to the sink to get my water. My heart began to beat faster. I turned on the faucet. I weighed my options about what to say. I could do nothing. I could let this water cup fill up and return to bed.

The water began to overflow onto my fingers. I let it for a minute. Then I shut off the water, turned around and took a deep breath.

"Can I–" I paused not sure where to go next. Lately, I noticed this thing happening where my sentences seemed to be running off a cliff. I couldn't always think of the right word in English if it was one I hadn't used in a while. But this wasn't that. This was fear. But I was in it now.

"Can I help?" I asked.

Michelle didn't turn to me.

"I don't think they liked me," her voice was quiet and faraway.

"Of course they did," I said. I stepped around so I was next to her. "They all did."

"Did you see the way his aunt looked at me?" Gianna had been more reserved than Bruna.

"You know she was eyeing Gaetano, too," I said. "I heard her tell Duccio's sister that she never travels south of Rome. It was a total dig. She's just a snotty northerner who hates southern Italians. She probably hates anyone who isn't in her *contrada*."

I was hoping we could identify a common enemy and go to bed.

"Do you think his mom liked me?"

"Yes," I said, emphatically. "I do. She called you *joia*. Did you hear that? You bring her joy? I didn't get that."

Michelle smiled at me weakly. "That's because you have a simple Italian name. Gabriella."

I smiled at her exaggeration of the syllables in my name.

"But, Michelle, *joia*, I think she really liked you. Like a lot."

Michelle nodded and bit her lip, hands still clasped. I took a sip of water and followed her gaze to the fridge. She sighed.

"*Che c'è*," I asked

"I can't stop thinking about that cake." The leftover *torta della nonna* was in the fridge.

"It was good cake."

"I thought I had this under control," she said. Her eyes filled up.

"You do. You will." I tried to sound more confident than I felt.

She shook her head. I had to figure something out.

"What if we just, I don't know, what if we each just took just one bite? Just one. Then stop. *Basta*. We could really savor it. And then we both go to bed."

She didn't answer for a long time. It felt as if we were both holding our breath.

Then she nodded. I sighed this time with relief. I opened a few drawers in the kitchen before I found two spoons. I got the cake and unwrapped it on the counter beside the refrigerator and not in front of Michelle on the kitchen island. I spooned us each two generous bites. I wrapped the cake back up and put it away.

I fed Michelle first and then myself. She wasn't going to unclasp her hands. Maybe that was for the best. The cake was still good, colder now, but you could taste the vanilla bean in it, the light lemon zest, the cream like mother's milk. In truth, I could have stood there and eaten the whole rest of the cake, but I didn't need to. This was enough.

"Okay?" I asked. "*Basta?*"

She nodded.

I unclasped her hands and held one.

"Water?" I held up my cup. She took it with her other shaky hand and drank. I tugged her back toward the bedrooms. Earlier the boys had snuck into the room we were supposed to share and put the situation right. She laughed as Duccio pulled her to his room, leaving Gaetano with me. I thought everything was okay, but it wasn't. I hoped it was now, but I didn't know.

"Are you okay?" I asked when we got to the corridor where we needed to go our separate ways. She squeezed my hand and then she hugged me for a long while. I thought she was going to thank me, but she didn't and I was glad. Friends don't need to thank each other.

She was smiling when she pulled back. "We smell like *uomini*."

"We do," I said. "*Buona notte.*"

"*Buona notte*," she said. I watched her walk to her room.

I crawled back beside a sleeping Gaetano and lay on my side. I couldn't fall right to sleep. Tonight was already a memory, a happy one at that. Even finding Michelle in the kitchen hadn't made it bad. I had other happy memories, but those had been tinged. I wondered if there would ever be a time when I could return to a happy memory and enjoy it for what it was. I couldn't imagine there would ever be a time when I could look back and take just one bite without going out of control. I wondered if I would ever forgive and move on. I wondered if I could ever truly let go.

But I wasn't going to try just then. I wanted to be there in that moment. Someone sleeping beside me, someone in the world, believed I was *favolosa*. I wasn't exactly sure of the translation, but I liked the sound of it. I wanted to try and let myself believe it, too.

24.

Olivia was done with school. She waited outside my door in her tank top, her arms turned brown from days studying in the park, trying to avoid her depressing apartment with Suzie. She raised an eyebrow when she saw Gaetano holding my hand.

Gaetano kissed Olivia hello and said that he would see us for dinner. He left me to explain the new developments between us. Olivia was full of *I told you so's* and *lo sapevo's*. And I laughed at every one and let her have her moment.

We ate toasted eggplant panini outside a café near Santa Caterina's church. We faced a view of the zebra-striped Duomo, the salmon Torre, the whole beautiful orange-and-pink skyline. We were holding on to this in our minds. We will never forget this, we vowed, and we never have.

Now that her was semester done and Suzie was back at home, Olivia was going to the Tuscan island Elba for a few days with people from her program.

Then, she would come back for the choosing of the *contrade* and we would start our big trip. I considered going with her, but I still had too much to do. *I'll have plenty of time to travel*, I told myself, and Olivia was coming back in a few days. Besides, it was too soon to leave Gaetano.

The day that all of our papers were due Janine insisted that we have a final dinner together as roommates. She dressed up for the occasion as usual, wearing a cute pink sundress that she bought at the *mercato*. She blew out her hair and put on a lot of make-up. She looked like herself or like the image she wanted to leave us with. She turned herself on that night, and she was kind to everyone, even to Lisa. She was all about image, only an image

I didn't want to be a part of any of it anymore. I served my time, and I didn't want to know Janine or Lisa anymore. I wanted to move away from them, to have my time with Gaetano and not have to do this. I didn't like who I was with them. I no longer wanted to be that way. But Michelle was being a good sport about it, so I stuck it out. It is only one night, I told myself.

After dinner, Janine brought out a good bottle of Vin Santo and *cantucci*. Michelle caught me rolling my eyes and shot me a disapproving look. I nodded, resigned to the fact that I had to stay. I wouldn't have to suffer much more of this. Michelle was moving out tomorrow. Olivia and Kaitlin were coming the day after for the choosing of the *contrade*. This was the ceremony where it would be decided what neighborhood competed in the Palio race in July.

"I would like to make a toast," Janine said, holding

her glass up in her newly manicured hand. "To us and our semester abroad."

"Here, here," Lisa said as we clinked glasses.

"*Chin-chin*," I said.

"Cheers," Michelle said.

"We couldn't have lived together better," Janine said quite seriously. I swallowed the Vin Santo, praying it went down the right pipe, and I felt Michelle kick me under the table. When I looked at Michelle, she winked at me. Michelle popped a *cantucci* in her mouth. Her healthy appetite made me smile.

It has taken me years, decades really, to realize that maybe Janine was right. We couldn't have lived together better. Maybe that was the best it could have been.

It was a hot day when Duccio, Gaetano and I helped Michelle move into Lucy's apartment. I said goodbye to Lucy, who went to the airport having never made any headway with her butcher crush.

On a run back to Via Stalloreggi, we stopped in Crai to buy some drinks. On line in the store was Kaitlin. Gaetano saw her first and picked her up, so she dropped her groceries as he kissed her.

"What are you doing here?" I asked.

"I forgot when I was supposed to come, so I left Paris, since I couldn't get in touch with you."

"That's so like you," I said laughing and kissing her. Back at Via Stalloreggi, Lisa and Janine made annoyed faces at Kaitlin when she arrived. Last night's harmony was over.

"And Olivia is coming to stay here tomorrow?" Janine asked with a smirk.

"Maybe, since we're all packed already, we should

stay at your place." I said hopefully to Michelle. I was just saying it, not really expecting it to work. That would mean I would leave Via Stalloreggi just like that.

"Do it up, G-dog."

"I could get a room," Kaitlin said. She could see I hadn't really thought this through. But it was the obvious choice. I no longer had to stay and deal with my roommates. I had options.

"C'mon, K. We've got to save money," I heard myself saying. "It's almost better to do it like this. This way, I don't get all emotional about it. It's a big deal, but you know, it's better to just go with it. *Andiamo*."

I went into my room and threw the last of my stuff into the bag. If I stayed too long looking at the view, I knew I was going to cry. And so with one glance over the roofs to the countryside, I said goodbye to the room and the little bed that had been my home for five months.

Then we were outside the walls, drinking on what was once Lucy's balcony. There had been no time to write to Kaitlin about what happened with Gaetano, but it became obvious when he kissed me goodbye.

"Oh," Kaitlin said, nodding. "I get it. You took my advice. Good girl."

I ignored her and asked Gaetano to stay a little longer.

"I should let you and your friends hang out tonight on your own."

"Yeah," I said. "I didn't know she was coming today. I'm sorry."

"We'll meet up tomorrow in the *campo*."

Once Duccio and Gaetano were gone, we sunned ourselves, drinking white wine. It was easy to just be with Kaitlin and Michelle. In the morning Olivia was coming and we could watch the choosing of the *contrade*.

"So you guys both got yourselves Italian stallions, huh?" Kaitlin said teasing.

"There's still a chance for you, don't worry," Michelle said.

The next morning, after we met Olivia at the bus stop, we went to a crowded *campo* where people were gathering. The sun shone on the piazza, making everything seem golden instead of pink.

The announcer began to name names of the neighborhoods that would race in the Palio. Gaetano explained to us in slow Italian so Kaitlin could understand why certain *contrade* were more excited than others. There were long standing rivalries and neighborhoods that hadn't won in a long time. There was energy in the air, the bursts of excitement when the *contrade* were chosen. Only ten neighborhoods got the honor of having their horse race in July. Seven would have to wait until the August Palio. Three neighborhoods got to run in both.

"You can feel it," I said, holding out my goose-pimpled arm to Gaetano.

"Wait until July for the Palio," Gaetano said. "You will never feel anything like it."

Duccio wasn't with us but standing with his *contrada*. Michelle decided to stay with the Americans, but we all exchanged kisses with Duccio's mom who seemed to think it was cute that we supported our adopted *contrada, leone*.

Janine was standing with Andrea's *contrada*. Her blonde hair stood out against the brilliant colors in the piazza. She was wearing a bright blue sundress and smiling. She waved over at the *stranieri* like she was genuinely glad to see us but just couldn't pull herself away from being Andrea's arm candy.

"She's as fake as a three dollar bill, isn't she?" Olivia asked.

"Yep!" Michelle said and then cheered loudly when Duccio's *contrada* was selected, drawing looks from our neighbors. She feigned being a confused American.

"Are you doing that for him or his mom?" I teased. But then I cheered when my *contrada*, or the *contrada* of Via Stalloreggi, the *leone,* was selected. Everyone just wanted to belong.

After the presentation, Michelle insisted on getting gelato.

"For Gabi is tartufo, for Michelle is gelato, for Olivia I donno what is," Gaetano said to Kaitlin.

"*Pane proscuitto*," Olivia said.

"*Brava*," Gaetano said. "Kaiti, what is for you?"

"I don't know yet," said Kaitin winking, up for a challenge. "Maybe I can figure it out over the summer. Hey, Gabriella, can we climb the tower now or what?"

I almost forgot. I handed in the last of my papers. I was no longer a student, at least not in this country. I could climb the tower without bad luck.

"I have to go get the *vespa*," Gaetano said, following Kaitlin's gaze. "And I still haven't graduated."

"I'm still taking the language class until the end of June," Michelle said. "I'm paid up. It can't hurt to continue."

I looked at Olivia. "You ready?"

She shook her head. She was afraid of heights. "I'm not sure."

"C'mon," I said. Then I quoted her back to herself. "Just have fun."

So the three of us climbed the tower. It was the first of many tourist attractions the three of us would see together. We stopped at each of the windows to look out over the piazza and beyond Siena into Tuscany. There were 306 steps and we went slowly. Kaitlin and I held onto Olivia.

When we reached the top, we could see everything. I felt triumphant. Not just because I was no longer a student in Siena, but also because I had made it through the whole semester. I had learned a new language and more. I wasn't sure when I was going to go home to the states. I didn't know what lay ahead, but for now, I let my worries float out over Tuscany. For tonight and for as long as I could, I was going to go with the flow. I was going to just have fun.

I would live and make choices and decisions and never be certain of the outcome until it was too late to undue. But that was okay. I would follow my life's path. I would play my cards. I hoped to make the trains I should and miss the ones that I shouldn't catch.

I had finished my semester.

Later in the evening, we all met back in the piazza. The sun set over the pink bricks. We American girls wore sweatshirts over our denim skirts. We refused to wear pants. We had lived through the cold winter, and now was the time for smooth bare legs. We were drinking supermarket wine and eating panini.

The feeling in the *campo* was so perfect that I didn't ever want to let it go. Everyone was drunk. We were going to drink the American way. The die hard Sienese were decked out in their *contrada* colors. Some people were even dressed in medieval costumes of multicolored tunics and tights, singing songs that had existed for hundreds of years.

Duccio teased me that I should be a horse jockey for the Palio. Michelle told Duccio and me a story of the first time she was on a horse. She was speaking Italian better than I thought that she could. She used the imperfect to describe something.

"Michelle, wow!"

'What?"

"You just spoke so well," I said. Duccio laughed and kissed Michelle.

"I teach 'er good, no?" he asked in English.

"Yeah."

Then he kissed her again. I smiled at their love. Michelle was never going to leave Siena. She was going to keep putting off her departure. She was never going back to school. She was going to prove Lucy wrong about being with the person you love at nineteen or twenty.

Michelle, who couldn't speak a word of Italian at the start of the semester, would surpass any of the *stranieri* in her language skills.

She would choose her English carefully when old friends came to visit, but even her English would be punctuated by Italian gestures and expressions. She would give herself over completely to this country. I will never know if she has stopped doing damage to herself or if she still carried her pain into the darkness, but I like to believe that she really has found another way.

That night in the *campo*, all of the *stranieri* from my group were coming up to hug Michelle and me goodbye and discuss our plans for the summer. Several of them were returning home, but many were staying in Italy or traveling through Europe like us. I felt like

313

all the world was in the Piazza del Campo. And anyone who wasn't there should not have mattered to me.

My little crew of American girls was getting giddier and giddier. Michelle couldn't stop kissing Duccio. Kaitlin was enjoying random men in the piazza who loved her red hair. Olivia was flirting shamelessly with Dino.

Italy had changed all of us. There was that confidence in the way Michelle let her r's roll. There were friends of Gaetano's that Olivia knew, and she kissed them on the cheek casually. I felt my walk had almost returned to what it once was. I didn't feel like my old self again, though. I felt like I had become someone else who I could almost like.

Around one, Duccio had to get back so his mother wouldn't worry. He wanted to give us all ride to Michelle's place, but she wanted some time alone with him before we all went back.

"*Andiamo*," Michelle said over and over again. She kept winking at Duccio. They went off and the *campo* started to clear out shortly afterward. The diehards were still there. They would sing until the sun rose because they were happy their *contrada* could race.

"I think it's time to head back," I said to Olivia after another hour.

"We do have to get up kind of early tomorrow," Olivia said. "And I think we've given Michelle and Duccio enough time."

"It's not going to happen for you and Dino tonight, is it?" I asked as Dino was starting to kiss us goodbye.

"No."

"Maybe when we come back." I offered. But she

shrugged. For her it was all good. Whatever happened would be.

The best thing to do about getting Kaitlin, who was the most drunk, home was to put her on the back of Gaetano's *vespa*. Olivia and I could follow behind on foot. Kaitlin smiled and her teeth were stained gray from the cheap Chianti. She wrapped her arms around Gaetano and tried to tell him things in Italian.

When Gaetano zoomed off, she was barely holding on. It was frightening, but we heard her screaming "*sessoooooooo.*" Halfway down the Via Martonioni, Kaitlin's sandal came off, and Gaetano stopped further away. Olivia and I ran down the street to get the shoe.

"Just keep going," I shouted at him. "We'll give it to her when we get back."

Michelle was standing on the balcony when we got to her house. We waved up at her, whistling. Olivia helped Kaitlin with her shoe, trying to steady her.

Gaetano parked his bike. He and I stared at each other. This was it. Even as he was kissing Olivia and Kaitlin goodbye and wishing them a good trip, he was looking at me.

"We're going to go up," Olivia said.

"Okay, I'll be right there," I said.

"You sure?" And I nodded. I wanted to make sure Kaitlin was okay. We had to get up early in the morning to catch the train. I watched them close the *portone*. I knew that above me, Michelle went back inside.

Gaetano sighed and said, "*Bella.*" I didn't want to do it. I wasn't quite ready to say goodbye to him. I left my apartment in a hurry and it didn't feel too bad. Maybe I could leave him quick, too. I was going to see him again.

"It's only a month," I offered.

"Yes, so you've told me."

"It's true."

"You want to go check on Kaiti."

"Yes, and I don't want to say goodbye."

"Okay, so go check on Kaiti."

"But you seem sad," I said.

"Because I am."

"Gaetano," I let my voice ring in a bit of a whine.

"Go," he said. I kissed him and then I hugged him and then I kissed him again.

"I'll call you when we get to Nice." I said, trying not to let my voice shake. He didn't look at me as I let him go. My chest was tight. I whispered *ciao* as I closed the door.

Michelle was sitting up in bed. Kaitlin was lying on a pillow in the other twin bed with her hands over her eyes. She was moaning.

"I thought you'd have taken a little longer to say goodbye," Michelle said.

"Me too," Olivia said.

"How is she doing?" I asked, nodding toward Kaitlin who had taken off her skirt but not her sweatshirt.

"We're keeping a basket by the bed," Olivia said.

"It's under control," Michelle said.

Outside we could hear Gaetano trying to rev up the *vespa*.

"You okay there, little Kaitlin?" I asked.

"Uh-huh," Kaitlin groaned weakly.

"Maybe you should try to throw up," Michelle said. She caught my skeptical look. "C'mon, sometimes it works. You're going to sleep with her?"

"Ughh, yeah, you are," said Olivia, climbing in bed with Michelle.

I went by the window. The bike started, it was idling outside. Gaetano glanced up at me and looked back down.

"Guys, would it be wrong of me to go with Gaetano tonight?"

"No," Kaitlin yelled from the bed.

"I was wondering why you even came back up," Michelle said.

"There will be plenty of time for bonding," Olivia said. I looked at the three of them, my friends who would be by my side in one way or another for the rest of my life. Olivia smiled at me. "Anyway, worse comes to worse, there's always another train. Just. Have. Fun"

"It will clear up the sleep issue." I pushed open both doors onto the terrace. I called down. "Gaetano."

"*Dimmi,*" he said looking up. He was already smiling.

"*Vado con te.*" I will go with you.

"*Allora, vieni,*" he said, smiling. Come.

Through the darkened city I ride with the man who is a true friend. What will happen between us in the future is not important. What we have is now. I am almost twenty-one. I am as young as I will never be again. I know this and appreciate it. My youth is mine to treasure. I close my eyes and tilt my head as the man driving the *vespa* goes up one of the hills in a city I think of as home. Tomorrow I will leave for the first stop on a voyage that will have many stops. But before that he is driving me through the night to his room.

My name is the same but accented differently now, and I answer to other names depending on who is calling. I am no longer running away. I love this beautiful medieval solace of a city.

My past is behind me, my future ahead. Nothing has changed. Nothing has disappeared. I might still see ghosts lingering against the tall reddish buildings. I might never be rid of all my ghosts but tonight that is quite all right. Because I am here.

The man on the *vespa* drives through the city. He stops at the gate of the monastery, turns off the *vespa*. He's moving in slow motion. I touch his cheek.

"Don't be sad," I say. "It's only a month."

"I know," he says, he looks away. Then he looks back at me with shining gray eyes. "But will you come back?"

"*Pazzo*," I say, kissing his lips. "Of course."

I make no other promises about the future because I do not know what train my life will take. But if I am able, if I can find a way, I will always return to Italy.

Basta così.

Grazie
Like some of the characters in this book, I believe you don't *need* to say thank you to your friends. I also know that sometimes a little acknowledgement is nice.

To my dear group of girlfriends: for inspiring my characters, supporting my endeavors, checking in and the constant cheerleading you all do so well.

To Kelly Blair: As always, yet as never before, you put your heart into this one. What Celine says is true. I just hope to tell you in the perfect smelling spot some day.

To Kristy Leissle: For late night DR sessions, reminding me that fun is NOT an intervention and informing every character since the D-evolution.

To Lynn Messina: For returning my constant volley of emails with your own strong serves, for emergency cheese and for being a dynamo.

To Karen Oh: For making my online life prettier and my real life MEATIER. Bronche!

To Corby and Lundgren: For photographing, calming and summer of funning.

To Aunt Anita: For all your thoughtful gifts.

To my dad, Rocco Papa: For surviving a very different trip when you were "barely twenty" with your spirit intact.

To YOU: For supporting this independent author.

And "credits" to my team at Papa Mike Publishing HQ. From the mascot who teaches me about the finer things in life to the intern and junior associate who respect when the day is done and it's time to punch out so we can really get to work. But most of all thanks to the editor-at-large who not only encourages me to go beyond the red rooftops, but helps me find ways of getting there.

www.ingramcontent.com/pod-product-compliance
Lightning Source LLC
Chambersburg PA
CBHW020335180626
46812CB00001B/217